To Peg ~
A most awesome
& caring friend ~
Love,
Dy

ECHOES THROUGH THE MIST

DYANN NEES

America Star Books

Softcover 9781632491688
PUBLISHED BY AMERICA STAR BOOKS, LLLP
www.americastarbooks.com

Printed in the United States of America

To my brother and friend, Dale T. Nees,
whom I love dearly for all he has been and is in my life.

Acknowledgements

I want to thank my cousin and friend, Pat Webers, for making this possible. She has typed and edited my work and I can't begin to tell her how much this means to me or thank her enough. Also my friend, Janis A. Elsen, for her endless support and contribution of the cover design through her photography. I would also like to thank my friend, Carmen A. Lueer, for her loving support and friendship of years. All three women are instrumental in helping me to feel and know that "I can!"

CHAPTER 1

Spring was not quite ready to descend its warming hands upon the dense woodlands of the great Sierra Nevada range. Heavy sleet cascaded upon the windshield leaving Malory Douglas nearly blinded. She hardly noticed. Malory felt the distant lights prying, drizzling in on her private world. Inattentively she flicked the wipers on. The piercing glare of the icy pavement did nothing to relieve her throbbing temples, and her eyes were still swollen with tears.

Each thick flake collapsed against the glass shattering Malory's already disconnected thoughts. Once again she was not in control, and very little time was left to regain her composure. *How could she assume command?* She zoomed the window half way down and let the brisk air fill her nostrils. Then she gently turned the stereo system on and slipped in a soothing CD. She was certain that only a short distance ahead, the renowned Melrose Resort, held the key to her happiness.

Earlier this morning, Malory had still been plagued with misgivings. *Was this the best way to cure obesity?* She hated that word, but doctors insisted on tagging it to her and she herself had tired of the yoyo syndrome she was famous for. Once and for all the fat would melt away, destined to leave her forever. She had not discussed with friends or co-workers why she had taken a month leave of absence. She was too embarrassed, yet in her young life of twenty-four years, she hadn't been able to properly abolish her pattern of binge, diet, binge, diet. Melrose was expensive for her meager income, so it damn well better be worth it.

Malory had leafed through the ten page brochure during every meeting, lunch, and planning session that Sacramento's Monument Social Services had demanded of her. It seemed hypocritical that she, a therapist trained to help others through a crisis, could not regulate her own. Lately she was extremely cognizant of everyone raising eyebrows at the delightful chef salads that she so painstakingly packed. They seemed to be screaming, "Do you really believe *that* salad has only a few hundred calories? Come on!" Malory also noted the ridiculing glances she was sure were directed at her each time she'd yank out a light meal or new diet cuisine. She was sure they expected that it was only her hors d'oeuvre and the *real* meal would follow shortly. It never did though.

Malory had the time coming and would not stall any longer. Immediately following this Friday's work day, she hopped into her new *black BMW* and began her northward ascent into the rugged mountains. She had fully planned to take her metabolic curse and let Dr. Drake Melrose and his wife, Thedy, disband its evil effects.

Malory hugged the wheel tightly as the car veered left, well aware of the frozen patches periodically whirling her left back tire. She was used to California mountain driving, but knew all too well that many travelers of this road weren't. Malory stayed to the inside, far away from the almost non-existent guardrails. She always wondered why the Highway Department bothered at all. If doomed, you'd either slide under, over or through. The thin metal barrier certainly couldn't be capable of halting a moving vehicle.

The wind expressed its increasingly hostile attitude, as the towering redwoods whistled in protest, whipping their branches to and fro. Malory shivered uneasily as she sank back into the leather upholstery. To her right, the giant Sequoias spattered the countryside, some of them well over a thousand years old. Malory readjusted her speed to exit onto one of the few turn-offs within the mountain range. This was the last stretch before the resort and she sensed something odd.

Probably the queasiness she felt was natural. She had obligated herself to this endeavor and planned to hand over thirty-five hundred dollars for a four week stay. Once again she tried to push back the apprehension and think of its glorious outcome... weight loss.

Ahead Malory's gaze fell upon the rustic, yet majestic manor which before she'd only seen on paper. She was astonished at its natural beauty, nestled in this vast acreage surrounded by snowcapped pines. The main building was truly exquisite in its attempt to capture the intrinsic elegance of the redwoods and still captivate a totally contemporary design. The profuse cinnabar lumber notched together to form a gigantic U-formation anchoring several long rectangular panes of Tiffany glass across its front. Below the panes, impeccably placed, were rounded evergreens packed in pine chips. Below, the burnt sienna brick flower pots that encircled the pines, were softly becoming filled with white dust. Even beneath the flurry blanket, evidence of unique landscaping was present as Malory noted the tops of huge cement figures peeking out, each strategically placed.

Taken in by the beauty, Malory swerved the car to the right practically forgetting her purpose for coming there. She parked in a compact angular space designated for visitors. With infinite care, Malory glided herself out from behind the driver's seat, glad she hadn't had to contend for too long with the squalls of snow still tormenting the area. Snow often had a gifted way of looking gentle, but feeling threatening. The drive had been less than two hours, yet daylight was nowhere to be seen. Her only consolation was that the days were somewhat longer and at this time of the year the snow was apt to melt quickly. Still, tonight it blanketed the earth and Malory slid all the way to the arched stucco-encased wooden doors ahead of her.

Once inside, Malory stomped her feet and tried to suck her gut further into her screeching jeans. Perhaps they wouldn't notice the bulges.

"Can I help you?" The question came from the tiny dark-haired girl who sat behind her tidy little desk.

"Yes, I'm Malory Douglas. I'm here to check in for your four week program."

"Have a seat," the girl peered over her glasses, adjusting them slightly.

Cold as ice, that one. Malory noticed her name plate which said *Trixie*. Hadn't that name gone out with Bosco? Whew, she sure hoped the rest of the resort's staff was nice. She had no intention of paying good money to be snubbed.

It wasn't too long and Trixie said, "Malory, you can fill this out." Then Trixie slapped the pad onto her desk for Malory to fetch. Ruff!

Just then a short, slightly chubby red-headed woman stepped out of the door directly in front of Malory.

"Oh," she giggled, "You must be Malory. Come here, dear. We've been waiting for you. Put that away, Trixie," she pointed to the pad. Trixie shrugged her shoulders and rolled her eyes.

"Yes, I'm Malory."

"Good, I'm Mrs. Melrose but do call me Thedy."

Thedy breezed around the desk wearing a long Hawaiian print garb that draped her body loosely. She stood a few inches shorter than Malory, but nonetheless swung her arm around Malory's neck, pulling her gently toward the office door.

Thedy then looked at Trixie. "We have Malory's application, so please just get her key. We'll be back in a minute."

With that, Thedy led Malory into the spacious anteroom ahead of them. She motioned for Malory to sit.

"Tell me about yourself. Why are you here?"

Was she kidding? She looked serious. Malory was stunned beyond words and fumbled through her purse, as her mind searched for the right answer.

"I'm sorry," Thedy began warmly, "I mean why *this* place? I know you want to control your eating habits."

Before Malory could respond, Thedy went on, "You know, my hubby, Drake that is, has such a great place here. There's everything right at the tip of your fingers. Everything that is, except the *wrong* food. That's very important, dear. You didn't bring any food, did you?"

"No, I…"

"That's okay. They'll check. I shouldn't have asked, dear. My husband says I talk too much, but I really believe…"

For once Thedy didn't get to finish. A tall distinguished looking man entered. His blue eyes twinkled as Thedy tip-toed to kiss his cheek. He smiled and winked at her. Very quietly Thedy teetered out of the office.

"You guessed it," he began in a deep tone. "I'm Dr. Drake Melrose."

Malory stood up to shake hands with the boss. He had wavy gray hair and a mustache. He sat his tall lean muscular frame into the armed brown leather chair.

"I apologize for my wife. She often comes on a little strong, but she's a good woman."

"Yes, she's very nice." Malory's bundle of questions were stuck somewhere between Broca's center and her medulla. She couldn't think of another thing to say for the moment.

"Well, let's not waste any time," Drake took over the stunted conversation. "I'll get your key, the schedule, and someone to carry your things in. Trixie will do the paper work, and you can come down later to pay, once you're settled."

Could he sense her frustration? Malory hoped not. She sat stupidly staring at the décor. Definitely not Thedy's touch. It was too dull. Thedy was colorful to say the least. Certainly not Trixie's taste either as there were no icicles hanging from the ceiling. It was far from ordinary though, paneled half-way up with wood, stained a shade too dark. The carpet was maroon and windows were dressed with beige vertical blinds with hints of maroon threaded through them. The furniture was brown leather and the paintings mounted on several walls were mountain landscapes... masculine... appropriate. Up above, the wall was lined with pewter plates, set at gated intervals on a carved oak rail.

Malory did an about-face, realizing now she'd been addressed. "Thank you. I'd like to get settled in first."

Drake pressed a button and soon Trixie bounded soberly through the doorway with Malory's room number, key and schedule.

The exorbitant content and layout of the building she stood in, led Malory to believe that soon a perfectly uniformed, muscular, good-looking bellhop would appear to assist her with the luggage. She couldn't wait. But instead, a scrawny, bent over elderly man with wisps of white bristly hair, limped over to greet Malory.

The old-timer offered his tiny wrinkled hand to Malory, "Hello, Miss. I'm Mr. Tom Tinnley. Call me Tommy."

Tommy didn't appear able to carry as much as Malory had in tow, and the German Sheppard that trotted at a slow pace alongside of him, also looked in need of a cane or similar walking aid. The dog sat still for a moment as Tommy looked eye to eye at Malory.

"Hello, Tommy. I'm Malory and I guess we are off to room 358."

Malory smiled and began to lift the largest of the three suitcases and the carry-all bag, feeling somewhat sorry for the sweet old geezer.

"You needn't do that maam', I'll manage." Tommy bent the rest of the way down and with ease pulled the medium blue valise up high, tucked the smaller blue matching make-up case under one arm, and then gently relieved Malory of the large suitcase she had intended to carry herself. She was amazed that he was capable of lifting that amount. Both Malory and the dog, Brisket, tagged behind Tommy as he led the way down the freshly painted enormous hallway.

Malory thought the place looked homey, yet antiquated. The heavy textured plaster swirled in circle effects and all doorways were arched to give it a sense of Spanish ornament. The walls were lined with oil paintings framed in thick hand-carved oak. At regular intervals, large brass flower pots were placed and each held a variation of a miniature palm. In between each set of paintings, old brass kerosene lamps were hung. They were newly electrified, and each gleamed from a mixture of polish and lacquer. The carpet was not plush as it had been in Drake's office, instead it was a heavy burlap weave with a sparse brown-spackled design running through it.

Tommy mumbled what Malory thought was an updated weather report.

"Yes, I do hope it improves also… soon. I must be at the end of the building."

"Yep, all the way down, then up three flights."

Forced exercise, Malory thought sarcastically. Could the old man do this? Malory wasn't at all sure she wanted to watch someone drop dead on the steps struggling with her luggage. Yet, Tommy really didn't seem to be struggling. She wondered just how old he was. Periodically, she noticed room doors open and someone would smile at her. A friendly place… she liked that.

The taffy-colored dog seemed to retaliate now, as if he had his fill for the day. He began to whine.

"Ssh, Brisket. C'mon boy." The dog quieted.

They neared the end of the hallway and Malory was preparing for steps but there were none, only escalators. *Thank God*, Malory thought. This was much better for the old guy, and it wouldn't hurt her either.

As they glided upward, Tommy spoke. "You're in a real nice section, missy. Nice folks there, Jade, Dani," he wobbled his head, "Yep, really nice folks."

Malory tried to listen up, Jade? Was he mumbling about jewelry now? She thought he said something about nice people. Couldn't he just turn and face her? This conversation would be so much more fruitful.

I'm glad. Are we almost there?"

"Yep, here you are," Tommy motioned to the door.

Malory glanced down the hallway noticing several doors opened, but continued to try and fit her key in the lock. Finally the handle turned and Brisket bounded through the door first.

"C'mon boy, back here," Tommy directed. Brisket bounced on Malory's spread and then leaped back to his owner.

Tommy set the suitcases down near the brass pot at the door. He turned to Malory and nodded, "You have a nice stay, miss." He winked at her and vanished. What a nice old codger.

Malory sat for a minute before she began to unpack. She hoped this was the right decision. Sitting there, she became aware of the immense room she was going to live in for the next month. She was sure it was bigger than her entire apartment. The ceiling was a high cathedral style with beautifully reddish-tinted wood beams, so common of the area. Walls were painted a deep terra cotta, bottomed by an ecru plush carpet. She sat in a caned rocker which was perched next to the lofty fireplace engulfed in a natural colored stone hearth. In front of the fireplace laid a large rectangular fringed oriental rug, filled with a mixture of beige and pale blues. Across from her rocker sat a sand-colored puffy leather couch with various rust throw pillows strewn about. This cozy little nook was just Malory's taste.

As she looked across the room two sets of paneled windows, each with three panes, decorated the walls. The middle pane was permanent Tiffany glass, while the two outside panes were clear glass and had crank handles. Under each window casing were wide low oak dressers loaded with drawers of various sizes, and in the center of the two dressers sat a queen size brass bed. The spread colors coordinated in a sprawling flower design. Above the bed was an old-fashioned cross-stitched picture framed in oak and on either side of the stitchery was a pair of hanging brass candlesticks, filled with creamy colored candles. The adjacent wall housed a writing desk and chair, and in the corner still another overstuffed chair. A crystal chandelier dropped sparkling prisms to the center of the room.

The desk and dressers each held singular lamps, Victorian in style. The mixture was unique and awesome.

By now Malory felt that she had to nose around a bit to see what was on the other side of the wall that held her couch; besides she had to unpack. She felt exhausted but knew it had to be done. Around the corner she found a walk-in closet. As the doors unfolded, one side had a long rail filled with brass hangers for long items, while the other side had shelves galore, complete with a built-in shoe rack below. Still, next to the closet, was a large bathroom. There was a linen closet, built-in tub and shower with sliding glass doors, two sink basins with massive mirrors above, and of course the main item in question, an aqua toilet. The tiles were ceramic squares with diamond designs in aqua and cocoa. The same design and coloring ran through the wallpaper which covered every square inch. Throw rugs were thick and fancy stitched towels lined the racks… all the luxuries of home… except food.

Malory was more than half unpacked when she heard giggles and a loud knock at her door. She opened the door to meet her new neighbors.

"Hello, I'm Dani Ellison. I'm right across the hall from you," Dani extended one hand for a shake, and held out a plate of vegies and dip in her other hand. "I brought these from the cafeteria. I thought we could all get to know one another." Dani's voice was soft with a hint of Bostonian accent, Malory guessed.

"And I'm Jade DuPont, right next door to you," she pointed as she spoke. Jade would stand out in a crowd and not because of her weight either. She was beautiful with long soft curls of raven black hair and huge, almost round, chestnut colored eyes. She had a raspy voice and a wide smile, teeth perfectly aligned. What a knockout! Malory knew she shouldn't stare, honestly, what was wrong with her?

"Come on in. I'm Malory Douglas and I'm glad to meet both of you," Malory finally managed. She led the two women into her little nook by the fireplace. They sat on the sofa, set the tray of vegies on the coffee table, and soon the three were like old friends.

"Dani, if you've been here for three months, how much have you lost? Are you soon going home? How did you do it?" Malory couldn't get the questions out quick enough.

"Whoa... you sound like my hubby now," Dani joked. "Well, although we're not supposed to think in terms of pounds, I've dropped one hundred and thirteen of them. I still will be here another month though because I have twenty of the hardest yet to lose."

"That's great! You mentioned your husband. How'd you manage to get away for so long?" Malory questioned.

"That's what's so wonderful," Jade popped in, "You leave them for awhile and they're much more appreciative."

The girls all laughed. Malory couldn't help but feel like she was at a good old slumber party with best friends... and she loved it.

"Really, my Richard and the girls come here often. I miss them terribly. My daughter Kristin is twelve, and Heather is nine. I think they understand that mom had to do this. Besides, I'm almost done now. We originally came from Boston and now settled in Sacramento. Richard's a computer analyst." Dani's green eyes lit up as she talked of her family in a motherly tone. Malory sensed this was not easy for her, just necessary. Dani's short blonde curls bounced as she bent over to reach for more broccoli.

"Bon Appetit," she smiled at Malory and Jade as she crunched away at the nibbles.

"What about you, Jade?"

"Well my dear, you can see I have lots to go here," she snickered. Malory really hadn't thought that at all. Jade must be almost six foot tall, well-proportioned and big-boned. Although she probably could carry an awful lot of weight and it wouldn't show. Jade looked very stylish in a pair of Gitano khaki-colored cotton pants, a tailored long-sleeve beige silk blouse, and a brown paisley vest.

Jade continued, "I've just lost sixty pounds, but I have fifty left."

"Well, I only plan to be here a month. That's all I can afford, but at least it'll get me started," Malory informed them.

Jade and Dani looked at each other with disbelief.

"That's what we all plan when we start, but this place has a way of changing one's mind," Jade told her.

What did she mean by that? Even if Malory wanted to remain at this luxurious resort, she couldn't afford it and bills, too. And of course, there was her job.

"Well, I guess it's getting late," Jade spoke as she glanced at her watch. "Did you check your schedule yet? We've got some really great people working here. And the scenery down the hall isn't too bad either," Jade raised her brows.

"What do you mean?"

"I mean our neighbors, Paris and Nick. Come with us to breakfast, Malory, and we'll introduce you."

"Sounds good. I'll see you in the morning then." Malory walked with the girls to the door as they said their good-byes.

A new surge of excitement filled Malory from head to toe. She couldn't wait to get on her weight reduction program. She practically forgot about Trixie's cold-shoulder treatment, as her new companions filled the air with warmth and friendliness. Malory couldn't wait to meet the men down the hall, after all she was free. She also felt a burst of energy radiate through her body while thoughts of exercising, swimming, and playing tennis in this gloriously designed paradise seemed almost too good to be true. No work, just fun and relaxation... and no food. She wasn't too sure about that part yet. Malory remembered now that she was supposed to have gone back down to pay. She was too tired now so she'd do it first thing in the morning.

Malory finished putting her things away in an organized fashion and then got comfortable in a long flannel nightgown. It wasn't so roomy now, but wait. She vowed that soon it would hang and sag as she melted away to practically nothing. She brushed her long red tresses thirty times or so after she snapped the combs out of her hair. They kept it from falling into her eyes. Then Malory brushed her teeth and put eye drops into her bright baby-blues. She planned to snuggle deep under the inviting covers and sleep sound so she'd be ready to greet the new exciting day.

It was only now that Malory became aware of the one thing that was missing in her room... curtains. How foolish, she thought. It really didn't matter much here in the middle of nowhere. Yet she felt funny standing in the center of the room with only a nightgown on. Oh well, on the third floor, who'd see her? She convinced herself to turn off the last of the three lamps, but couldn't keep herself from staring out the window just to make sure. *Make sure of what?*

She was sounding like some of her clients... very doubtful. Curiously she scanned the back grounds, realizing that the snow was falling lightly now, very gently over the flat rooftops. She recalled from the brochure that the long back set of buildings housed the gymnasium, spa, sauna, exercise mats and machines, as well as the tennis court. Overhead far beyond the buildings, she could see gigantic redwoods as they descended down the mountainside.

Malory's gaze fell upon a particular path leading into the density of trees. Her eyes focused, then refocused through the mist of snow. She felt a shiver of fear fall upon her. She was sure one of the figures she saw was bent over, while the other figure's head flopped backwards, dangling, nearly into the drifted snow below. Malory froze for a moment, then quickly cranked the window, letting it fly open. What could she do anyway? She tried to scream, but her voice choked off. Surely that far away they wouldn't hear her. They? The second figure was dead, she was sure of it. The moving figure was limping deeper into the woods, leaving a fading quality to what must have been an apparition. At least, Malory hoped so.

Terrified, Malory toppled back onto the bed. She felt flushed so she left the breeze from the open window fall upon her. Malory felt her heart's rapid beats. She was tired and wondered if she could be sure of what she'd seen. But then she knew… she was *very* sure and just didn't want to believe it. She saw someone toting a dead body into the woods. Now what? As she laid there, Malory heard the echoes of the wind tunnel through her muddled mind. For a moment she thought she heard voices, too. She felt dizzy and soon drifted off to sleep.

CHAPTER 2

He had only a short distance to walk and he was glad because she was heavier than he expected she would be. His head was throbbing in silent agony as it always did at times like this. Feebly, he trudged on well aware of his lack of usual strength. Must be the headache, he thought. He felt weak.

He stopped for only a minute to rest, as if this would help to replenish his last reserve of energy. He tried to gulp a few deep breaths as he let her body slump into an unnatural position. He could hear her throat clicking and that made him angry.

He continued to edge the rear boundary of the property as he glanced nervously toward the building. Was that a light? In a frantic state, his brain could not seem to absorb its input. Yet even through the dusty light, as snow filtered past, thereby impairing his otherwise perfect vision, he was sure it was coming from the third floor end room. He couldn't remember now who occupied that room. In fact, when he checked yesterday he was sure no one had. But he'd find that out without a doubt. He was also certain that he just saw a woman peering out... a typical nosey fat woman.

Rapidly he began to shove his way through the virgin snow, but was unable to keep his eyes from darting toward the lighted window. When he looked again it was no longer lit... all was dark. The outside lighting at the resort, although dim, offered a faint flicker that allowed him to see that now the third floor windows were open. Could the woman really see him? Did she think she'd yell at him? Despite his aching temples, he wanted to laugh at her. Did she think she could stop him? If he wasn't so weak, he'd have produced a belly-laugh. As it was, he stumbled toward the opening, vowing to check out the window and its owner later.

Oblivious now to the outside world, he gave her feet a sharp tug, pulling her inside with the others. He groped through the cold darkness, touching lightly the dank cavern walls, to find his trusty lantern.

"Here it is, just where I left it," he pulled her deeper into the recess now filled with rays resembling sunlight.

He continued to rattle on as if he expected one of them to answer. "Yes indeedy, it's much warmer now. Here you go." He jammed his hands under her armpits and yanked her to a sitting position. Now she was lined up with the rest of them.

"Feels good, right girls? Hey, if you don't want to talk it's fine with me." The glorious rush of adrenalin streamlined his veins and he felt refreshed. His head was somewhat relieved.

He hoped Liza would keep her word and meet him here again. He giggled when he thought of poor dumb Liza. He knew every inch of this cave, just as he knew every inch of her body. She was a dumb blonde for sure, but again tonight, he needed her. How many times had they made love on the other side of this wall and she had no idea what he was up to? The mere thought sent a ripple of shrill titters through him. She came here out of love... how touching.

"If Liza comes girls, I'll have to leave. Yes indeedy I do, but don't worry, Beebee will take care of you."

He talked directly to the new body, "It's okay. Don't you fret. Just put your hands behind your back for Uncle Beebee."

He cuffed her hands behind and then joined her to the heavy chain bolted deep into the earth and rocks.

He left the new body sitting limply, blew the lantern off, and inched his way now with a flashlight back toward the mouth of the winding cave. He started with the basic A-frame to build a cozy fire, as he shook and fluffed the blankets against the limestone, the flames began to radiate warmth. He wanted Liza to feel comfortable.

*****

Liza knew Beebee had his strange ways, yet she couldn't believe she was stomping through the snow with her new all leather boots no less, just to spend some time with him. Love did funny things to a woman, Liza agreed, but the cave again? This was ridiculous and she knew it.

Beebee said he was a mountain man, born to live amongst nature. Liza would have preferred a cozy apartment or motel room, rather than the mulchy earth covered with blankets. Although she did admit Beebee would make it warm and comfortable for her. She really loved the man, his lean muscular body and brown curly hair. Nevertheless, she couldn't understand him. She wasn't allowed to tell anyone at the resort about their affair. He was very firm on that and she wasn't about to cross him. And then there were his temper tantrums. Well, she couldn't expect him to be perfect.

The flakes landed directly on Liza's eyelashes which annoyed her. She just revamped herself this morning at the shop by gluing a beautiful new pair of lashes on, manicuring her newly designed nails, and cutting her bleached-out hair into a new short bob. She knew she looked extremely feminine, just the way Beebee wanted her.

21

Liza's eyes refused to work in this obnoxious weather, but she was sure the entrance was only a matter of feet away.

"Beebee, I'm here," Liza announced. She didn't see him but went to rub her nearly frozen fingers over the blazing fire.

"Hi doll, I've been waiting," Beebee was always very direct in his approach. His green eyes pierced right through her as he reached around her tiny waist, pulled her forward and kissed her long and hard.

It was then that Liza was certain why she came all the way back to this place so late at night in this godforsaken weather. Already the heat was apparent.

Liza dabbed at his lips with her slithery tongue and watched the man unthaw right there in front of her eyes.

"Where were you when I came in?"

"Oh, just beyond here in one of the small compartments, only a path away. Want to see?" he asked.

"No way. You know I want to see my way out of here. And I don't like critters, thank-you. This is far enough into any cave for me," she rubbed her hands up and down his back and buttocks, gradually bringing them around to his front side to unbuckle and unzip.

"Yes indeedy, I love the way you are a woman of few words. And so time conscientious," he fumbled for her huge breasts as he spoke softly to her.

Liza giggled. Her fingers coiled around him carefully, not allowing her long nails to cause him any pain. She didn't want to spoil it.

"I didn't see you at all today," she told him.

It was too late. He didn't answer. He never talked during their sessions, almost as if he was in a trance and that bothered Liza, but what could she do? That was Beebee. He'd only get mad if she brought it up again. So she laid there submissive to his demands, making only a few of her own. He always obliged her that way. As he rocked away, she usually found herself counting icicles, rather stalactites, above. She giggled at the thought of her taking time out to count. As usual Beebee interpreted her giggle as satisfaction and pushed at even a more impossible pace. Finally in a frantic rush of motion, he came.

Even if she wanted to, Liza wasn't allowed to leave for a couple of hours. She had to hold and comfort him. He would rest for a while, then awake dreamily. After that he was usually ready for conversation. Tonight he seemed a little distant, but she didn't mind.

Liza gently pulled the army green sleeping bag over the two of them as they settled under the thickness of it. She hadn't planned on it, but suddenly her eyes felt heavy, swollen, and gritty and soon she drifted off to sleep.

*****

Beebe had forced his eyes closed, hoping as it happened that Liza would fall asleep. He had no intentions of lying there all night. He felt jittery as a trapped rabbit as thoughts of the third floor peeper crept into his mind. Just what had she seen? He rolled over slowly so as not to disturb Liza. The last thing he needed was more uncertainty. He felt compelled to find that wench. He had to know who she was, before he'd know what he should do. Beebee's mind was hazed with fatigue. His face felt tensed as he awkwardly shimmied his sweater over his head in silent apprehension.

Beebe wondered if he should lean over and kiss Liza, but instead he flashed a sultry smile her way and said, "Good night, bitch." His temples creased his eyes narrow and he felt an unmistakable urge to laugh as he thought of Liza waking up all alone out here. For a moment he was skeptical, then without further hesitation he left.

He was breathlessly chilled by the time he reached the back entrance of the resort. The snow had stopped, but the wind had gained speed. He hadn't bothered to button up or even slip on his gloves. Pausing briefly, Beebee began to rummage through his jeans pocket to find the right key. He had to first unleash the security system. As he stood under the designated room, he noticed the windows still wide open. He fit the keys in the lock, irritated with the jangling sounds they were making. He really had thought that room was empty. Perhaps he'd have to check Trixie's files again.

He slid gently inside and relocked the door behind him. With each careful breath he drew, he rode the escalator higher, sweating profusely from the anxiety building within. Beebee had always been able to handle planned activities, but this was far from planned. Women seemed to have a way of launching surprise attacks and that's exactly what he despised about them. He was beginning to feel the need for sleep. His legs felt like jelly under him as he exited his swift moving ride.

Yes indeedy, he suddenly felt ill. Beebee twisted and turned the doorknob not knowing himself what he'd actually do if she came to the door. Thank God, the rest of the hall was dead. He could barely hear but identified it as moaning and groaning beyond the door he was presently trying to knee in. What kind of person was this? Moaning, groaning, peeping, and still an open window on such a wintry evening? He had no choice but to go directly to Trixie's files.

With renewed skepticism, Beebee headed toward the main offices. He just couldn't understand the framework of the world... supposedly a man's world. Huh! He felt little consolation in that assumption, as it was women who ruined it. They had such a conniving way of spoiling and intruding that it angered him greatly. At times he'd try to feel close to one, but she'd always do something to sever his trust. He was waiting for Liza's imperfection to sprout any day now. He was sure it wouldn't show up in the love-making department, but it would unveil itself. It always did. Women were like chameleons in decision-making and cobras in personality. They just never seemed to know what they wanted, but they'd bite to get it. It all came down to not being able to rely on them... and Beebee knew he never would. The hate Beebee felt made his teeth ache. He clenched his jaws like the grip of a Pit Bull, as memories etched a trench through his mind as raw as the sharp-edge of a butcher's blade.

Beebee tip-toed past the cafeteria and cocked his head to the side straining for any cautionary noise. He didn't deserve to be caught. He was distracted by a scratching sound as he leaned full-force against Trixie's door. Shortly, a familiar whine was audible and he was certain it was only Brisket.

Beebee clipped his voice to a sharp whisper, "Ssh, ssh, Brisket – lay down."

Brisket obeyed.

"Yes indeedy, Brisket. It's only your old pal, Beebee," he shifted his voice into neutral. "You just lie there and look stupid. Pay no never mind to me."

Brisket shifted into a curled heap, staring stolidly at Beebee who was now paying him no attention whatsoever. Brisket acted indifferent, but surely he could see the glazed look of insanity brush across Beebee's eyes as he searched fervently for papers that indicated a definite name to him.

Then he saw it. *Bingo!* His eyes were fixed in an unfaltering steady gaze upon the perfectly aligned sheets held tight under

25

Trixie's Millefiori paperweight. Beebee picked up the piece of antique glass that reminded him of looking through a kaleidoscope. He turned it again and again, repositioning each shapeless color, while he let his mind twirl along with it. He felt an odd sensation swelling up inside of him. Perhaps he just needed rest. He snatched the top sheet of paper and took it out the door with him.

His body was overtaking, demanding total control. In its uncompromising state, Beebee knew he'd have to give in to it. The girl would be safe for yet another night. He was sure the rules according to Hoyle or somebody say 'when you gotta, you gotta.' And Beebee had to give in to the nagging weariness. He had to succumb to his body's want of one of its basic needs, sleep. Before he could put his mind at ease though, he had to examine the paper one more time for the name he had to know. His eyes trickled blurry waves of light onto the sheet he white-knuckled into his fierce grip. He could barely read the small print, but in bold caps he was clearly able to make out the name, MALORY DOUGLAS.

CHAPTER 3

Malory's body was drained of its prior enthusiasm. Earlier last night she felt motivated, but the latter part of the evening left her weak with a dull ache across her forehead. She wondered now if it was all a dream… yet somehow she knew it wasn't. Rather than energy, she anticipated extreme fatigue. She wasn't at all sure she could even make it down to pay her bill, much less through breakfast and then exercise. Maybe she'd feel better just talking to Jade and Dani. She was doubtful that she'd share what she had seen with them. They'd think she was crazy. Besides, her sleep had been endlessly invaded with images of death. She had awakened several times to imaginary noises outside her window and door, and she felt too exhausted to even discuss it.

With little eagerness, she reexamined what she knew her eyes had witnessed. It had kind of a nightmarish hue to it as she recounted the two figures etched in her mind, the live bent over one and the hanging dead one. She shivered. There was something that kept nagging at her, but her… mind refused to let it surface… something she'd seen and wanted to remember. Great, when her clients had selective memories, she called them on it.

Malory forced herself to shower, brush her teeth and pour herself into her new aqua sweatpants and matching hooded sweatshirt. It was the recommended daytime attire. She

27

slipped her running shoes on over her tube socks and fished in her coat pocket for the rectangular beaded barrette she had just purchased to hold back her mop of hair. Rest assured, Malory could not get through the day feeling like she did. She'd have to perk up and remember her reason for being here.

Starting out the morning with Trixie was no way to brighten it.

"I understood, Miss Douglas, "Trixie sat straight up and glared at Malory, "that you were supposed to have taken care of *this* last night."

"Yes, I'm sorry. I got busy unpacking and meeting people. Well you must under--."

"Yes, and I'm busy now, too. But you see even though I'm busy, I'll take care of this because it's my job. I'm supposed to do this, and so I will," Trixie turned away from Malory.

Trixie flipped through the stack of papers under her Millefiori paperweight. She seemed unable to find the one she needed. She scowled at Malory, "It was here last night, but you weren't." Then Trixie bent back over her desk and scribbled out a receipt for Malory.

Malory tapped her foot incessantly, trying to decide how many years she'd get if she leaped over the desk and choked the lady. Too many... Trixie wasn't worth it. Malory rubbed her temples in despair and finally snapped the receipt from Trixie's hand. She could do without any flak from Trixie.

But Trixie couldn't let go, "I trust you'll thank me for my trouble, Miss Douglas?"

Where did this lady come from? The Twilight Zone?

"Yes, thank you. You'll have to excuse me. I have a headache." Malory wanted to ask Trixie what her excuse was, but instead she turned and walked away. Enough was enough.

As Malory entered the cafeteria with all its festivity and beautiful décor, she almost let herself surrender to its beauty and allow the horrible vision of last evening to disappear completely. She spotted Jade flagging her down and motioning for her to come and sit.

"Hi, Malory. Let me introduce you. This is Paris Lullo and Nicholi Hardin, but we call him Nick."

"Hi," Malory shook hands with both men and slid in the booth next to Nick. "This place is unbelievable," Malory continued, "Wow, a real tree?" There in the middle of the room was a live growing redwood.

"Yes, it's real. Dr. Melrose says living plants make the environment healthy," Jade imitated Drake Melrose's deep voice.

They all laughed.

"Say, do the rest of you have trouble with Trixie? Or is it just me?"

"Oh, Trixie our little pixie?" Nick asked sarcastically. Paris smiled as Nick ranted on, "You mean that friendly receptionist? That emotionless piece of rock sitting behind the desk? Yes, I've had a few run-ins and let me tell you what you need to do, Malory. Get from me a list of all the times that Thedy is in their little office and enter only then. If you go when Trixie's there alone, it's 'enter at your own risk'."

Again the group giggled. Malory felt relaxed again and was glad for that.

The cafeteria was a series of material-covered booths, in blue and rust tones, surrounding each rectangular redwood-topped table. The tables were heavily stained and varnished. Table settings consisted of crystal plates and glasses and good silver, placed on top of cinnamon colored placemats with blue linen napkins on the side. A hanging pewter lamp with a glass chimney centered each table. The floor was a rust colored brick, brightly polished. The walls held the same décor of kerosene lamps, pewter plates on rails, and oil paintings throughout. Wainscoting came halfway up the wall topped by chair rail and country blue and rust small print wallpaper covered the top half.

Each guest was served their choice of tea or coffee, a half of grapefruit, and a plate holding a bed of lettuce with a thin wedge of ham and cheese quiche. One could have all the water they desired, mountain iron on ice. Yick! Malory thought it was a very tasty meal, yet when she finished, her stomach was still growling.

The atmosphere was wonderful and with Malory's time consumed with new surroundings, company, and diet, she was almost able to dismiss last night's terror. Should she mention it? No, she wouldn't.

"Why isn't Dani here yet?" Jade turned to Paris. "I really hadn't figured she'd be this late or I would have dragged her out of bed myself."

In all of the new excitement, Malory had completely forgotten about Dani.

"Maybe she's sick today. I'm sure she'd have answered your knock otherwise. She'll probably be down any minute," Paris attempted to console Jade.

"Maybe she needed fast food and checked out of this joint for awhile," Nick teased. When he noticed Jade's disapproving eyes, he tried again, "I know she wouldn't go off her diet. Maybe her alarm just didn't work. We'll check on her after."

Dessert was not heard of at breakfast, instead each dieter was given a small doggie bag of healthy midmorning snacks to take with them.

Jade seemed anxious now thinking about Dani. She was much quieter and kept turning about in her seat to check all entrances. The cafeteria had three doorways to the front, one on each side, and three to the back, which was poolside. They sat far away from the pool now, so Malory wasn't able to check that out. She knew she was scheduled for a dip later. She was not able to relieve her mind of Dani either. Why wasn't she here?

"Do you guys go to the gym first?" Malory asked as she glanced at her schedule.

"Oh yes, Malory," Jade answered. "We all have the same schedule so follow us. We're scheduled according to the wing we reside in, which is really kind of nice. That's how we are able to meet everyone. We're together all day long, like it or not."

"There are six separate schedules, equally divided according to Drake. I like ours particularly because we end up with the swim at the end of the day. You were placed in with the best," Paris smiled. He winked and Malory couldn't help but notice how his beautiful brownish eyes seemed to match Jade's. Paris also had brown hair although it was a few shades lighter than Jade's. They could be brother and sister because of the close resemblance. Now that she paid more attention she wondered if they were close... certainly they were attracted to one another. That was obvious.

As they left the booth and headed toward the gym, Paris put his arm around Jade, confirming what Malory had suspected.

"I'll be right down," Nick said. "I'm going to run up quick and check on Dani."

At the end of the main hall was a shaded glass walkway which connected the main building to the gym, spa, and tennis courts. This was most convenient in the mountains where one never knew what the weather would be.

Paris told the girls to stop and wait as he ran out of the door. Malory was surprised and confused, but Jade seemed to know where he was headed.

Both Nick and Paris reentered simultaneously.

"Dani's room is empty," Nick furrowed his brows and for the first time Malory saw that he had a serious side to him.

"Empty?" Jade's husky voice was almost a screech.

"Not only that, but there's no white Mercedes in the lot."

"I can't believe this. She would have told me. I'm sure of that," Jade insisted.

"It does seem strange. She was so happy with this place last night," Malory added. Something kept buzzing in Malory's head, warning her that this situation was not right. She took a few deep deliberate breaths to try and clear her head. What was going on? She felt weak again, like she had earlier. She had hoped to rid herself of this nonsense. Yet the vision of last evening invaded her mind again, as if to tell her something.

"Are you alright?" Nick asked Malory.

"Yeah sure. I'm fine," she lied.

"I'll actually go to Trixie myself, later," Nick informed them, "to check on Dani." It was settled.

The four walked through the tinted glass to the gym and Malory noted that last night's demon weather had subsided. In fact, it was rather sunny and the snow had already melted on the blacktop, although it was still piled plenty high in many spots. She found herself glancing nervously beyond the buildings. At this height she wasn't able to see over the rooftops and that bothered her. Malory scanned the grounds for footprints even though she knew it was foolish. It wasn't even here, but much farther back, beyond the buildings they were now entering that the sight she saw sent fear rippling through her body. Once again she tried to shake the image. But there was something that kept nagging at her and still she could not seem to pull it.

"Looks like my third floor crew isn't exactly ready for a workout. Who's your new member?" the instructor, Paul Winnette, asked. Paul was in charge of both the gym and track area.

Malory was then introduced to this gorgeous muscular blonde. Paul's hair was wavy and he had big green eyes. He reminded her very much of Nick except that Nick had a mustache and still had a flabby belly.

At the spa and sauna, Malory became acquainted with an absolutely gorgeous shapely instructor named Tia. Not only her name was unusual, but Malory couldn't quite figure out her heritage. Her skin had an olive tone and she wore her black hair long and straight. She seemed very soft spoken and caring, perhaps oriental, yet she had the widest blue eyes Malory had ever seen. She moved in long sleek strides and even though she had a great sense of humor, she kept her customers moving in a grinding whirlwind fashion. She also spoke of Drake every few minutes. That set Malory's mind to wondering. They had two classes with Tia. One was aerobics and machines, and the come down of that was the spa and sauna.

After that they had a break period and then they went for a few rounds of tennis. At the inside courts, their instructor was Bart. Malory was beginning to get the picture. All of the instructors were lean, muscular, and trim. She guessed it was purposeful. Bart also fit this mold of lean with wavy hair. She was starting to think she ought to run over to the shop this evening to get curls on her head. It seemed to be the 'in thing'.

"Come on, Malory. You *got* to move," Bart spoke directly to her. His mouth wore a smile, but his tone did not.

"I'm trying," Malory was nearly in tears. Tennis was never an interest to her, and even less of one right now.

"Lay off, Bart. She's new you know," Nick spoke up in Malory's defense.

"Sorry, Malory. You can rest if you need to." Malory resisted a strong urge to argue with the man.

Something in Bart's smirk sparked Malory's Irish and she chose not only to stay in the game, but to win it. That was one instructor Malory felt she might buck heads with.

Finally their relaxing pool session came. This was free and unstructured and they all seemed to enjoy the relaxing atmosphere. The lifeguard on duty was Barry.

"Malory, let me quickly explain the rules. Besides the common safety rules which are posted, we prefer twenty minutes in and ten minutes rest, two times. I'm here at all times if you need me, but basically you're on your own. Do make use of the way your body can benefit from the water exercise as its losing weight," Barry told her.

Malory was taken in by Barry's sexy smile and while she floated along she couldn't help but stare at his perfectly shaped legs that hung out from the chair high above her.

It felt good to be able to relax and reflect the day she had. She met a lot of new people and worked hard. She should be exhausted, but instead she felt revived. This was good because after supper, nutrition classes were still to be held.

Malory seemed to float endlessly, periodically opening her eyes as she floated by life-size tropical palms, intricately designed chaise loungers, and setee type furniture. The color scheme was blue, matching the blue ceramic blocks that surrounded the pool itself. Blue had a calming effect and it seemed to work as Malory actually let herself nod off for a short time.

Unexpectedly, fragments of a far away lost reality trespassed into Malory's dream. It was an unfocused scene through a white mist of snow. She heard voices, and then she saw it again... the dangling body.

"Are you alright?" Nick was alongside of her now.

Malory's face felt flushed and her stomach upset. Was it too much exercise? She was afraid and Nick must have sensed that.

"You screamed. Are you alright?" Nick tried again to break the blank stare that engulfed Malory's face.

"I'm fine." Malory shivered a momentary odd tingling. Then her heart raced at a wild uncountable speed as she lurched forward, away from Nick, trying to grip the pool's edge. She had to get out before she sank to the bottom in fear.

Her appearance exuded color and Nick reached out to grab the chalky white figure again in front of him.

"You'd better sit," he told her as he grabbed hold of her arm, helped her up the ladder and onto the nearest lounger.

"Yes, I'd better."

It was only minutes and Jade took hold of Malory agreeing to see that she made it to her room to rest. Malory knew they were frightened for her. They assumed it was the exercise. She wanted to tell them it was her mind that was weakened and terrorized, not her body, but when she tried to talk her tongue was too heavy and her lips felt pinched.

Jade led Malory to her room and got her half-sitting, half-laying on her sofa.

"I'll be just down the hall. If you don't' perk up soon, I'm calling Dr. Melrose. Why don't you leave the door open so I can hear if you call me. Malory... Malory?"

"Sure, Jade. Thanks."

But when Jade left, Malory used every ounce of power to oust herself off the couch to lock the door. She had to… she was petrified. What was going on in this place? Didn't anyone but herself know about it?

Malory was confused as she plunked herself back down onto the cottony cushions. She wrinkled her pert little nose trying to envision what it was that was harping away at her insides… something she had to remember. She contemplated with many unsuccessful attempts to recreate the scene. All day she'd pushed it aside and now she dared it to billow forward.

Still drenched in her pool attire, Malory lost all knowledge of her other senses. Only her ability to see… to remember, seemed to matter. She panted as a mounting sense of desperation encased her every thought and she let the image brush past her in living color.

Then she was interrupted. Was it Jade? Her ears were attentive now as a buck in danger. The knob on her door pivoted back and forth.

"Jade, is that you?"

There was no answer.

"Nick? Paris?" Malory tried any name she could think of as she watched the knob jump in a state of frenzied velocity.

The phone… she could get ahold of Dr. Melrose. But would she get Trixie first? A lot of help that would be! She requisitioned her stubborn fingers to dial. What would she tell them? Someone was after her? That was silly. Or would she tell them that she could now identify who she'd seen? They wouldn't believe her. Perhaps she should talk to Jade instead.

The last vision kept hurdling through her mind intermittently with the booming at her doorway. Both echoed in Malory's eardrum, ready to burst with excruciating pain. First she'd hear the knob... then see the blonde curls dangling... then the knob... then the curls... the curls. It was Dani! Malory had to tell someone that she saw Dani dangling at the feet of some ravaging maniac.

CHAPTER 4

She slumped over trembling. Something was locked in her throat far behind her tonsils. The air was dense and Dani felt short of breath. She could no longer hold back the deluge of slippery tears. Her cheeks puffed up like a packed squirrel as she filled the air with uncontrollable sobs. Her restless mind worried as it replayed bits and pieces of last night's horrible excursion. It might have been fooled if not for the forcible restraints that now burned her wrists like branding irons.

A shudder zig-zagged through her tender frame as she figured out that she was trapped in a terrible nightmare. Dani squirmed into a sitting position as thoughts whirled around her head filled with a mixture of uneasiness and fear. *What crummy place was she in? Why? Who brought her here?* The locomotive inside her came to a screeching halt. *Who cared why? She had to get out!*

Dani winced as she tried to jiggle forward. The hot liquid trickling from her wrists must surely be blood. She was so tired... so unfocused... so much in pain. As she thought of it, the overload of exhaustion forced her eyelids closed.

It was only a matter of minutes and Dani's eyes rolled open again. She sniffed the air well aware of the distinct odor it held... somewhere between shit and death. She was still bothered by her throat, positive an oversized licorice stick had lodged itself vertically from top to bottom of her esophagus.

She kept gulping as her body experienced an intangible stiffness that reached out to every limb. She could not seem to get it in motion just yet.

Dani's mind was not on a logical track yet, but it had to get there soon. She had to free herself, that much she knew. Maybe someone could hear her. She wanted her voice to shriek blood-curdling sounds but all that escaped were raspy spurts of resonance, hardly comparable to minor utterances. She was actually surprised that much came out. Besides being parched, her throat was swollen in fiery grips of pain. Then it came to her... his hands. His hands were tight about her squat neck. They left no room for air. She tried to pull them away she was sure. But he was forceful. She wanted to retch as thoughts of struggling and lack of oxygen came roaring back to her.

She couldn't rely on her voice. She'd have to free her wrists even if she had to pull her hands off and was left with only stumps. She'd have to try. What if she bled to death? Dani's mind fogged with gloomy thoughts as she tugged her tormented wrists away from the sharp metal. Then she relaxed her hands, still not making any gains. It was more than she could bear. Tears streamed her forlorn cheeks as she thought of the resort, Jade, and most of all home. Was someone out looking for her? *Please, dear God, let that be true*, she begged.

Stiffness seemed to be gaining speed, and she kept trying to startle the fatigue away... sort of a surprise attack. If her body wasn't aware of its weariness and aching, perhaps it would keep moving regardless. Maybe if she'd sink back to the muddy earth, she could roll herself free, or at least as far as her chains would allow. Although she couldn't tell, she suspected that wasn't very far at all.

Dani had all she could do to slide herself back down to her elbows, her wrists screeching in disapproval underneath. For what seemed to be hours to Dani, she'd been staring at the rocky décor in front of her full aware that she had to be deep inside a mountainside cave. It was only now that the full gamut of what that actually meant came to a head. Even if she freed herself, she wasn't home free… she had to find her way out of a cave which she knew nothing about. She'd been in the area long enough to know that instead of going out, she could very easily go deeper in. Her mind was racing ahead again and she had to stop it. Getting out? Right now she didn't even know if she could turn over.

Dani rocked back and forth trying to gain enough momentum to make a complete turn to the left. Finally she gave herself a push and off she went. Even at one roll, the chains tugged uncooperatively and Dani felt one more brick wall being placed for her to hurdle. Her body was inflexible it seemed, but she didn't suppose it had to be overly supple to force it to roll again, this time in the other direction. She'd try the chain's allowance one more time. Dani heaved her body over not expecting to come face to face as she did with a cold, rigid, decaying body.

"Oh my God," she didn't recognize her own throaty words.

Dani stared at the vague pair of eyes in front of her as her own bounced all around the area ignoring any and all throbbing neck muscles. She was in a panic as each shallow breath she took, felt like her last. She knew that body… she was sure.

"Where's Jade? I have to tell Jade. Help," she moaned in futile discontent.

Shivering, she jerked away and sobbed in desperation. A radiant flood of warm fatigue filled her marrow. She felt more helpless than ever. Even in its unnatural state, she recognized the distorted face as Jill. She hadn't had classes with Jill but remembered now that Jill was on a second floor wing. When Jill checked out a few weeks ago, Dani remembered some of her friends seemed unaware that Jill had intentions of leaving at that point, but quickly the talk cleared and life resumed at the resort. The uncertain facts jostled the evidence now in front of Dani, and a certain statement by a friend of Jill's echoed now through Dani's left hemisphere… "I know she would have told me if she were leaving." So, Jill hadn't planned on leaving and neither had Dani. Dani was frantic with disbelief.

Beyond Jill, gazing with her aching stretched muscles, Dani could barely make out a few, maybe three, maybe four more bodies. And in an awkward clump in the distance, she suspected a few more. Was she supposed to be dead, too? If she were capable, she'd scream for what little good she realized it would do. Dani's neck and throat pulsated with rapid apprehension. Selectively, each distended vein decided to relax at its own pace. Dani slunk back into a curled frightened fetus. She was unbelievably tired again and soon her thoughts sank into a dreamless mist of oblivion.

*****

Nick was not in favor of the action he had to take. He didn't recommend it for Malory, nor for himself. Addressing Trixie at any time could be life-threatening, but especially after a long tedious day, it was like pure uninterrupted suicide. Yet, he had to do it for Dani's sake. He'd hoped he could slide right by her and check for himself, but there was no sneaking by old eagle-eyes.

"And what can I do for you, Mr. Hardin?" Trixie's curt trite question came with her usual tone of annoyance. She kept right on working as if she'd hoped he'd change his mind and leave.

"I need to know if, and when, Dani Ellison checked out of here?"

"Just what makes you think you have any right to the access of private records and information? Perhaps Mrs. Ellison would not want you to know anything about her. After all-"

Nick tried to remain docile, but with Trixie it became an impossibility. "Look, I've asked a simple question. I want a simple answer. If I wanted any of your frightening philosophy, I'd have asked for it."

Nick half expected Trixie's face to flare red. It did not and her voice remained monotone.

"If you're going to get wise, Mr. Hardin, I'll not answer a thing. I don't need your help, excuse me, interference with my work. Now that we've settled that, good day."

Trixie swiveled her chair away from Nick and continued to type. Nick was brittle, an inch away from snapping with anger. Just then Thedy came in.

"Well, hello, Nicky dear. What's on your mind this afternoon? Would you like some coffee, dear? You know a nice hot calorie-free, caffeine-free, sodium-free drink is what the doctor would order." Thedy never awaited anyone's answer, except perhaps Drake's. She traipsed over to the steaming stainless steel pot and poured Nick a Styrofoam cupful.

"Here you go, Nicky dear," she handed him the cup and began to walk toward the office door.

"Wait, Thedy. I do need something. I need to know when, and if, Dani Ellison left."

"Well, dear, that's really in Trixie's domain, but I do believe we got a note from her early this morning. Isn't that right, Trixie?"

"Yes, maam."

"What do you mean a note? What kind of a note?" Nick wasn't about to give up.

"Trixie, do you have Mrs. Ellison's note?" Thedy questioned.

"I'll look," Trixie purposely avoided Nick's glazed eyes.

Her non-committal attitude was eating away at Nick. It was even worse than usual. Hadn't that woman a heart or any compassion whatsoever? How could he make her know this wasn't a joke?

Nick walked around to greet Trixie eye to eye, "Truce?"

"I *said* I'm looking."

It was no use and he really didn't care. He only wanted to know about Dani.

"Here it is," Trixie announced. Then she began to read, "Dear Dr. Melrose and Thedy, I've enjoyed my stay and am happy with my loss. Perhaps someday I'll return, but right now I feel I'm needed with my family. Thanks for everything. Sincerely, Dani Ellison."

"Geez," Nick was truly perplexed as Trixie handed him the note to examine, "what a snap decision..." his voice trailed off into thought.

"It's okay, Nicky dear. She just got homesick. It happens," Thedy offered.

"I suppose. Thanks."

Both women stared as Nick gently set the note upon Trixie's desk and quietly walked away.

He'd relay the message to Paris and the girls, but he was certain they'd have their doubts as he did. Why wouldn't she have taken a few extra minutes to write Jade a note also? They've been like sisters. Or rather than a note, shouldn't she have stopped to see Jade? Unanswerable questions continued to zoom as Nick worked his way back to his room.

Nick didn't know why he felt so unsure. After all, Dani had every right to make a decision to leave. There was something else about it that bothered him. He guessed it just didn't seem like a tactic Dani would use. She had been so warm, friendly, and motherly that it was out of character for her to depart unannounced, without seeing that everyone was taken care of, without an exchange of addresses, and without directions on what she expected of them. Perhaps that's why he felt lost.

Nick had a good workout earlier and should have been energetic and refreshed, but somehow the old zing had left. He couldn't help but agonize over how he'd break the news to Jade and Malory. He knew Jade was a strong person, surely she'd take it in stride, maybe give Dani a call or whatever. He was more concerned over Malory's weakness. Perhaps she couldn't handle pressure. She seemed almost as upset as Jade, and Malory really didn't know Dani all that well. Nick was distraught without choices. He boldly shuffled along, determined to leave the answer to Jade.

*****

Dani stirred slightly, thudding her face against the murky damp earth below her. Every square inch of her body ached as if she were the football tossed, squeezed, dropped, and trampled on by the L.A. Rams. She had hoped that if she awoke again, things would have changed. The pain was still present and freedom was a word from her past. She supposed she should be thankful she had her mind, yet if she hadn't, she wouldn't be aware of the horrible figures that surrounded her. *What kind of person would do something like this?*

She continued to surmise for a few more minutes. Then her thoughts were derailed by the high-pitched soprano voice she heard getting closer and closer to her.

Dani squeezed her lids shut and listened.

"… in came the doctor, in came the nurse, in came the lady with the alligator purse. Yes indeed, I'm here, girls. It's Uncle Beebee time and it's not worth a dime…" the voice sang until it screeched its highest note.

Dani knew immediately the deep danger she was in if she so much as moved a freckle.

Dani slit one eyelid open. She knew she should recognize the figure, but didn't. And the voice… although shriller than normal… was one she was sure she'd heard before.

He was slouched over the gigantic bag made of thick alligator skin. From the back, she wasn't sure, but he seemed to be blotting his forehead. He cackled and talked away as he swatted at the air and hurled items from his bag at the primitive wall in front of him.

"Yes indeed, it's Uncle Beebee showtime. Where's Liza when I need her?"

Liza? Dani knew Liza. What did Liza have to do with all of this? Dani felt ill.

"It's okay, girls. There's no one here but us. Don't be shy. Yes indeed, no need to be shy. You're amongst friends, don't you know?"

He turned slightly, but Dani still couldn't see his face. There was something odd between his words, but she couldn't quite make out what that was. He wore old blue jeans and a forest green hooded sweatshirt. She continued to lay in tight-lipped silence. He strode toward the pile of human carcasses. He kicked the top one, allowing it to topple resembling a plank of wood.

"Oops! That's what you get for jumping on the bed!" He chortled at the top of his lungs while he swished his right index finger across his left, indicting what a naughty body she was.

"Shame, shame on you. Don't get Uncle Beebee angry now." He turned quick and Dani rapidly flushed her lids together. She had an eerie rumbling in her gut. She hoped she didn't heave all over.

"Ahh--look at the new little missy. Don't be afraid of Uncle Beebee."

God, was he talking to her? She didn't so much as move a strand of hair as she prayed for dear life that he'd keep his distance.

She could feel his presence closer and knew he stood towering over her. Surly he could tell she wasn't dead. Beebee was there several minutes and Dani was sure she would start to cough or sneeze shortly. The mind seemed to force involuntary reflexes onto the body when it shouldn't. The very urgency of it not happening, always seemed to imply that it would. Luckily, Dani was able to hold off and Beebee walked away.

Dani remained still. She was sure it was Beebee who began whining like a dog. She knew her own vocal chords weren't capable of such a noise. She slit her eye open again and saw the man picking up every item he'd flung earlier, and very carefully placed it back into his alligator bag. The sound didn't seem to be from him; it was getting closer. He paid it no mind. The familiar taffy colored canine came strutting in and went directly to Dani. Brisket. How could Brisket help her? The man never turned to greet the dog and Brisket seemed to ignore the man also. But Brisket didn't ignore Dani, sensing she was the only other living body around. He began to lick. Dani cringed as Brisket's long slimy tongue graced her face from top to bottom. God, how she hated licking. Please Brisket, help me, but not this, she pleaded with bated breath.

Brisket continued to whine as he turned and left. If only Brisket would have stayed, Dani might have cleared her mind long enough to think of how he could help her. It was too late.

Now the man, who called himself Beebee, snapped up his huge bag and again began to rant.

"Just remember girls, it's only over when it's over. Uncle Beebee will continue to take fine care of all of you, yes indeedy."

Dani could tell he was facing her and wanted so badly to get a good look at his face, but didn't dare. She knew the voice. It really didn't matter though. The only thing of importance was that she wanted to get out of here alive. Maybe Brisket would return.

"Bye ladies. Hope you enjoyed the Uncle Beebee show… time to go. Out went the doctor, out went the nurse, out went the lady with the alligator purse."

Dani could still hear him far beyond her immediate space. It had been more tiring than she thought trying to figure out who he was and trying to stay alive. She couldn't think or try any longer. Her mind crept deep into a cushioned unconsciousness so it could mend for a short while.

CHAPTER 5

Liza toed the floor nervously as she snipped away at Thedy's wet ringlets. The red hair dropped in clumps while Thedy babbled on as usual.

"We checked in a really nice girl last night. Her name is Malory. Have you seen her yet? Oh, you probably will. *That* one has really long hair. It'll get in her way eventually, I'll just bet you. Liza, you're quiet today. What's wrong, dear?

Liza was not particularly used of having enough of a break in Thedy's conversation to respond. "I guess I'm just angry. No big deal," Liza curled her bottom lip to a pout.

"Oh, oh. Must be boyfriend problems. I can spot them a mile away. Maybe I can help. Drake and I have had our ups and downs like everyone, although mostly I adore the man. Sometimes he's a little bossy, but we usually come to an understanding. Men need to be coddled, babied, and just loved to death."

"Yeah, well sometimes women need that, too!" Liza countered with yanking a bit too hard on Thedy's tender head.

"Ouch!"

"Oh, I'm *so* sorry, Thedy," Liza's eyes teared, "I just can't seem to concentrate today."

"It's okay, dear. But, if I were you, I'd get that man off my mind for now. I'd like my perm to turn out just right."

"Yes, maam."

Liza rolled the last tress and generously squeezed the apple scented solution onto Thedy's head. She wished she could talk to Thedy about Beebee. Actually, she wished she could talk to anyone about him. Her temper flared when she once again thought of waking up alone and freezing in that ugly old cave. Liza was so furious she was glad Beebee was nowhere in sight. She was afraid of making a scene.

"Let me make a suggestion, Liza," Thedy sensed Liza's distress. "Cool down and then go home tonight, and prepare a candlelight dinner along with some fine wine, and everything will work out great. I promise you that."

"I'm sure it will, Thedy," Liza lied.

"Who is this charming young man anyway? Anyone would be lucky to have you, dear."

Liza was thankful for Thedy's thoughtful comments but she knew full well that Beebee was not a candlelight person. The mere thought was preposterous and almost sent Liza into a full roar of laughter. Besides which, she wasn't quite ready to dine with Beebee anywhere after the stunt he pulled last night. She had a half a notion to go yank him right now from his job and give him a good piece of her mind. She knew it wouldn't do any good.

I'll just get you padded here with cotton for the drips and then put you under the dryer for a few minutes. Tell me more about this Malory." Liza really didn't care about any of it, but she was certain that she had to sway Thedy's thoughts away from Beebee.

"Oh, she's a nice young lady. A therapist from the Sacramento area. I'm coming, I'm coming..." Thedy felt a tug upon her sleeve indicating that Liza wanted her to move to a new chair.

The heat intensified on Thedy's crown leaving a wonderful warmth upon it. She had been chilled all morning, but now was content and relaxed watching all the 'ins and outs' of the salon. Drake's idea of having all this pampering available suited her just fine. He believed so in mental health and beauty was only a part of it.

While she enjoyed moments of peace and serenity, Thedy marveled once again at her flare for decorating. What would Drake do without her? The salon was contemporary in tones of mauve and gray. It had a cheery atmosphere and Thedy felt satisfied watching the smiling faces and happy conversation at each station in front of her. It was a busy place, her favorite kind. Liza seemed disturbed today and Thedy hoped her suggestions would help. She especially liked Liza.

Thedy continued to scrutinize as Liza prepared for Thedy's return to her station. Beyond Liza, Thedy spotted a young man staring through the large tinted pane of glass to Liza's left side. It was difficult to see much, but he seemed to be staring at Liza. He looked vaguely familiar to Thedy as she squinted to get a clearer view. Gosh, who was he? Didn't Liza see him? Now he was bobbing his head up and down and from side to side, trying to get her attention. Must be the young man she's in love with. Thedy was sure he worked at the resort, but where? She just couldn't quite place him. She'd have to check with Drake. It wasn't like her to forget a name, but this man she was sure was fairly new.

Liza came to Thedy now. "Yep, you're ready. Come on over," she said with a smile.

Thedy looked again and the man was gone.

"Didn't you see him?" Thedy questioned.

"What are you talking about?"

"That man. I'm sure it was your young man. He kept looking at you through the window. Gosh, it was hard to see through that glass, but I'm sure it was you he was after."

"Oh, look at the curls! Time to neutralize," Liza purposely avoided Thedy again. Beebee wouldn't be that stupid, would he? To come around here?

"Well, if this doesn't beat all," Liza now turned to see Beebee motioning her to come out into the hall. She quickly slapped the neutralizer on Thedy's head, threw her a towel and went out the door in a huff. Thedy watched.

Just looking at Beebee made Liza's insides screech and stomp with outrage. Visions of her waking up frightened and alone in that dark and freezing cave tore through her. And the pitiful moaning she'd heard... was awful. Beebee would never believe that. He'd say she was off on a feminine tangent, but Liza knew better. There was something back further in that cavern. Liza wondered if Beebee had an animal of some kind with him, but she wasn't about to bring that up now.

Liza flew into the hall, "What do you mean leaving me alone? And what are you doing here, now? I'm working on *Thedy* and you don't want anyone to know about us!"

"They might not if you'd calm down. Christ, Liza, act casual."

"Casual? You... you..." Liza began to cry.

Why wasn't Beebee holding her? Instead, he looked annoyed.

"Here, don't be so stupid. Look like I'm giving you money or something. Tell Thedy you've been giving me a lift here or something... as a friend. Stop your whining," he directed. Beebee's voice had a way of cutting right down to the bone.

Liza stood up tall, biting her bottom lip. "Well, what did you want anyway?"

"Meet me there later."

"I will not. I'm through with that dumb cave of yours. Are you alright?"

Beebee kept twitching his nose, staring back at her through his bloodshot eyes.

"Of course I'm alright. Just getting a cold. Hey," he grabbed the upper part of her arm snuggly, "you'd better be there. Say, tenish."

Liza pursed her lips and turned away from the shop's view as Beebee left her standing there.

"Where's Thedy?" Liza was astounded as she picked up the five dollar tip left on her dressing table.

"Said she couldn't wait. She wanted to air dry. I finished her up," Mona told her. "Don't feel bad. She made her next appointment with you. It's alright."

Liza felt faint and scanned her surroundings as they began to zoom around her. She clutched the arm of her chair and sat for a moment.

"Boyfriend troubles?" Mona asked.

"No... no... nothing like that," Liza quipped. "I just feel nauseous."

The next customer came and Liza was quickly back on her feet trying to forget Beebee's demanding ways and the blank stare in his eyes. Why were they always so red lately anyhow? He was so fit and trim physically and yet always seemed on the verge of a cold with all his sniffling. It just didn't make sense.

*****

One snort never lasted long enough for Beebee. He could tell he needed another line... and soon. Satisfied with the orders he'd placed on Liza, Beebee strolled into the men's room. He really wanted a faster high but it was too risky at work. He gave his nose an extra shot of nasal spray to soothe the irritation as he prepared for the next round.

He perched one foot on the blue porcelain below and artfully pinched the small mirror between his thumb and finger, resting it on his knee, as he chopped the powder even finer. He felt restless and needed the burst of energy to get him through the rest of the day. Last evening was long and draining. This, his mainstay, would enable him to carry on. He puffed out a short breath and flared his nostrils as he inserted the tooter for a last-stitch effort at glory. The cool tickle led to a burning that made his eyes water. It didn't matter though. In a few minutes he'd feel renewed.

Beebee's break was almost over. He hoped Liza wouldn't disappoint him this evening. He needed her as well as any money she could be talked out of. Beebee was just about to open his stall when he heard someone enter.

"What could possibly be wrong with her? Our day wasn't that bad, Nick."

Beebee recognized Paris' voice.

"I don't really think it was the exercise at all. Something else is bothering Malory and I intend to find out what that is."

"I guess you're right. Jade said that last night she'd been totally enchanted by this place, and yet this morning she really didn't show that enthusiasm."

"Paris, did you see how white she was in the water? She seemed to be dreaming about something. She was so bothered by Dani's disappearance and I just don't understand that. She really doesn't know Dani. Just the same, I want to help her. This wasn't a very positive start to the program."

"That's for sure. Perhaps this evening she'll be better."

Perhaps this evening she'll be dead, Beebee thought. Their voices trailed off and Beebee knew it was safe to come out. The other girls had gone so well, and now this time with Dani, Beebee found himself cursing out his own stupidity. Maybe he was just lucky before, but the last thing he needed was a witness. Either way, he was stuck contending with this bitch, Malory. Even in his now euphoric state, he hated her. She'd have to pay for being in the wrong place at the wrong time. He couldn't afford to take chances. If anyone started to suspect him, it'd open up a whole can of worms. He had no choice but to go for Malory, perhaps even Jade if he had to. He did not want any run-ins with the law ever again. If they locked him up once more, he'd go crazy for sure. He was accused of being nuts as it was, he didn't want to give them any more cause to believe it.

It always seemed to happen this way. Only a few months at any one place and he'd be in trouble somehow. He didn't understand it. He thought this time he'd conquered it by not renting or living near people. But always… always… always there was some stupid woman. And this time her name was Malory. Worst of all, he didn't even know her. It didn't matter though. There seemed to be a Malory on his tail everywhere he went. Always there'd be someone he'd have to dispose of for peace of mind.

He had to go back to work… they'd miss him. And yet he had to go to Malory. His heart and mind were racing and for a second Malory almost didn't matter. After the initial pump however, reality hit once again and Beebee realized that Malory had earned herself top priority on his list.

Beebee's body felt refreshed and ready to move, but his mind hazed with thoughts of how to handle the mess he'd managed to get into. He knew so well that timing was important. He must have fouled up his timing with Dani, and this was the outcome. So, it was most imperative that he cleared his head of its confusion and create a plan. A plan that allowed him to remain free… a plan that would include the elimination of Malory.

CHAPTER 6

"Malory, open the door," Jade screamed.

Malory boosted herself up and into total consciousness, so relieved to hear the familiar voice.

"Oh, thank God it's you, Jade. Is it only you out there?"

"Of course it's only me. Come on, open up! I've been worried half to death about you. Open up!"

"I'm sorry. Come on in."

"God, at least you have a little color now. Do you feel some better? If not, tell me. I'll call Drake up here. You're still shaking, Malory. What can I do to help?"

"Listen… Jade, just listen, please," Malory's voice breezed its cool demand.

Jade sat back and tried to follow Malory's instructions.

"Listen, it's really important. You've got to help."

"Why are you locking up? I'm sure Paris and Nick…"

Malory's voice climbed to a deplorable squeal of frustration. "Please, Jade, please. I have to talk and I don't want you to think I'm crazy."

"Okay, okay, settle down."

"This morning, no, not this morning… last night. Well, I feel this now, because of last night. It has nothing to do with today's activities. I… I saw something and I really couldn't explain it well until after today."

Jade was totally confused, but said nothing.

"Just stay with me, Jade, I know this is hard to understand, but it's about Dani."

"Dani? What do you know about Dani?" Jade jolted to a stance.

"Now *you* settle down, please."

Jade sat again, regaining shaky control.

"I'm sure, before I fell asleep last night, I saw someone being carried out into the woods. The body looked dead, Jade. And now, I'm positive that body was Dani's."

Malory held out her hand to secure Jade's shoulder.

"Did you hear, Jade? I'm sure it was Dani."

Both girls stared blankly for a second, neither knowing what to say or do.

"Where did you see a body?" Jade asked calmly.

Malory led her to the window and once again attempted an explanation that Jade could accept.

"I know this seems unreal, Jade. I really thought it was just me, but now with Dani missing, I'm scared. I mean really scared. It's not the first time I heard someone at my door. This place has frightened the liver right out of me and I hope you'll help. Jade, do you think I'm nuts? I've never felt like this before. Right now I feel so helpless."

"I honestly don't know what to think. Yet all of this sounds so familiar."

"What do you mean?"

"Just a few weeks ago, there was a girl, Jill. She stayed on the second floor. Her friends insisted that she was missing. I don't know if they ever found out about her or not. I didn't really give it much thought... but Dani... I know Dani wouldn't leave without telling me. I hope you're mistaken, Malory. But, in case you're not, I'm with you. Nick should be coming any minute to let us know what he found out."

Malory sat somewhat contented, with half the burden lifted to another body. She couldn't help but wonder if she should trust anyone at all. Malory was aware of Jade's painful expression. Dani was her good friend. Perhaps she'd been too blunt.

Outside the sky was heavy with blotches of gray and Malory couldn't help but wonder if snow would embrace the twilight one again. The air hung just as weighty between the girls, neither having the inclination to move or to talk.

Following the brief uncomfortable silence, there was a thumping sound outside of Malory's door. Both awaited in stillness, gripping their seats with fear. Malory waited until the noise abated and then carefully opened the door. Jade instinctively placed herself within the phone's touch, ready to dial. In the distance, Malory saw Nick and Paris heading their way and as she went to greet them she tripped over her gym bag which had been tossed directly in the path of her door. By whom? Why didn't that person knock?

"Wait until you girls hear what Nick found out from Trixie The Bear," Paris grinned.

Nick briefly relayed what Dani's note had said.

"We thought you girls would be happy to hear that it was Dani's decision to leave," Nick said sincerely, although he was loaded with doubts of his own.

"Go ahead, Malory. Tell them what you told me," Jade encouraged Malory to speak.

Malory once again gave a detailed account of last night's terrifying experience.

"Well, that's enough for me," Nick concluded. "I say we call the cops."

"Whoa, slow down, Nicky," Paris rubbed his brows intensely.

"I think he's right, Paris," Jade added, "I think we need help out here. I'd go check the woods myself if I thought it would help, but I'm really afraid of what I'd find. Don't you guys remember that Jill girl from the second floor?"

"Let's not go overboard," Paris warned. "If we start with accusations like that, the cops will think we're all nuts. They'd probably think we've been losing brain cells as well as fat cells."

Paris' attempt at humor didn't even bring a chuckle and he guessed he really didn't think it would.

"I'm sorry guys. I'll go along with the consensus. All I'm saying is we should move slow. Let's let them investigate Dani. If we bring too much into it, it'll bomb."

"Who wants to call?"

"I don't really want to," Malory said, "but I am the one they'll question for what I saw. I might as well do the honors."

Malory picked up the receiver and dialed.

*****

Captain Saul Keller had heard of the Melrose Resort for sure. But it was better known to him as the fat farm up in the hills and it was the last place he ever expected to hear from. The girl, Malory, had sounded on the verge of tears, so he guessed it wouldn't hurt any to take a ride up through the bluffs and talk to her. He couldn't help but wonder if it'd cause a bit of a stir to see a man in uniform wandering about.

Saul had heard Dr. Melrose speak at the University several months ago and it was inconceivable to him that this resort could stage a setting for a crime. Yet, in his profession, he knew better than to make idle assumptions. A murder could happen anywhere, anytime, to anyone.

It was already past suppertime and Malory had said she'd be free until seven-thirty when she had to attend a nutrition class. He didn't have much time and thought about calling her back and holding her off til Monday. Wrought with anticipation on what fat farm people all in one spot looked like, Saul decided to spend the next portion of his Saturday shift checking it out.

Musing for the moment at the beauty of the Chatel Pine Bluffs, Saul found himself attaching special importance to the fact that these people were obese. Why? This should make no difference whatsoever to their credibility, and because it filled his mind with a mixture of discontent, Saul was displeased with himself. He had never had a weight problem and was satisfied with his height of six foot one and lean appearance... not skinny by any means, but muscular in a novel sort of way. Saul knew it didn't make him better than anyone else and increasingly became annoyed for even worrying about anyone's body build at all. It would have nothing to do with the case, if there was a case.

Still, Saul had no idea what to expect as he drove along gazing at redwoods tangled in second growths, trenches and several rock formations. He couldn't help but notice all the paths that cut through the pines in zig-zags leading to who knows where. As he drove on, it became more apparent of the possibilities that these woods could hold for unknown and unwanted activity. He felt insidious and stupid. Saul had lived amongst this beauty all of his life and never once, even amid all of the crimes he had seen, thought of nature surroundings as being capable of disguising evil. A shutter ran through him. He knew better. It wasn't nature, but people, that posed a problem. Malory had sounded so sure and so afraid. Saul could relate to some of that fear for the first time as he plodded on through the vast area, seemingly all alone in his effort. He actually wished he'd brought one of the crew along.

It was often that Saul felt he was an intruder. The building stood serene in its effort to house and educate, benefitting human beings with the knowledge of how to help themselves. And quite by accident he was called upon to disturb and interrupt an otherwise calm structure. It bothered him yet it was his job.

Saul walked directly to the front office.

"Could you direct me please to Malory Douglas' room?"

The woman jerked her head up with disbelief at seeing the official man in front of her.

"Sure," Trixie swallowed hard, biting back her tongue, wanting desperately to know why he was here to see Malory. "Just go straight down the hall, up the escalator to level three, and room three-fifty-eight will be right there, sir."

For the moment Trixie lost her defensiveness and it was probably a good thing.

"Thank you, maam," Saul tipped his hat off his brown wavy head and left. Trixie couldn't help but notice the honest look in Saul's deep green eyes and rugged handsome face. It'd been a long time since a man caught her eye in such a way. Trixie felt relieved that he'd gone quickly and couldn't see her blush.

Saul was quickly impressed with the decorative aspects and design of the resort. He found it easy to see how one could come here for the sole purpose of weight loss and obliviously lock the rest of the world outside of its doors.

His visit seemed timed to perfection, for as he was about to knock on Malory's door, a tall beautiful woman was about to exit.

"Oh," Jade was startled as she eyed the officer from head to foot," you must be Captain Keller."

"Yes," he extended his hand, "just call me Saul."

Jade opened the door wide to allow his entrance and promptly introduced Malory.

"I'm so glad you're here, Captain Keller," Malory began.

"Saul."

"Yes, Saul. I'm happy you could make it. I'm so afraid that I'm beside myself. None of us know what to do."

Short of time, Malory hastened to explain all that happened since her arrival. She felt on the verge of hyperventilating and was glad when Saul stopped her.

"I guess, Malory, I'll begin with a look around the resort and surrounding grounds. I really don't think you need to worry about your own safety. Sounds like you have a network of close friends."

"I'll just bet Dani didn't think she had to worry either," Malory snapped.

Immediately Malory felt awful. Here this wonderful man was trying to help and she wanted to get sarcastic with him. What was wrong with her? Her eyes teared and Saul gently put his arm around her.

"I think I understand how you feel, Malory. But, let me reassure you. I will check all of what you have said. Then, get back to you and your friends. I promise."

Saul couldn't speculate as to why, but he felt a special attraction to this therapist from Sacramento. He'd always had an interest in red-headed women. She really was very pretty and right now very insecure. He wanted to help her.

Saul accompanied Malory, Jade, Nick and Paris to the second floor room where their nutrition class was about to begin.

"I'll check back with you sometime tomorrow, Malory, after I have a chance to complete my search around. Remember, if you have any problems, call," Saul winked at her as he slipped a card with his phone number into her hand.

"I will, Saul." Privately, Malory thought she'd like to call him for other reasons also. How could she be thinking of her own selfish attraction like this when perhaps Dani was *dead*? She could hardly even think the word.

Saul was reluctant to tell Malory his already existing thoughts, which were neither comforting nor desirable. One had to know the building existed first of all. Its obscure entrance did not point to an outside perpetrator. Dani was more than likely apprehended while asleep, inside of the building. And with the security system Saul had noted, the place seemed real tight. More than likely he would have to look 'in house' for a suspect... if he found any suspicion of a victim. Also, before he left the office, he had called Dani's home. He spoke to her husband who hadn't seen his wife and didn't expect her home. Malory's worst fear was sufficiently loaded with reality.

*****

Malory wasn't able to concentrate during her first nutrition class. Another new instructor, Neely Orth, had introduced herself and Malory was sure Neely was stocked with useful information about food in relation to the body's use of it, but there seemed to be no way Malory could keep her mind from straying.

Although Neely presented the image of wholesomeness herself with much vivaciousness, enthusiasm, and a trim figure, Malory continued to lapse in and out of the conversation at hand. Malory paid special attention to Paul Wynette, her gym and track instructor. She couldn't think of a reason why he needed to attend and wanted to ask Jade if his presence was usual or not. On top of that, he kept side-glancing Malory's way... she was sure of it. Malory put great effort into ignoring Paul's ricochet eyes, although she remained bothered by them. What *was* his problem? Once she thought Jade was aware of it, too. Malory chose not to ask Jade about Paul at that moment. Instead, she leaned her tired arms with palms extended up onto the table in front of her, making certain to cup her chin before it dropped down to the table out of sheer mental fatigue.

Malory's gaze kept fluctuating from Paul, then to Neely. Finally, she got up and went out of the room to splash her face with water and get a long drawn out breathless drink. She felt thirsty as well as a need to clear the lump that now seemed settled in her throat. If she'd failed to understand her client's anxiety up to this point in her career, she'd have clear sailing for a wide birth of insight to it now. Malory was not at all happy with her profound symptoms.

Why hadn't she thought of it before? As Malory tilted her head to an upward angle, she spotted a pay phone. Certainly by now they could just call Dani. Inside, Malory knew the call wouldn't really help, yet perhaps, just perhaps she was mistaken and if Jade would give the phone a try, maybe they'd find Dani cuddled snug in her bed, safe at home. Possibly it was all a big misunderstanding. Malory was not appeased by the thought, but anything was worth a try.

Jade noted Malory motioning to her and managed to muddle through the crowd. Malory's expression tensed as she watched Paul do a double-take upon Jade's exit.

"What's the matter?" Jade questioned.

"How stupid could we be? Look, we should have tried to call Dani hours ago, instead of worrying about ourselves," Malory pointed to the phone.

"I can't believe I didn't think of this either," Jade responded. "Dani's probably home... or at least Richard could help," Jade sounded a little doubtful.

Jade moved frantically, pulling her cell out of her suede satchel.

"You know," she told Malory, "I had said this earlier and then we were so caught up in everything, then Saul came," Jade rubbed her face as if the worry would fade away. "Everything moved so quickly and to be honest with you, Malory, I'm a little afraid to call."

Soon Jade had the line ringing and tilted the phone for Malory to listen along. At the door, Malory was sure she had seen Paul staring at them. When the answering machine finally let the ring abate, it was Dani's voice they heard on the recording. Malory could feel the bristly hair stand like gooseflesh on her arms. It was a chilling voice, not the Dani she'd met. Jade looked disappointed as she gently pressed the phone off.

"I feel defeated, but perhaps they just went out to dinner."

"You might be right... a reunion dinner," Malory agreed.

"I hope so, Malory. I'm going to try again later. It doesn't seem like Dani to have her girls out this late. I thought maybe we'd even get a hold of a sitter or something. Well, no more speculation."

"Yeah, I thought so, too."

The girls returned to the meeting disheartened.

Later in her room, Malory checked all the locks on the door and windows. She felt foolish but insisted that Nick and Paris accompany her while she also checked closets and under the bed. Malory felt at least seven years old as she went through the ritual. Making sure the phone was in working order, the four of them agreed to call each other if anything came up. When they left, Malory took out sheets to tack up to her windows because she knew the pain they would cause her all evening. She also continued to try Dani's number, only to get the answering service repeatedly.

While Malory laid wide awake in her huge brass bed, thoughts of Saul came floating back to her. He was a looker and she couldn't help but feel secure knowing he'd be there in the morning. He represented hope, and good-looking hope on top of it. She tried to fill her mind with thoughts of the two of them, anything to fill the space so that horrifying thoughts could not prevail. Then she started to wonder if he'd already checked the path behind. What if he had and he was in trouble? What if he never showed up tomorrow? What if... what if... Malory needed to spare herself of the 'what if' game. She knew better than this. Yet, no matter what, she couldn't seem to get tired enough to drift off to sleep. Malory kept fighting off the urge to roll off the bed, onto the floor and gently roll under her bed. Nope, she wouldn't give in to that kind of fear. Dani's voice on the machine kept resounding in her head and at last Malory rolled over and carefully pulled just a slight corner of the sheet back. She had to look at the path. It was etched in her brain and she had to know if it was threatening again tonight. She poked one eyeball up to the glass. Could it be true that she saw someone out there again? She couldn't really distinguish a figure, just a faint flickering of a small light that seemed to maneuver itself deeper and deeper into the distance.

CHAPTER 7

Richard lathered himself from top to bottom hoping to wash away the latent apprehension that was beginning to surface. What had Captain Keller meant about Dani's friends reported that she was not at the resort? There must be some mistake. Keller said not to worry; he was certain that when he'd go out to Melrose everything would work out. Or else he'd let Richard know. *Know what?*

Richard had to attend his sister's anniversary party last evening. After all, it was her first and she'd met her husband, Al, through Richard... his best pal. Besides, Kristin and Heather had stood up in the wedding. If not for that, he'd have headed north last night.

Richard wondered if he should call Drake first but decided against it. It had been hard enough to sit still and quiet last night. Shortly they'd be on their way and he'd find out firsthand what was going on with Dani. He'd just spoken to her Friday evening, so he couldn't imagine what Keller was talking about.

"Dad, can I wear this pair of jeans? Do you think Mom will notice that they're new?" Kristin bounced in front of him, as he walked out of the bathroom wrapped in a blue terry cloth towel.

"They look fine. And yes, Mom will be sure to notice," Richard didn't dare tell the girls about his bothersome call.

"Daddy, can we stop and take Mommy some flowers?" Heather inquired.

"We'll see. We're going to leave right away, so grab your jackets. I'll be ready in a minute."

The girls were anxious to see their mother and Richard had no idea what he'd say to them if this Keller guy was right. What if Dani wasn't there? Where would she be? Richard would feel reassured once he saw Dani. Why hadn't Jade called if Keller were right?

Richard had completely forgotten to check the answering machine. He glanced now at the number in bold print. It read seventeen. He listened quickly as the girls situated themselves in the back of the silver wagon. No messages. Why wouldn't there be any messages? Richard found his stomach pulsating to a tropical drum. Could it be that Dani *was* really in some kind of trouble?

The drive seemed forever and the girls were unusually quiet. They seemed to detect Richard's tightness and responded appropriately. He couldn't deal with any whining or bickering at present. The word *missing* played over and over in Richard's head and he felt a little sheepish for not heading this way a darn sight sooner. What if Dani really needed him?

After a considerable distance, the thoughts that crossed Richard's mind of what he might find when they got there became progressively more distorted. He needed to talk to his children and take a load off.

"How about if we play the road games," Richard tried to put enthusiasm in his voice.

"Okay," Kristin agreed, "let's start with the ABC'S. I see *A* on that sign- Sacramento."

"*B* on the license plate ahead," Heather joined in.

"*C* in juice on that truck," Richard added.

They played for miles and Richard was thankful that the girls were so cooperative. They were good kids.

Finally, they edged the gate that began the long driveway into the resort. The girls cheered and Richard's heart fluttered. As they neared the building, Richard hunted for his wife's white Mercedes. He couldn't see it anywhere and like a crazed mechanical wind-up toy, he veered his car in circles around the lot to reaffirm what he already knew... the car was gone.

Richard did not hesitate to pull the girls through the doorway and confront Trixie. Personally, he saw no use for the woman, but at least she was a little more tolerant of the children.

"Hi Trixie," both girls chimed in unison.

Trixie looked up, half scared out of her wits, "Well, I'm surprised to see you girls here today!"

"Why? It's Sunday. We come almost every Sunday," Kristin told her honestly.

"But, well, it's different now. Isn't it?"

Richard had never seen Trixie in such an unsure state. If it wasn't so serious a matter, he'd have teased her incessantly. She didn't leave much of an opening for that even now. Instantly her expression slammed shut like a hardcovered book.

"I'll get Dr. Melrose."

"Why? We're just checking in. We don't need to see Drake."

"Please, have a seat. I'll be right back."

Trixie shot out from behind her desk in a flash, leaving no chance for Richard to dispute her direction or disappearance.

Just a second and a half later, Thedy breezed through the doorway and Trixie followed in puppy-dog fashion. Trixie emerged in front of Thedy, grabbed a Bic pen and looking downward, jotted something in large scribbly loops onto a five by seven file card. Richard glared at Trixie wondering how she managed to escape any proper form of etiquette through the years. Certainly she should have picked up some manners along the way.

"Richard, how nice to see you and the girls," Thedy's voice was a warming welcome, so opposite Trixie's tight little nod of recognition.

"It's nice of you to greet us, Thedy. But we really just came here on our usual visit to Dani. Trixie seems a little upset. I don't quite understand…"

"You know, Richard, we don't quite understand this either. Trixie, could you please find Drake and the note that Dani left for you? You know, the one Nick was asking about yesterday."

Obediently Trixie poked through a stack of folders and fumbled as she snaked around some untidy bundles of index cards. Satisfied that she had the correct folder, she then picked up the microphone and pressed a button in front of her.

"Dr. Drake Melrose, please come to the front office."

Kristin's eyes widened and Heather sat up tall at the official crisp sound of Trixie's summons.

Trixie flipped to a fresh page and then addressed Richard once more, "If you would please sign here, they'll be happy to go over your wife's file with you."

"I need to know what's happening here. I don't give a shit about my wife's file. Where's Dani?" Richard's ears were six shades of scarlet and his otherwise unruffled personality spit laser beams of force directly piercing from his icy blue eyes.

Thedy continued to smile, "Please, Richard. Perhaps you'd like to come into our office and wait for Drake. I'm sure Trixie will entertain the girls."

Thedy led Richard into the office. He still felt firmly in control of himself but stopped for a minute to pray it would continue. Richard sat somewhat unwilling and dabbed away at his lips with his clammy stubby fingers. Anger did not have top priority here, Richard was suddenly scared to tears.

*****

Tia was always there for Drake. It was never that he wanted to hurt Thedy, in fact he hoped that it never did. Thedy was a wonderful wife but there were times when Drake couldn't suppress his desire for Tia's sleek body and long raven black hair. She was beautiful and gentle. Tia was so experienced in her young ways, it was easy to forget she could very well be his daughter.

Drake gripped his fingers into a fist and gently knuckled her second floor door. Surely she was awaiting his visit.

"Come on in, Babe. Lock the door behind you," Tia called soothingly.

"Hi sweetie, how are you?" Drake's deep voice was not indicative of the mild tremors that ran through his lean body like a pack of startled mice. He probed into Tia's blue eyes and found his urge uncontrollable. Often he became incognizant of his own limits.

He leaned over to kiss her, very aware of her nipples raised in desire beneath her sheer blue camisole. They awaited his touch. He hungered for her, his tongue darting in and out and all around her supple unblemished flesh. He wished he could give Tia the time she deserved. He always felt so rushed, so guilty.

"It seems like forever, Drake. I wish we didn't have to hide like this."

"I know darling, I feel the same way. Please don't make me feel bad about this."

"I'm sorry, Drake. I don't ever want you to feel bad."

He delicately slid the elastic band down each hip, not interrupting his endless kisses.

Tia Jovan understood their relationship fully, only desired it to be more. Tia liked Thedy and often found it difficult to face her. But Tia was a victim of unyielding love. She loved Drake in a way that she'd never loved another man. He was so sure of himself, so secure and intelligent. She couldn't resist.

Drake slowly inched his way into her private domain until slowly and heatedly they became one. He was extremely annoyed that in the midst of his enjoyment, he had to hear Trixie's shrill call. It was almost enough to make him lose his erection. Thank God he was able to ignore it and continue with his business.

A few minutes later a more demanding Trixie called again.

"Damn, there she goes again. There must be some kind of trouble." This time he couldn't ignore it.

In a frenzied state of embarrassment, Drake withdrew and began to fumble for his clothing.

"It's alright, Babe. Later." Tia massaged his shoulders and kissed his back as Drake mechanically began to pull his pants up and grab for his shirt. Why now? It damn well better be important. He was irritated to say the least.

"I'm really sorry, Tia," he kissed her forehead and turned to leave.

*****

Drake scrambled into the office, beat red in the face and still straightening his tie.

"What's the matter, Trixie?"

"Oh, Thedy would like to see you. She's in your office with Mr. Ellison."

"Well, call Dani down. Why does Ellison want me?" Drake snapped abruptly in an uncharacteristic tone.

Wasn't Drake even aware of Dani's disappearance? Trixie wanted desperately to listen to the next room's conversation but could not manage to distract Kristin and Heather and inconspicuously listen in. It just wouldn't work.

"Oh, Drake, you remember Richard Ellison don't you?" Thedy noticed but said nothing of Drake's rustled and flushed appearance.

"Yes, good to see you again Richard," Drake's voice glided into a strained welcome.

"Good morning, Drake."

"I meant to show you this yesterday, and well things got so busy around here. Not only that but sometimes you're a hard man to find," Thedy lovingly handed Drake Dani's file. An overwhelming sense of guilt made him wonder if the last statement was for his immediate benefit.

"Dani left?" Drake's brows rose as he spoke.

"Look, I'm really confused here," Richard piped in. "Does anyone know where Dani is?"

"Generally speaking," Drake took over the conversation, "we're all very aware of who comes and goes. That's because our guests use the conventional method. They register with us and they let us know when they plan to be through with our program. You know that, Richard. Dani was pledged here for another month and for some odd reason she must have gotten homesick. She left this note and then left herself. Isn't that correct, Thedy?"

"Yes, dear. As I said, it all happened so quickly. Evidently Dani left this note on Trixie's desk Friday night and took off. Her car's gone. And this is Dani's writing isn't it, Richard?"

Richard examined the note more closely. The signature was definitely Dani's.

"Yes, it appears to be her writing... but... well I spoke to her on Friday evening and she said nothing about leaving. In fact she was all fired up about the next month. It just doesn't make sense to me."

Richard felt defeated. He gently laid the note back on top of Drake's desk and sank into a nearby chair.

"I can't imagine then why she wouldn't be home," Richard added.

"I feel really bad about this, Richard," Drake's sour words vibrated Richard's now throbbing head. "I just don't see how we could have stopped Dani anyway. She is a free-willed and quite spirited adult. However, if there's anything we could do to help, we'd be more than happy to."

"Yes," Richard responded immediately. "I'd like to see Dani's room, talk to Jade and also have that Captain Keller come back out here."

"Who's Captain Keller?" Drake's voice rose to a shrill note.

"Calm down, Drake. Captain Keller's that nice young man who was here last evening. He came to see the new girl, Malory."

"Was I on vacation or what? If I wasn't aware of my own two feet standing on this carpet, I'd swear that I had died and left you and Trixie in charge. Was Captain Keller's a social visit, or do I get to guess what he was here for?"

Thedy was horrified at her husband's sarcastic pitch. Obviously he was not happy. Why hadn't she gotten around to telling him these things sooner? Christ, it just didn't seem like that big of a deal.

"Honey," Thedy gently put her hand to her husband's shoulder, "let's let Richard go and see Dani's room and you and I can then go over all the details."

Thedy gestured impatiently for Richard to go ahead and leave the room, anxious to tell him all she knew and to get to the bottom of his distress. Surely he couldn't be this worked up because he wasn't shown a note. It didn't add up and Thedy was worried about him.

Richard left unhappily and Thedy apologized in tearful pleas. Drake was torn between anger and guilt, each tugging at one end of his torso like a taffy pull.

"I'm sorry, Thedy. It was awfully embarrassing being confronted by a man whose wife we're sort of in charge of, and I wasn't even aware of her disappearance. Even *that* wasn't so bad, but Captain Keller?" Drake grew red again and balanced his head in the palm of both hands as he agonized over what he should do.

Thedy sat in maddening silence as she awaited her husband's decision.

"Well, I guess one thing for sure, we should call Captain Keller back. At least we'll look interested in our customers."

Thedy was afraid to tell Drake, but she had to.

"We don't need to do that, dear."

"What?" Drake was near the explosion point.

"He's on his way."

CHAPTER 8

Beebe stood watching the clatter and commotion in and out of the office. He was glad there were no classes today. It gave him this glorious opportunity. Trixie was so naïve. She actually kept telling Dani's children that there wasn't a problem and their mom was fine. She was no great shakes with words, but those definitely set off the trigger of his funny bone. Yes indeedy, if he didn't know better, Trixie could be an awfully disturbing person with her stupid words of wisdom.

The effects of his White Lady were beginning to wear thin. After hearing talk about that cop, Beebee knew he'd have to smoke a little crack, get feeling good and then get out to the cave… carpe diem, make use of the day. He'd have to make a few changes for smart ass Keller. Yes indeedy, he'd have to throw a few stumbling blocks into the path of Mr. Smart Guy.

Beebee slid through the cafeteria and helped himself to a few snacks for later. He stuffed his pockets full of raisins, dried apricots and a bag of bran flakes. He had no time to waste because he told Liza he'd pick her up at elevenish for brunch. He really didn't feel much like a huge meal, but after reconsidering Friday evening, he figured he owed her one for the way he left her out in the cave. At least he planned to cooperate with her… she was his only ally at present… the only one he could count on. Besides, it wouldn't hurt him to take her out just once, he guessed.

Right now his head zoomed with plans. How could he take care of moving the bodies further back and create a blockade of sorts, some simple type of deterrent to stall Keller off? He wanted the cave to appear natural in a sense. Maybe Keller would not even see it... or see any reason to come back to it.

Beebe trudged through knee high brush still moist with winter residue. The snow had mostly melted but the ground was thick and muddy. He ebbed toward the entrance feeling somewhat satisfied that it was partially hidden. He figured Keller might spot it, but no Californian in their right mind would enter a cave that they knew nothing about. That was one point in his favor.

After he uttered a single growl of contempt, Beebee separated mounds of thicket and brushed away any loose surface soil. He made a careful entrance into the cavern chanting and singing as he wiped his soggy hands on his tattered pair of jeans.

Beebee was feeling good. Not Liza, Keller nor Dani's family were going to put a dent into his high. The heck with all of them. He shuffled past the heap of bodies which he'd already decided to bury. He'd only keep the latest two, Jill and Dani, for his pleasure.

Easier than excavating an opening large enough to dump the bodies, Beebee recalled a stretch of the cave a little farther south that declined with a deep trench just a few feet from an underground stream. He headed that way carrying one body at a time.

At times like this Beebee marveled at his own strength. It was a good thing he had learned control. His body was in shape and capable, which was very important to him. He laid them in a long row, shoveling some side dirt and clay over them. He could always add more later. Next, he unleashed

Jill's stiff, partially decomposed remains and dragged her to the new location. Just the anticipation of feeling lifeless cold flesh sent a warm current through Beebee.

Beebee darn near blew a gasket when he unchained Dani's body. Definitely a live body. The circuits of his wired body scattered like a short wave terminal at the very thought that this could happen to him. What would he do? The very idea seemed to fill his throat with titters and bubbles, but the reality of it terrified him right down to the chilly bones. Now what? Beebee was truly baffled. She was unconscious while he gripped her underarms and dragged her all the butt-bumping way below. He fumbled with the heavy chains and cuffs he was now forced to tote along.

By the time he neared the stream, Beebee was comfortable with Dani's predicament. If she wanted to suffer, that was her business. She'd have never found herself in this situation if she'd have died like he planned. He'd just leave her bleed and rot; it made no never mind to him. Perhaps a return conversation from his little menagerie wouldn't be so awful either. Besides, if she became too much trouble, he had a few ideas as to how to make sure she popped off next time.

In the meantime, Beebee could take no chances of Dani emerging from her state and honking off her big mouth. He had no choice. In came the doctor, in came the nurse, in came the lady with the alligator purse. Beebee pulled out a needle just right for injecting a young woman. He'd have to do a little speedballing on her and if she overdosed, so be it. He knew where Thedy kept her valium and he'd prefer that effect, but this would have to do until he could get ahold of Thedy's medication. Anything to keep her quiet.

Satisfied with his actions and decision about Dani, Beebee decided to fold up shop for now. He'd check back later. In the small entrance right before his new premises, he pushed several good sized rocks. They'd be easy enough to move, but why would anyone do it without reason?

*****

Beebee drove into Liza's driveway honking the 2010 white Mercedes.

Liza couldn't believe her eyes! What the heck? She had demanded to be treated better, but this was way beyond what she figured Beebee was capable of. She knew he said he owned an old blue Honda that sat in the resort's parking lot. She'd never seen him drive it. But a Mercedes?

Liza didn't plan on spending time worrying about it. It was off to brunch and she was elated... Beebee was finally taking her out. She couldn't help but wonder what other surprises he had in store for her... flowers maybe?

He honked again and she grabbed her new mint green spring jacket. She was the picture of perfection as usual for Beebee. She had not forgotten her anger, but decided to put it aside. At least he was trying now and he didn't seem to be carrying a grudge over her not showing up at the cave last evening. Liza still felt threatened by that place and even its thought brought about some odd sensations.

"Wow! This is something. I just can't believe it," Liza leaned over to kiss Beebee as she slid across the front seat to snuggle close to him.

"Hi, Babe," he returned the kiss. "So, what do you think? I'm really cruising in this machine. It's a trial. I'm not sure if I like it enough to buy it."

"Who's car is it?"

"A friend's. He has no use for such a big car anymore. Hogs up too much gas, he tells me. Oh, listen to this."

Beebee shot the CD up loud and wrapped his right arm around Liza's shoulders so they could huddle close. It was as though they never had a disagreement at all.

"It was nice of you, Beebee, to go to all this bother just for me. You don't know how happy it makes me to go out to someplace nice instead of that icky old cave."

Beebee kept his eyes on an even keel at the road ahead.

"It's no bother at all, Babe. The car just sort of came my way and anyone would be happy to take out such a beautiful young lady like yourself."

Liza couldn't help but notice how charming Beebee could be when he wanted to.

"Your friend must have little girls, hey?"

"What do you mean?" Beebee swallowed hard. He felt his face flush and quickly put the window down an inch or two. He needed air.

"Well, look at the dolls and doll clothes back there," Liza turned and pointed. She read the side of one doll case and it said *Heather*. Some vague tinge of recognition rippled through Liza like a vibration, but left her just as quickly.

"Don't worry about it," Beebee told her.

The weather was decent at least more so than Friday evening had been. The sky was actually blue and the breeze mild, not like the harsh chilling biting wind of dead winter. There seemed to be inconsistent hope for spring after all.

All of the ingredients of the day started out good to Liza and now suddenly Beebee seemed annoyed with her. She leaned closer to kiss his cheek and made up her mind to ride in silence for a while. She knew better than to ask him any more questions. He never did like to answer them.

The meal was great once Liza turned the conversation away from that blessed car. Beebee was more at ease. As they sat cozily in the booth, Liza's eyes would sway to the parked vehicle. Where had she seen that car before? It became increasingly hard to pay attention to Beebee's words.

"What about later?" He sounded irritated with her.

"I'm sorry. What did you say?"

"I *said*, I've been lonely. I need you. What about later?"

"Well, now that you have this fancy car, why don't you come back to my place around seven or so?"

"I don't have this car!" Beebee barked the words. "Besides, I want you to come out by me later. I won't leave you there again, honest."

"Please, Beebee, don't ask me to come to the cave. I don't think I can. As much as I want to see you, I don't think I can do it. All I keep thinking of is hearing that awful moaning and groaning. It was sick, like someone dying or in pain."

Dani! Maybe he had made the wrong decision. Why didn't he just strangle her again? He knew women were nothing but trouble. Later… he'd think about her later. He could rectify it easily.

"It was probably an old owl or something," he quickly reassured her.

"I don't know what it was, but I couldn't take hearing it again. I don't think I could handle the cave, Beebee. Please."

"Stop your whining and sniveling. You know I hate that in a woman."

"I'm sorry."

Liza sat up tall and perky as the waitress brought the main entrée. She started out ravishing, but as the thoughts of the cave, the moans and the car nagged at her, Liza's appetite diminished. She had to eat or Beebee would throw a tantrum for sure. All her preaching about taking a lady out would go to waste if the lady didn't try to enjoy. Liza wondered how Beebee would react if they ran into someone from work.

Beebee noticed Liza's distress.

"Not hungry?"

"Oh sure," she lied, "I'm just waiting a minute or two for the appetizers to settle. I should know better than to eat all of that first." Liza smiled what she hoped didn't appear to be a phony attempt.

They continue to eat, each lost in thought and periodically popping back into the real world to make a stab at small talk. Liza couldn't feel as good as she expected. Beebee was totally out of character here and something was wrong... dead wrong. A hazy memory tried to surface each time she'd glance in the car's direction. Why couldn't she quit being a ninny? She forced him here and now she was spoiling it for him. Liza simply couldn't manage to get these thoughts out of her head and it was ludicrous to sit here and try.

Beebee muttered something to the waitress about a doggie bag and she was glad they could finally leave.

The ride home was quiet though Liza cuddled right next to Beebee wondering where his thoughts led to. She decided to give in to him once again.

"OK. I'll meet you there. Isn't seven kind of early?"

"Yeah, make it eight or so, it's dark by then."

"I'm really glad we did this, Beebee."

"Yeah."

Liza was sure Beebee would be in better spirits later. She would have to force herself though to do the same, because somehow she couldn't shake the ominous feeling that she acquired about that place. Why did she feel so suspicious? Certainly there was no reason for this new unpredictable wave of discontent. She loved Beebee and wanted nothing to interfere.

Beebee was uncomfortable with Liza's silence. Yes indeedy, he was sure of one thing… he won. She agreed once again to meet for a little escapade. So, all was well again… Liza would be there.

*****

Beebee knew he should have known better. A car can bring just as much trouble as a woman. They are similar in so many ways; both expensive, both demanding attention, and both get to the point where you just can't use them anymore. Dani's car had to go. He was actually taking a chance as it was being seen with it, so enough was enough.

Beebee's heart was beating fast as he drove the car off of the main highway and through the thicket of trees just bordering the land which the resort filled. He edged the car slightly to the curve. Below, thousands of feet, Beebee could barely see the pine tops. He exited the car, leaving it in the neutral position. He stood gallantly behind the auto ready to heave-ho. The car seemed heavy, but Beebee was determined. With a third big shove the car was in motion and Beebee lost his balance along with it. He clung to the slippery stray bunches of weeds for dear life as he watched the car plummet to the bottom of the earth, swallowed whole by thousands of green swaying needles that seemed to suck it quickly out of sight. Beebee continued to hang tight, watching for a puff of smoke, explosion or fire. But he saw nothing. It was as if Dani's car never existed. Yes indeedy, it was long gone.

Beebee struggled and pulled at the browned grasses below him, fearing a slide to the lowest depths himself. He'd forgotten how gushy and uncertain the mud below his feet could be. Clumsily, he pulled himself to safety and was able to attain a sense of security even though he was still trembling.

Beebee took one last look at the vastness below him making sure it didn't heave the white object back into sight. On a childhood whim he let out a beller, just to see if the air would echo it back to him. It was an eerie billowing sound that reverberated.

The air was weighted now and the haze settled low to create a sluggish film over the stretch of land he now had to walk. The white pillows above had escaped and the sky was no longer blue. It now hung in steel gray sheets that threatened to lose Beebee and every other living soul. Beebee's steps were slow in an attempt to regain his composure, but hastened when he realized all the drudgery he had left to finish. He felt undone as a newly sketched canvas, waiting for details to complete him.

Slow motion turned to an escalating pace as a new surge of excitement renewed Beebee's soul. He knew now how to end this uncertainty with Dani. He knew what he had to do, and with Keller on his tail, he had little time to waste. Beebee jumped in delight and ran with wild hysteria full speed ahead directly toward his beloved Melrose Resort.

CHAPTER 9

Saul Keller had slept restlessly as thoughts of Melrose Resort, Malory and a missing woman, Dani, tossed over and over in his mind all night long. Certainly Malory's fear seemed real, so she must have seen something. He had a special liking for that girl and hoped it wouldn't impede his normally objective viewpoint. Her story did seem rather far-fetched though, and still Dani Ellison had to be somewhere... but where?

He was somewhat bothered by Malory's ability to see so well on such a wintry night. Yet, she didn't say she saw it perfectly, rather she spoke of mist and snow and of having difficulty seeing. Regardless, he'd take his walk around like he promised. He really wanted to speak to Richard again, so he would check that with Dr. Melrose after his tour.

He began in the west parking lot, scanning each vehicle and taking particular notice where Jade had told him Dani's reserved spot had been. He saw no unusual, or for that fact usual, objects in the near vicinity... the blacktop was merely damp now, so no prints of any kind were apparent. A pretty dry run.

Saul followed the lot out back along the tennis court and beyond it. He was not in uniform today, but was glad he'd chose walking boots and jeans for his attire. The weeds and brush were moist and high, some almost up to his hips. He wasn't too squeamish but surely hoped he could avoid various critters and snakes so common of the area. He saw several paths and tried to choose one running in the direction Malory had pointed out. She had offered to come along but he nixed that idea.

The sky above was baby blue though the forecast did not indicate that it would remain that way for long. The incoming front was expected to be one of sleet or perhaps rain. The path he chose continued southeast and he could see several others where the brush was also trampled down. Saul gazed at the pines that filled his nostrils with a wet holiday scent. The odor leaned to the musty side because of the dampness. The deeper he went, the heavier the air.

Saul was just about ready to turn back or at least jut to the outskirts when his eyes fell on an opening partially hidden by rocks and excess timber. His stomach sank when he realized it was probably the mouth of a cave. It seemed vital that he check it out, although his boyhood phobia tried to take precedence. Well, maybe he could manage to walk next to it, make sure he was correct, and then high-tail it out of there. He kept heading toward the entrance, stepping over roots and fallen limbs along the way. His lips suddenly felt loose and shaky as he pulled some brush away and saw the first glimpse of an almost hidden cavern. Could it be? His face twisted in a bizarre mask of horror when the rank odor hit him like a whip across the snout. Momentarily he froze as reels of ten vintage Boris Karloff films ran past his mind in the fast forward mode. And he was sure a bat swooped down overhead… he was only missing the vampire and didn't plan to turn around to see that.

His imagination was unrelenting, holding him in an unkind sense of doom. He was certain that he could hear a mournful voice echoing pitifully deep inside. Saul's hands shook violently and he began to run, slipping and sliding in the late winter run-off below him.

Once about thirty feet from the entrance, Saul stared back almost amusingly perplexed. He felt foolish. How could he allow his own stupid aversion to interfere with his job? He looked again at the damn opening and became angry with himself. There was nothing there to fear. What was wrong with him? Surely it was just a dumb old cave, of which there were most likely hundreds around that one could explore within the entire Sierra Range.

He could hardly report to Malory that he was so frightened he froze and heard voices. How manly would that sound? Saul continued to scold himself all the way back. He felt much better once he had two feet on the solid blacktop nonetheless. If he felt a need to go out there again, by God he'd create an excuse to take help. He didn't see anything strange, so perhaps the eerie path wouldn't have to be dealt with again.

Saul knew he'd fare quite better inside of the building, so that's where he headed, still trembling but not visibly so.

*****

Richard sat back in the main office, shaken by the fact that every stitch of Dani's clothing and personal belongings were gone.

"Oh good. Captain Keller, can you come here please?" Trixie called to Saul.

Richard jumped right out of his seat.

"So, you're Captain Keller? Just the person I've been asking for. I'm Richard Ellison," Richard extended his right hand out to grasp Saul's in a shake.

Saul noticed Richard's teary eyes through his unshakable exterior.

"I'm glad we could meet face-to-face, Richard. Let's sit and talk."

Saul turned now and spoke to Trixie, "Is there a place where we could speak to each other privately?"

Trixie knew he meant without the girls and so she responded, "Sure, use Drake's office."

Trixie directed the two men.

Saul checked his watch, noting it was almost noon.

"I'm assuming by seeing you here alone that you haven't heard from your wife yet?" Saul began.

"No, of course not. That's why I've been insisting on talking to you. What can be done? This is ridiculous! I can't believe..."

"Whoa, slow down. I have a few questions I need to ask. Some information here to gather and then we'll see where we sit on the subject."

"Sit? What are you talking about? My wife's disappeared."

"Please, I know you're upset, but if you cooperate, this will go much smoother."

"Go ahead. Ask anything. All I want is Dani back."

"I know that, Richard," Saul said sincerely. "That's what I want, too."

Saul began by seeking statistics on Dani first and Richard answered to the best of his ability.

"Now, when were you first aware that Dani was not here?"

"I told you, when you phoned."

Richard could see that Saul meant well but was irritated to have to repeat things. Especially to such a young man. Was Saul really capable?

"Just bear with me, Richard. When you got here today, please tell me exactly who you saw and what was said to you."

Richard recounted the morning's unfruitful events rather excitedly.

"And then," Richard continued, "they showed me the note Dani left."

"Dani left a note? Do you have it?"

"No, but it's in her file. God willing, Trixie will get it for you."

Trixie curtly brought the note in handing it to Saul, ignoring Richard completely. At least she respected the law. Frankly, Richard hadn't expected that much from her.

"Is this Dani's writing?"

"Yes, I believe it is, but…"

Saul interrupted, "Do you suppose Dani would have gone anywhere else?"

"What are you insinuating?" Richard was white with anger.

"I'm not insinuating anything. Please, what about other family, girlfriends, or perhaps male friends?"

"I knew it! *No*, I don't suppose she'd go anywhere else. Look, Keller, Dani's in trouble and you better find out about it."

"Richard, you really need to settle down here in order to be of any help. I have to ask these questions, and for Dani's sake you need to answer them."

"Ask Jade about Dani."

"I have."

Richard felt boxed. "I'm sorry. Check with family and friends. I wish you would. I don't believe she had other male friends, but check on that, too. Anything to get my wife back."

Richard took a deep breath and sighed a tired fatigued gasp of air. He couldn't believe this was happening. He didn't know which way to turn.

"Have you told your girls, Richard?"

"Our girls. No."

"I think you should at least let them know that their mom has left here and we're looking for her."

"She hasn't left. Someone took her. I can't afford to lie to the girls."

"You can't afford not to tell them, or it will be a lie."

Richard was overwhelmed with grief as well as fear and he, too, could see no other alternative. The girls had to be told that Dani was missing and it was one job he dreaded.

"Before I go and hurt my children, tell me what you will be doing to find Dani."

"Well, I've already conducted a search of the grounds and found nothing. Next, I'll put an APB on Dani's car which should help considerably. Then I'll check friends and relatives. If none of those things help and we don't have a clue, I'll start to interview people within this resort. From there on, I really can't predict. There are so many avenues to explore and so many possible answers."

"I don't see all of those options because I *know* Dani. She wouldn't just leave."

"That's why I'm the cop, Richard. I'm able to be more objective. I have to. I'm sorry that you feel so badly, but I think you're assuming the worst. Don't torture yourself like that."

"I'm not leaving here without Dani."

"The best thing for you and your girls is to maintain your normal routine and leave the detective work to me. Don't you have a job and the girls school?"

Richard was extremely agitated now.

"Perhaps you don't understand, Keller. Of course I have my normal routine of work. But, Dani's my life. I couldn't leave here knowing she could be in trouble and I didn't even help."

"She left a note. You have no reason to believe she's in trouble. Obviously she's not here, but that doesn't necessarily mean trouble."

"Yes, it does. It may be Dani's writing, but it's not Dani's note. And that frightens me even more."

*****

Saul had an uneasy feeling after speaking with Richard. Richard was a determined man and definitely worried. He tried to play the suppose game and nothing seemed to work in his favor. Suppose Dani left and was too tired to drive, so she checked into a motel. She still should have been home by Saturday noon. Suppose Richard didn't listen well when they spoke and Dani told Richard other plans. Still, Jade or someone else would have also known of Dani's other plans. And besides her note said differently. Scratch that. Suppose her car broke down. There weren't many stations between here and Sacramento. Somewhere a state patrol would have called that problem in. Suppose Dani wasn't happy at home. It didn't add up with what character witnesses described.

Forget it. Saul decided to step out the front door for some fresh air before he'd tackle another rough conversation. He sincerely felt bad, and people never seemed to believe that cops have feelings.

The air hung low which defeated Saul's purpose of stepping outside. The blue sky had turned to an unnecessary gray and haziness surrounded the parking lot in suffocating clumps. Saul noticed someone running toward the side door of the resort, a young man. Probably out to get his exercise. He supposed weather would not stop a determined dieter.

Saul was anxious now to see Malory. His job for today was pretty well completed, although he still would like to make some phone calls later. He looked forward to seeing this redhead again and hoped that she was less distressed today. He'd like to be able to reassure her, but he didn't think that what he had to say would be very consoling. Instead he'd try to pick their brains and see if Malory or her friends could give him any clues as to people he may need to contact for Dani's whereabouts.

As he drew closer to her door his anticipation grew. He tried to divert his attention and remind himself of his purpose for being here. Still when she opened the door, he smiled soft and genuine.

"Hi, Saul. C'mon in."

Malory seemed less tense. She wore her hair long and natural and donned a pair of mint green sweats and a matching sweater.

"Did you sleep better last night?" Saul began.

"Actually, no. But I'm getting used of that. It's one new bad habit to add to my old ones. Here, sit down, please."

"How about your other friends? Have you seen them today?"

"Oh yes, they're waiting for you, just like me. Did you find anything out there, Saul?"

Malory jumped the gun, she knew, but she couldn't wait any longer.

"Malory, these things usually take longer than one look around."

Her heart sank because she knew what that meant.

"How long do they take, Saul?"

"I'm sorry, I don't know. I'd like it if your friends could help with the names of people, friends or relatives, that perhaps Dani had spoken of. I need a list, somewhere to start."

"So, there was nothing out there," Malory's voice sounded far away. She got up slowly and edged toward the window. "Oh, maybe because it's so foggy."

"The fog just came up. But, I'll check again, Malory, soon."

Malory was grateful for Saul's assistance and didn't want to be pushy. He was warm and friendly and had his job to do.

"Well, I'll call Jade here for you."

While they waited Saul turned the conversation.

"So, you're a therapist. Did you take a vacation from your job to come up here?"

"Yes, actually it was a leave of absence. I just felt it was time to conquer my problem. I listen daily to everyone else's and I really love my work. But I needed time for myself."

Malory wasn't sure if this was standard questioning procedure or if Saul was trying to get to know her.

"I go to school two nights a week, Saul offered. "And most of the time I work second shift. You happened to catch me on a weekend favor to one of the guys."

How lucky could I get, Malory thought. Saul's skin looked flawless and firm. She guessed him to be over six foot tall. Malory couldn't keep her eyes from staring at his wavy medium brown hair. It laid full on his crown and sides in a salon perfect fashion. She couldn't help but wonder if the waves were natural or not but didn't dare ask. She wanted to tell him he fit right in with curls out at this place, but decided not to offer her opinion either way. He had impressive eyes with lashes that Malory would kill to have. Had she stared a little too long? Her cheeks flushed.

Soon Jade, Paris and Nick strolled in. Saul relayed his futile findings to them. Jade was able to list a few relatives, the same ones Richard had already volunteered, and other than the three sitting in front of Saul, she knew of no other friends, male or female.

They left, promising to return for Malory later to go to the cafeteria with them.

"I'm sorry if we didn't help much, Saul."

"I have a few names to check and then I believe I'll put an APB on her car."

"I think that's a great idea. Please keep in touch, Saul. I'm really feeling insecure here. I know you're doing all you can, but I can't get the scene or noises out of my mind."

"I'll call and come out. Don't worry, Malory. Oh, by the way, would you be interested in going out some evening that I don't have to work?"

He immediately hoped that he hadn't come on too soon, too strong.

"I'd like that, Saul. But maybe we should get this thing with Dani settled first."

"As quickly as possible," he grinned.

Saul left feeling good about Malory and the hours he'd spent here. He couldn't release the eerie feeling about the cave, but was certain it was his own silly fear. And then there was Dani… he had to find Dani… for Richard and the girls… for Malory and her friends… for his own satisfaction… but most of all for Dani. She really should have shown up somewhere by now. Since she hadn't he also feared for her life.

CHAPTER 10

Dani was certain her body was bruised from head to toe, front and back. If Beebee hadn't yanked her arms out of their sockets by dragging her, then they must have twisted out on the drop down to the sullen earth. Either way, they ached and resembled long rolls of misshapen bread dough, rising in puffs of yeast a little at a time. Besides the overall swelling, flushed mountains of skin peaked in several spots. Dani began to feel like a gigantic fermented hive. She wondered how much abuse the body could handle before it expanded beyond all recognition and burst like the Fourth of July fireworks. This time Beebee chained her arms to the front. She almost wished he hadn't. Before she wasn't able to see the bulging purplish joints she thought to be accurate with her wrist placements, screeching for a bit of air. Before she could only feel the pain... now she could see it.

It took every ounce of courage and residue of determination left for Dani to hoist herself from her slumped position to one of a stiff doll jointed only at the shoulders and hips. Anything in between refused to bend and Dani couldn't blame it. She wanted desperately to ease from this semi-alert state to one of total consciousness. She desired complete control over each body part, but somehow her mind wasn't able to convey that message. Dani tried to forgive herself, but it just wasn't her nature to concede. As long as she was still sure of breath, she had to try to leave. Dani was about to attempt another chug of her vocal cords, when her body collapsed once again for a much needed rest.

When Dani came to, her eyes took even longer to clear. She recalled now that Beebee knew she was alive. She vaguely remembered staring up at a face she should recognize. Most of all it was his voice that sent shivers of terror through her. It was a voice void of caring, shrill with enjoyment, but callously lacking any minute resemblance of sanity. Yet it was a voice she recognized. But from where? Dani did not feel together herself. Still she could perceive deep frustration in the turbulent situation she faced.

There was no mistaking that what was left to identify of the decomposed remains next to her belonged to Jill. If nothing else seemed conclusive, Jill's collection of unusual rings and jewelry were a dead giveaway. They were still intact. Although Dani had been certain at first, she tried to talk herself out of that conclusion; to reason with her own judgement so to speak. She now realized there was no reasoning involved. That was Jill, she was Dani, her abductor was insane and that left no rational explanation. She'd better wake up and stop looking for one. One's first response to an incorrect situation is to assess it, to evaluate its being and outcome. For Dani, this process was useless. It would only waste valuable time. Dani's energy would be better spent in gaining strength to mastermind an escape, God willing. The chance of it happening was bleak and Dani knew it. She simply couldn't bite through chains. The only conclusion she seemed capable of was that of retching. The putrid stench had finally permeated every square inch of previously unaffected air and Dani had no choice but to succumb to it.

Dani stared up blindly at the dirt ceiling, allowing her eyeballs to float endlessly. Waves of dizziness and nausea hit with force as she tried to comprehend, for what seemed the thousandth time, her surroundings. Where exactly was she? She knew she'd been moved to still another place filled with hollow darkness. In between the stillness, she could hear trickles of water flow near her. Occasionally she heard flaps of tiny wings. She feared anything that might live in this environment, and yet she had to admit she was living in it. At times even her own life felt questionable. Perhaps one still had thoughts when they were dead. Perhaps she was really dead.

Straight ahead of her, Dani noticed a dim light spilling into the clay cavern. Was that a way out? Or, was it only her senses playing tricks on her? She didn't see any other numb reminders that a world existed outside of her own body.

From behind the remote shadows of light floating in the background, Dani saw a familiar form trot through, Brisket… she'd forgotten about him.

"Come here, boy. Come on."

Even Dani's jaws ached, but she summoned until Brisket sat next to her.

"Hey, boy," Dani reached slowly to pat his head. "It's so nice to see a face I know."

The tears rolled freely upon Dani's cheeks. She had no time to cry. She rubbed her eyes and tried to think. Brisket was her only link to the outside and she needed him now.

"Stay here, boy," Dani continued to pet him while thoughts whirled at an unreasonable speed through her mind. How could he help?

"Oh, Brisket," she wailed, "why can't you just go and tell Jade and the gang that I'm here? Get me help! Do you understand?" Dani sobbed.

Brisket laid his head upon Dani's aching lap. He whined some and Dani found herself consoling the old dog.

"Where's Tom anyway?" she asked Brisket, as if expecting details. "It's okay boy, you don't need to whine."

Dani ran her swollen set of stubby fingers through Brisket's tired coarse fur. She almost screeched in pain when her thumb collided with his leather collar. Then it came to her! His collar. Should she take it off? Would Tom Tinley wonder where it was? She loved little old Tom, but was afraid that a simple missing collar wouldn't spark any sense of urgency in him. Could she write on it? With what? Dani's face tightened with frustration. She just had to think of something quick before Brisket became bored and her only hope trotted away from her. Then she remembered, she had a pad of paper in her pocket… if it was still there. Of all the pants to be wearing! She still had on her faded old blue jeans. She'd been so proud of the fact that she could finally squeeze back into them. Now that squeezing haunted her. She leaned back as far as she could, so as not to disturb Brisket. She was about to embark once again upon pain. Swollen fingers did not like being forced into a pair of skin-tight jeans. Dani shoved her right hand with all of her might, finally feeling the corner of her blue pad of stick-ups. Stubbornly, her fingers caught the pad and inched it out of her pocket.

"Oh, what's the use?" Dani moaned. Brisket glanced up at her and for a moment she actually thought he understood.

"Stay here, boy, please. I need you so badly."

Dani worked her fingers unmercifully to tear off one sheet of paper. She was beyond the state of pain. She bent her stiff torso over so she could dab her index finger into the wet earth. As if finger painting, she spelled out the letters of her name in crude mud art. Dani waved the paper slightly and then carefully, with Brisket in full cooperation, she folded the small piece of note paper and attached it to the metal prong that jutted into the hole on his collar. In spite of the cursing that her fingers did to her, Dani managed with a fierce urgency to slip the leather end back into position. Pleased with the outcome, she sat back and sighed... a slight ray of hope where before there had been none.

"Brisket baby, do your job. Please, go visit Jade or someone, please!" Dani gave the dog a gentle hug and then sent him on his way.

It wasn't until he left that it occurred to Dani that the wrong person could find the note... or perhaps no one at all would notice a little patch of blue. It could even fall off, she supposed, before Brisket got back to the resort. Dani had no idea how far away she might be. Yet, with Brisket near, she could only hope.

As the negative thoughts continued to work at outnumbering her previous confident ones, Dani became aware of the toll that the little bit of activity took on her body. Her lids felt weighted, and her body dripped with weariness.

*****

Drake hesitated before he took a longing look outside of his office window. He scanned the front grounds reminiscing happier times. He and Thedy had put so much time, energy, and money into this resort, his dream. They were younger and on top of the world. Today Drake felt all of his fifty-six years plus an additional twenty. He'd been successful and things should seem unruffled. Today they felt complex. There had been only Thedy and he was satisfied with that. Now he searched his usually moral and ethical values exploring an explanation for his inclusion of Tia into her otherwise protected world. He could find no reason except his physical attraction to her. It made him feel week to appease his urges in a way that he knew some day might hurt Thedy.

Surely his face paled as he continued to torture himself with blame. On top of that, he wasn't sure about Thedy's suggestion to allow Richard and his daughters to occupy Dani's room. His cynical speculations could only foresee trouble. His beautiful pride and joy, his creation of an exclusive getaway resort, filled with the benefits of weight loss and good health, would be blemished. Who would want to come here for peace and quiet if a missing person or even murder should enter the picture? He felt ruined.

"You look tired," Thedy came up behind Drake and gently rubbed his shoulders. "Let's go out and talk to Richard. He needs us and maybe we need him. He's not angry with us, you know. He's just upset. Let's give him the room. He's sure to stay around here anyway. I've called Tommy to come and help him with his things." Thedy tried to convince Drake.

"He actually has **luggage**? Did he plan this?"

"Dear, he just came prepared. He doesn't plan to leave without Dani. Actually, I think that's right decent of him. He loves her so. Some men would just leave, you know. They might look at it as a good opportunity to go home and be unfaithful. I give Richard credit."

"Yes, well. Let's go then."

Thedy sensed Drake's tenseness by his tightened neck muscles and clenched jaws. She wondered if it was only Richard that bothered her husband now.

Drake and Thedy accompanied Richard and the girls to Dani's room, Tom lagging somewhat behind.

"I really appreciate this, both of you."

Richard's sincerity sliced right through Drake's tough exterior. Perhaps he could do more to empathize with the man, regardless of his irritation at the situation.

"Anything we can do, we will," Drake responded and he meant it. "I do trust, however, that our clients won't be involved. We will accommodate you in any way possible until Dani is found, but please remember, our clients deserve their normal routine and business uninterrupted."

Did Richard dare to tell Drake that Dani **was** one of his clients?

"Girls, we have someone setting up another double bed just for you! I'm sure you'll love it," Thedy attempted to breeze over Drake's stifling statements. "Tommy," she called, "where's Brisket? I'm sure the girls would love to have a pet around."

"The old mutt took off earlier. Seems to have an interest out in the woods these days. He comes and goes. I'll fetch him though and bring him by," Tommy promised.

Kristin tried to look excited, but Heather's eyes teared. Both girls were exhausted with the news about their mother. The day seemed endless and neither could believe it was only afternoon.

Richard's shoulders drooped dispiritedly as Drake unlocked Dani's room door. For the second time, Richard shuddered at its emptiness, a feeling he was fastly becoming quite familiar with.

Kristin stopped just short of an object lying on the floor.

"Look, Daddy! What's this?" Kristin questioned as she bent to pick it up.

"Oh, my God!" Richard felt too weak to stand. He sat on the bed's edge white-knuckling the flowered spread as his eyes riveted toward the short glass tube that Kristin held. The whole thing was too much for him to bear. Could Dani be involved in drugs? Never. He resolved this immediately if not sooner in his head... must be the maid.

Drake eyed Richard coolly. "Did you know about this?"

"What are you saying?" Richard's face was a pinched expression, as if he'd been forced into a pair of jeans three sizes too small.

"Let me try this again," Drake's impatience was growing at a bumbling pace. "Did you know that Dani used drugs?"

"Drugs?" Kristin screeched.

"Stop it, Drake. You're way out of line. This is your God damn room. Don't blame what you find **here** on my wife. What kind of people do you have working for you anyway?"

Thedy pulled on Drake's arm. "Let's go, honey. Let them get settled. Please," Thedy begged.

Thedy eased Drake's stiffened arm out of the door. He tried to wrench free of her iron grip, yet he knew it was best to get out of Richard's sight. Abruptly Drake turned, knowing that both men needed a break.

*****

The entire ordeal was perplexing and Richard's neck muscles were as tight as angry fists. He had no idea what to make of the glass tooter he now twirled between his stocky fingers. He'd only seen this type of thing on television and it was inconceivable to him that Dani had anything to do with its presence in the room today. He certainly hadn't noticed it earlier and cursed the fact that Kristin was the one to find it. He wasn't at all sure his explanation to the girls sufficed.

Heather and Kristin looked angelic as they laid sleeping sprawled upon the bed Thedy had ordered. He couldn't help but notice Heather's resemblance to her mother. She had Dani's almond shaped eyes and her blonde ringlets fell softly over the edge of the bed.

Richard stared vacantly for awhile trying to relax the nerves that were buzzing through his limbs like a power saw. In just two days, his world had crumbled. How could this be happening? He wanted nothing more in this whole blessed world than to hold Dani in his arms and reassure her, let her know that everything would be fine.

The loud clatter outside of his door, jarred Richard's chain of thoughts.

"Richard, open up."

He hoped Jade wouldn't wake the girls.

"How are you doing?" Jade whispered when she spotted the sleeping cherubs. Malory tip-toed behind her.

Richard motioned for the girls to sit. He was certain that his weary eyes didn't fool either one of them.

"I guess I'm all right," Richard said with little enthusiasm. He assumed it was an appropriate response.

"I hate to say it, Richard, but you look awful. Who could blame you though? It's just that we have this favor to ask of you."

Jade leaned back, resting her entire weight on her left elbow.

"Go ahead, shoot. What do you need?"

"It's not that kind of favor. Malory and I want to help. We'd like to know if we could tag along with you. You know, wherever you go, we go. Check with Drake. That way we can keep an eye on the girls, make suggestions, or whatever you need. We'd like to…"

"Wait a minute, Jade," Richard interrupted in a sarcastic tone, "I'm already in a fix with Mr. Drake Melrose himself.

I'm not asking for another thing, even though I'd love the company and help of two beautiful young women. Drake has, in no uncertain terms, made me agree not to mess up any routine in his building. And absolutely for sure, not to bother any of you guys, **his** clients."

"That's strange. I wonder why? You'd think he'd be most cooperative. After all, Dani was his client, too," Malory thought aloud.

"Cooperative, mph!" Richard sneered. "The man doesn't know the meaning of the word."

"Well, he did let you stay, didn't he?" Malory questioned.

"You mean his wife twisted his arm. Probably so he wouldn't look like the cold fish he really is."

"That just doesn't sound like Drake," Jade raised her brows suspiciously. "Then again, this whole thing doesn't make sense. I'm very quickly acquiring some good old-fashioned fear and I don't like it. Do you know I was actually afraid to be in my room alone earlier? And when Paris came to the door, I thought my heart would pound right out of my chest. That's why I know I have to do something."

"Oh, I'll do something for sure. If Drake or Keller won't help, I'll go at it alone."

"Richard, don't do anything foolish," Malory warned. "We'll help and I'm sure Saul Keller can be counted on. It just takes time."

"I respect that. There's only one small problem. I'm not very secure with the fact that we have time. I have a sneaking eerie suspicion that time is our enemy and that Dani's life is dependent on my knowing this fact."

The three stared helplessly at one another while Heather unconsciously moaned the word *Mom* in her sleep.

*****

The lantern had died out and Dani's surroundings were once again pitch black. The light she thought was outside must have been a figment of her imagination. Dani sat straight up and pulled her weight against the chains. She knew better. It wouldn't help her to have a tug-of-war with metal. It was impossible for her to win.

Dani's mind ricocheted from her abductor, to Richard and her girls, and then back to the resort. Somehow she had to have faith that her friends and family wouldn't let her down. Deep in her heart she was sure they were near. Brisket... she prayed to God someone, the right someone, would come in contact with Brisket.

Dani's stomach churned and gnawed with discontent. She had to do more to help herself. She felt obligated to figure out the identity of her abductor. It was imperative for this information to unleash itself. She was positive she knew him. She knew the voice. It was like a dream, she knew the details, but they were foggy. She vowed to concentrate and defy all boundaries of imagery. She leaned her head back, determined to alter her state of mind; allow herself to surface this man's face. And then she heard it... in the distance... along with discerning a faint flicker of light, she heard the familiar, "Yes, indeedy."

CHAPTER 11

Beebee waited for the coast to clear. Snickers and titters bubbled in his throat as he realized that preparations were being made due to Dani's disappearance. So, dear Richard was going to stick around. Nothing wrong with keeping an open mind, Beebee thought sarcastically. He had really hoped Richard would be gone by now, although with Thedy clinging to Richard so, Beebee's next endeavor would become much easier. He watched them embark down the narrow bleak hallway and then with a precise turn he jogged vigorously toward the adjacent hall, heading for Drake and Thedy's suite. The Valium was a must.

Once inside, Beebee quickly gave his mirror of Stardust a gigantic nose-tickling snort. He squeezed his watery eyes tight and opened them with renewed enthusiasm. He thought it logical to head straight for the bathroom and probe the obvious wooden mirrored medicine cabinet. To his astonishment, there was only one bottle of coated aspirin to be found. Feeling the magic rush, he next devoured the rather insignificant contents of the bathroom linen closet. He was not unduly shaken when this also turned out to be a futile avenue. Now what? Beebee was somewhat reluctant because of the time factor, to search the dressers and such, but he was left with no alternate choice.

Beebee walked in front of the dresser mirror and smiled snidely into it. It was a pretty good feeling to know that everyone was jumping and hustling around because of him. It was the air of importance he thrived on. It often saddened him to know that he wasn't allowed the credit or recognition of it. He was the genius in the background, the creator... the one who pulled the strings. He made things happen by exercising the control he so successfully succeeded in mastering. Somehow behind the scenes, he worked well.

Bingo! How lucky could he get? There in the first drawer he pulled open, were forty or fifty bottles of various kinds of medicine. Some prescription, some not. All sizes and colors... what a gold mine! He rambled through each one, scrutinizing and desperately ready for the one that read Valium, or any similar compound. He was sure he remembered Thedy talking about her nerve problems more than once.

With aberrant pleasure, Beebee finally cast his eyes upon the pills he sought. Not only one, but **four** bottles stared him in the face. He poured part of the contents of three bottles of small blue pills into one, slipped it in his pocket and shot out the door. He'd count them later.

As if he applauded approval of his own accomplishment, Beebee practically danced down the hall. It wasn't often that he was filled with such merriment. He could just feel that things were going his way today. A little later he'd see Liza and the day would end as perfectly as it began.

*****

The day was dying a lingering death, sinking beneath the sheets of darkness like a squealing stuck pig in a sinkhole. With the disappearance of haze, came the first sprinkles of rain.

Beebee smiled vacantly as he trudged along to his destination, the cave. He was certain Dani would be alert and he'd have to take care of that before Liza showed up. He entered the cavern receding to the section he knew so well. Here the air choked off and all that was left was the rancid drenching smell of death. He strode beyond the littering of debris chanting his unnerving verse, speaking in familiar spurts long before he could see her. His flashlight danced about the dark walls as it pivoted to and fro, casting flickers of shimmering light. He wondered what had happened to the lantern he lit earlier.

"I'm here!" he teased Dani.

He could vaguely see her sitting in a stooped position, but felt sure she was awake. Beebee reached up to inspect that lantern. No good, out of fluid. He pressed a button on the battery operated one next to it and the room illuminated.

Dani's neck jerked up and down in place like that of a diligent woodpecker. This was unbelievable!

"Oh my God, it's you!" Dani managed to eke out.

"Well, well. I'm flattered."

"Why? Who do you think-"

"Shut up," Beebee snarled. "I'll be the one to ask questions, if in fact any are needed. Your only job is to listen. Understand?"

Dani nodded numbly as a faint chill ran up her spine.

"If I ask you to speak to me, sweetie, I'm known as Beebee around here. Make sure you address me as such. Yes indeedy, I'm Beebee and don't you forget it."

Whoever was he trying to kid? Dani sat for a short time in shock, barely aware of her dumb-founded fear. She watched as Beebee took an old rusty coffee can to the stream and filled it. He came and plunked the can of amber muddy water in front of her.

"Here you go. Eat and then swallow these pills."

He laid down some half crushed grimy looking packages of soda crackers next to her and handed her two blue pills. He couldn't possibly expect that she'd drink that stuff, could he? And what kind of pills did he want her to take? He had a look in his eyes that made him appear different… a demanding cruel look. Obediently, she tugged away at the cracker crumbs, her hands now shaking violently.

"I said drink."

Beebee grabbed her hair in a clump on the crown of her head and yanked it back. She tried to keep her jaws shut, but he pried them open and threw the pills back into her throat. It felt like more than two. Beebee gripped the muddy can and swished the murky water down her esophagus. Dani gagged but he kept pouring. The water felt slippery and she wanted to vomit. She convinced her head to keep the water down, afraid that if she didn't, he would surely give her seconds.

Dani was nauseated with crackers, water, and most of all terror. She knew him so well… at least she thought she had. She felt weak, dizzy, and confused. Finally, the blurred vision ahead of her melted into non-existence.

Morbidly fascinated, Beebee watched with casual flippancy as Dani struggled. Once again, he sloshed some water and pills in her mouth, knowing that subconsciously she was still able to follow his commands. She swallowed submissively.

Beebee now stood in the mouth of the cave, awaiting Liza's arrival. The chilling beads of rain lashed away at his face and arms relentlessly as the previous sprinkling hastened to a downpour. Beebee was well aware of his increasing anxiety accompanied by tightening muscles. His jaws clenched together locking his teeth like a forceful angry grizzly. He stood in the archway gnarling his fingers into stringent little hard-rocket balls.

In the distance, Beebee spotted a shadow coming closer. In his present state of mind, he couldn't trust his eyes that it was actually Liza; instead he wondered if it might be an optical illusion. As it neared him, he realized that no optical illusion could have Liza's figure. He was sure of that much.

"Did you order this garbage?" Liza threw the dripping piece of plastic over her head. She shook it up and down, whipping the water through the air like bullets.

For a moment Beebee looked at her quizzical and then began to laugh.

Liza stood straight up now, trying to ignore the musty old smell around her. The odors seemed to shoot invisibly from every angle, trying to conceal some private type of war. It was times like this that Liza could just shake Beebee. Where was his common sense? This was no place for a lady.

"You look beautiful," Beebee held her close, allowing some of his tension to ease.

"Except for this single dab of mud on your nose, you don't look so bad yourself." Liza gently wiped the smudge away and kissed Beebee full on the lips.

"That was nice. How about some more?" Beebee softly begged. The charm oozed out of him when necessary.

"Gladly. It's been such a long day. Why I just-" Liza's voice fell silent.

Beebee could care less if all the bats in the cave took a flying leap, croaked, or blew tin whistles. Right now he was going to demand Liza's undivided attention. Voluntarily, he admitted that he possessed a certain amount of insane logic. But there was nothing insane about the compelling force he had right now. In fact it was very natural for a man, and about the only real excuse he could find to have a woman around at all.

Liza continued to love Beebee in the way she knew would make him happy, though she couldn't help but sense something different about him. Something so obvious that it should jump right up and bite her in the face. Yet it was odd, she couldn't quite detect what his problem was; still it was evident that it was there and nagging away at him.

He held her indecisively for another moment, stroking her harsh dyed hair, lingering with his hands securely around her neck. Liza felt a sudden chill and impulsively pulled away.

"What's that for?" Beebee demanded, his brows raising in question.

"I'm tired, that's all," Liza lied, avoiding Beebee's glare.

"C'mon, Babe. Let's not start again. I'm not happy with all of our arguing lately."

"You're right. I'm not either. It's just that you seem so preoccupied or something. I don't know what it is. But lately when I talk to you, it's not really you I'm talking to. Do you know what I mean?" Liza was unsure of her own confusion. She knew if she asked Beebee flat out what was wrong, he'd only deny it.

"You're right," Beebee agreed. "These last few days, I guess I haven't been fun to be with. I'm sorry, Babe. Really I am. Work has been so demanding. It seems like everything comes together at once. Sometimes I get to feel like life's a struggle. Ever feel like that?"

"Yeah, every day. I feel like it's more monotony than struggle. No matter what it is though, some days it takes a lot, just to make it through. You're my bright spot, you know. If I didn't have you to look forward to some evenings, why I'd just burst, I'm sure." Liza's smile filled her face, but behind her façade the foul breath of reality was not being ignored. She suspected Beebee was in some kind of trouble.

They remained entwined for the better part of the next hour. Then suddenly, Beebee gave Liza the impression that he was trying to get rid of her.

"I really don't mind if you leave." He hastened to add, "I'll even walk you to the parking lot," as he cocked his head in an unnatural right angle.

Did he think she was stupid? She knew a brush-off when she heard one. Besides, usually he begged her to stay. She couldn't help but wonder if he had someone else in line. Who would show up here after she left? The very thought made Liza extremely angry. She was half tempted to turn around after he left and follow him back. Instead, she restrained her doubts, got in her car, and drove home.

Beebee hated to rush Liza off but he needed a snort as well as a few minutes to finalize his plans for the next few days. Somehow, he had let himself get side-tracked from Malory Douglas and it was no longer possible to do this. She was at the bottom of all this stir. And although he thrived on the attention, he was left with no choice but to pay her back for the inconveniences she had caused him. Perhaps there was still time to trap her, offer an explanation for Dani's disappearance, and get that cop off his neck. He had to try. It simply was none of her business and she had spoiled it for him.

By now Beebee's eyes were glassy but he didn't care. His nose felt irritated. Frankly, he didn't believe it was the Coke. Experts thought they knew it all, but Beebee was certain they didn't know their ass from a hole in the ground. He had an inkling that it was just a cold coming on.

Absently, Beebee checked in on Dani who was semiconscious once again. He commanded her to down some more pills accompanied by the stream water. He was confident they'd hold her over until morning.

For a fleeting moment Beebee felt as vulnerable as he knew Dani was. He envisioned the string of events over the past two days, concluding once again that Malory was to blame for its outcome. The facts as he saw them, supported his deduction that he would have to stop her clock… dead.

He giggled as he thought of Malory so pitifully stupid. As with most women, he could tell by her poise that Malory viewed herself as pretty, secure, and confident. Fierce dribbles of laughter loitering deep in his throat began to surface. As usual, Beebee thought she was way off her beam. One conflict with him would prove to Malory just how insecure and dispensable she was. Beebee's flawless belief in women as low-life human beings had grown steadily throughout the years, and now seemed to reach its pinnacle.

In his mind, Beebee visualized Malory's surprised expression. Surely she'd plead and beg his forgiveness. He'd chant to her and tell her to shut her mouth. He'd be totally enthralled with her stumbling torturous fear. He'd be in command. Yes indeedy… power.

The strength suddenly ran out of him and Beebee realized sleep was in order. He'd rest now, see that Dani gets attended to in the morning, and then place his full attention back on Malory. Beebee shrank back against the clay-like walls. Yes indeedy… Malory, watch out!

CHAPTER 12

Malory relaxed sprawled upon her huge quilted bedspread. She arched her back, letting her neck muscles relieve, and allowed her strawberry hair to flow to the carpet. The outside view was upside-down and she could discern blackness tinged with moisture as she watched the drops swirl patterns upon the glass of her window pane. Malory thought about the designs in terms of connected sprinkles. Did they join to form a playful kitten, a tall pine tree, or were the drips splashed in unrelated sequence... oh my God, all this just about rain? What was wrong with her head? Sure, it hurt... but that was no excuse to get so technical with raindrops.

Propping a pillow to hold her weary head, Malory reflected the last couple of days. The feeling was an unsettling one, working non-stop, hunting for the solution. At first she had felt a gripping fear accompanied with inability to trust her own judgment. She was certain at one point that someone was after her. That feeling had diminished some, yet she was uncertain as to just how much she should slacken her guard. Malory felt foolish worrying about herself. It was Dani she should be thinking about. It was all moving too quickly and so unexpected that Malory was finding it difficult to assimilate all that had happened.

She laid for the longest time speculating on a way that she could help mend the tattered pieces she had stirred. She could sense Drake's definite unhappiness, after all her story blemished his otherwise perfect resort. And then there was Richard's fear; certainly her rendition of the events caused him much distress. Jade was making good attempts to remedy the situation, but Malory could tell she wouldn't hold out for long. She supposed she may even have added a little misery to Saul's life, although she'd like to turn that into idle curiosity. She smiled what felt like the first smile of the day. There were many things Malory needed to check out, but undoubtedly after Dani, Saul would be given top priority.

It felt good to lay back and dream about the man in uniform. Saul's soft green eyes came into Malory's focus. What she looked for most in a man's physical makeup was his mouth, and Saul's fit her prescription perfectly. His sturdy jaw line led down to a superb set of pleasurable lips which, when parted, displayed his evenly aligned pearly whites. Her mind moved in succession down his muscular frame. Malory forced herself back into reality. This was absurd! She could not allow herself a smooth trip to dreamland when a real problem existed. She must activate her brain and get her body in gear for Dani's sake… and it wouldn't hurt her own mental state either.

Malory was interrupted by a voice at the door whom she quickly recognized as Jade.

"I talked to Richard again. He's still so upset about Kristin finding that tooter. I don't believe Dani had anything at all to do with that. I'm on Richard's side and I can't imagine Drake being so cold. I'm going to speak to that man shortly and he's not going to like what he hears. It's unbelievable to me that he hasn't turned this place upside-down."

"My sentiments exactly. I keep trying to figure out what we can do. Perhaps I can get some advice from Saul. Well, maybe that's not such a good idea. Even though our intentions would be to help, I suppose a police officer would have a different point of view. I don't know what to do. I only know what I saw. I can't change that."

"I wish you could, Malory. Believe me! I know Keller will do all he can. It's just that with something like this people want the answers sooner than they're available. Maybe I shouldn't say this, but it seems to me that you have an attraction for Keller. Am I right?"

Malory didn't mind Jade's question in the least. They needed something else to talk about to ease the distress found in not knowing what to do about Dani.

"I guess you could say that," Malory sat up tall with a definite glint in her eye. "You have to admit, he's much nicer to think about than the other thing that's been on my mind. My arrival here began on shaky grounds, I guess the image of Saul eases up on that a little. So, to change the subject again, you're not too happy with Drake? Frankly, I'm quite surprised at his indifference also. Do you think it means anything?"

Jade flopped on the bed next to Malory and pursed her lips.

"Well, I'm not sure. You just would think the man would put himself out a little. He did work with Dani for several months now. She has a lot invested in this place. It's kind of sad to think that after all that, he doesn't seem to give a rip. It corks my hiney, to say the least." Jade ended with a definite pout of disgust written on her face.

"It almost makes me wonder if he knows something that we don't. I guess that's sort of silly though, isn't it?"

"Actually, it's not silly at all. It crossed my mind several times today. I can't shake the fact that we've been through this once, only I didn't realize it. You remember, we told you about Jill. If I remember the incident, certainly Drake should be well informed. I'm tempted to ask him and yet there's something about him right now that says 'stay away'."

Jade looked at Malory for a rebuttal.

"Perhaps the best route for that information is through Saul, especially in lieu of the fact that Drake's actions do seem a bit peculiar. I'm inclined to think that Drake would not respond so well, and also that it is as good of time as any to inform Saul with any information you can about Jill. There isn't anything else that's happened that you might have forgotten about, is there?"

"Come on, Malory. This is hard enough as it is."

"I'm sorry, Jade. I don't mean to be pushy, but it's really important. Obviously, no one thought the disappearance of Jill odd enough to pursue it. Sometimes things are not as they seem at first. I thought maybe, just maybe, there might be other things that may have seemed insignificant at the time, but now with Dani gone, well, they might seem worth mentioning."

"I know your intentions are good. I'm tired though and confronting Saul will have to wait. I can't properly do any more tonight." With that, Jade stood up to leave.

Malory escorted Jade to the doorway and both girls vowed to get a good night's sleep and be ready for routine, as well as minor detective work, in the early morning.

Malory contemplated for quite some time what sort of a role she could take in helping Richard, Jade, and Dani. She did not want to infringe upon Saul's territory… still she was certain about what she witnessed, she could not let it fade with time. She had to act now, acquire any and all information that may be useful. She'd call Saul in the morning, but right now she had something more pressing that she had to do. With unrestrained anticipation, Malory hurled the contents out of her top dresser drawer. She had to find the brochure and the introduction packet that was given her. Surely something in there should give her a clue. It included several bulletins with background information on the resort, its instructors, and its owners. Malory planned on researching a bit about Drake Melrose.

*****

Thedy was glad to have a few minutes by herself. She felt a migraine coming on as well as an old familiar twinge of nervousness. A definite shakiness within had formed. She had no doubts that it was brought on by Drake's aloofness. Instead of bothering Drake with details of her symptoms, she decided to nip them in the bud before they bloomed into something uncontrollable. Thedy quickly headed for her suite where she could get her medication, Valium, to pacify the way she felt.

Thedy longed to know why Drake felt so angry. It wasn't like him to behave this way. Most of the time, she was able to mask her own feelings as well as his. It was a must, with such a business as theirs to be in charge at all times. Usually conversation worked well. She thoroughly enjoyed their clients and the notoriety associated with Melrose Resort. Right now, it wasn't important what she enjoyed. It was necessary to get her bottle with refills. She'd have Drake send out for them, which would make him well aware of what he had to contend with. He wouldn't ask questions and he wouldn't push her. Drake was used to this procedure. He'd cooperate. He'd get the prescription refilled, and then Thedy could once again feel secure. Whatever was troubling him would be put on the back burner. He'd tread carefully knowing that Thedy was on the verge of maybe even a breakdown.

Thedy rummaged through the many bottles contained in her top drawer. She chuckled when she thought of Drake telling her that she owned two businesses, the resort and a private pharmacy. He was right. Sometimes she felt like a junkie, but no apologizing for it. It was mandatory. According to her recollection, there should be four bottles, all partial and one with a notation for refills. Where was the fourth? As she poked further, Thedy realized that the three she held felt much lighter than they should. Thedy eyed the drawer even longer, exhaling her gasps of contempt. Was Drake capable of this? How could she even think that? Of course he wasn't. The bottle had to be around. Perhaps she left it lay elsewhere in their room. Thedy bustled in and out of each room, all the while trying to figure out who could be responsible. Besides the missing bottle, two of the other prescriptions had only three tablets left. Why there was enough missing to choke a horse!

Without further hesitation, Thedy took one of the few blue pills that remained with her. It would serve the purpose for the time being. Although Thedy's curiosity hadn't lessened as to where the missing pills could be, just the motion of swallowing told her brain that the calming could begin. She wiped the accumulated sweat from under her fringe of reddish bangs and, with a sweeping of her hands, straightened the flowing flowery material over her plump legs. Thedy was once again interested in who might have seen her pills. She decided to buzz Drake just in case he set them somewhere by mistake.

The mistake came in bothering Drake with one more missing thing. He was irate and Thedy supposed she couldn't blame him. She'd have to attend to this mystery on her own. Drake was very busy answering to various people about Dani's disappearance.

Thedy tried to imagine her last Valium encounter. Did she throw the bottle in her purse? Nil. Maybe it rolled under their bed? Nil. Was someone else in her room in the past two days? Nil. The only other person with a key was Trixie. Nil again. Did she know anyone with a drug problem? Couldn't think of a soul. An uncomfortable image popped into her head. The exchange between Liza and her boyfriend. At the time she thought of drugs. She cautioned herself. How silly! Even at the time she realized Liza was too sweet and innocent to be involved in anything illegal. Thedy wouldn't hear of it. There had to be an obvious explanation that she was overlooking. Thedy decided to take a walk and see Trixie. Even if Trixie couldn't shed any light on the subject, Thedy knew that walk would do her good.

Trixie didn't bother to turn at first. "Sorry, Thedy. But I'm absolutely positive that no one came for your key at all today. I was here every minute, and you know I wouldn't forget that."

"Yes, I'm sure you would know. I just thought I'd check," Thedy said.

"You know I keep that key in the safe so there's no mistaking at all. What is it you're looking for?" Trixie shook her head impatiently, letting Thedy know it was her designated time to leave.

"I seem to be missing some medication that I need."

Trixie nodded in understanding, but didn't respond. It was only minutes and Trixie had vanished.

*****

Malory's bed was blanketed with mounds of folded paper, but to her disappointment none of it seemed to offer what she was looking for... though she herself couldn't easily identify the details she sought. Hopefully at some point the list of staff names could help, but she was sure Saul already had those. Not enough background data was supplied in the short little blurbs on each person although if it seemed conflicting in any way, Malory imagined Saul would need to know that. She began to gather them into a tidy pile when a scratching sound outside diverted her attention. Was that on her window? Malory perked her ears up to listen to a mournful sound... almost like that of a dying dog. Her heart roared ready to burst right out of her chest cavity. Calm down, she told herself rationally. It could be any number of things, perhaps a wounded animal. An animal this high? Malory leaped off of the bed and flicked the light off. She wanted the advantage. She juggled the papers in one hand and the telephone receiver in the other to make sure it was working. Should she run and get Paris or Nick?

Malory felt as though she had suddenly gone crazy. She dropped the pamphlets and the phone, and slowly crawled to her window. She felt ridiculous. A helpless pit was forming deep in her gut. Was this what her clients meant when they said terrifying? There it was... another scratch. She hadn't noticed screens on her windows. Malory's fingers climbed up the lower wall, determined to let her eyes peek out. At first she saw nothing, but noted that the rain had quit, leaving a filmy chalky residue of haze. The temperature must have dropped. It was then that her gaze fell upon a black gloved out-stretched hand rising to the window pane. She was sure it was blood that twinkled between the fingers. Malory let out a blood-curdling scream and dropped to the floor. As she crawled to phone security, Malory heard the whimpering echoes drift through the mist below her, almost beckoning her to rescue them.

CHAPTER 13

Tia paced the floor, while she brushed her sleek black hair together at the nape of her neck and secured it with a tortoise shell barrette. Where was Drake? He had always come here much earlier. She pulled her pink sweat pants up as she gaped out the dormer at a day that couldn't seem to make up its mind. The haze was beginning to lift, leaving the sky pale. It appeared to be jacket weather, but it didn't matter to Tia. What would make Drake so late? Soon she would have to leave in order to punch her clock on time.

Finally Drake entered, his face filled with a cloudy expression.

"Hi. Sorry I'm late." He leaned over to kiss her with an unusual lightness.

"Hey, don't be so grumpy. There are other mornings, mister," Tia attempted a smile, sensing there was stormy weather ahead.

"I'm afraid not, at least for a while," Drake could hardly say the words in an audible voice. Seeing the hurt on Tia's face doubled his own. He continued to speak rapidly, "There's so much happening and so much to explain. I don't know if I can do you justice if I squeeze it in during these few minutes before work. It's not you. God, it's not you. Let me tell you briefly. The Ellison woman has disappeared, maybe you've already heard. It's going to mean police investigations, I'm sure. We're all very upset and I don't want this matter to get in our way, hurt you and Thedy, and perhaps have you dragged around the block with it. Do you understand? Please try, Tia. This is very difficult..."

"I do, Drake. I understand. Nothing will be said and we'll leave nothing to chance. Just for a while, a short while," Tia gripped Drake's muscular forearm in a discerning fashion. She kissed him gently on the cheek and left.

Tia did not show Drake her tears and disappointment. It wouldn't be fair. She was certain the matter was beyond his control. He'd be back. She knew he'd be back.

Nor did Drake expose his sentiments to Tia. It had to be this way, at least for the time being.

*****

Malory felt the heavy hours of the night. Security came along with Jade, and both reassured her that no one was or could be outside of her window. She'd sobbed, feeling foolish. The night was spent tossing and turning, acutely developing a deep sense of terror.

Still disgruntled from the lack of significant data in Melrose's brochures, and uncertain about the window episode, Malory dragged her near limp body out of bed. She planned to address the day as planned. She would give Saul a ring and continue with the day's activities as if zilch had happened. If nothing else, it would serve the purpose of a normal appearance. Lord knows Melrose could use that!

Weight became the issue at hand as Malory packed her body into another new jogging suit. Once again, she realized her true reason for coming to this place. The reason seemed so distant and trivial compared to all that had happened. Yet, standing at a side-view of her full length mirror, she had to admit that the reason still existed.

Malory dialed Saul's home phone number that he had given to her. She related the noises and image she had seen the night before, certain that he must think by now that she was crazy. There seemed no other explanation. Jade was not being cursed with visions, so surely he had to question hers. Still, he maintained a very even and concerned voice and seemed highly interested in seeing the brochures she'd spoken about.

"I'd really appreciate if you'd hang onto those and I'll stop by later to pick them up."

Waylaid by last evenings events Malory had almost forgotten her main reason she'd called Saul, "Oh gosh, before I forget. The main thing I wanted to tell you is about another girl named Jill. Jade recalls another client missing a few weeks ago. She said it passed over and she hadn't really thought about it until this happened with Dani."

"When did you know about this? And what's Jill's last name?" Saul's voice took on a professional tone.

Malory was hesitant, "Well, I did know about it the first time we spoke. Paris thought it best not to bring any other speculations into the picture. After all, none of us know that it's related. It's just that I have this feeling, Saul, and I thought it best you know. Her last name was Simon. Maybe she's home by now…" Malory was skeptical, as she crossed her legs and took a deep breath of air.

"Anything, anything at all, Malory, even if you're not sure, please tell me about it. And about last night, check with the custodians about the security of your windows. When I come by I'll bring a dead bolt for your door. Not that you need to worry," he added quickly, "but just to be on the safe side, we'll go through standard procedures."

Malory hung up feeling confident with Saul, but her thoughts were scattered every which way. No matter which way her mind trailed, it would endlessly hammer its way back to the awful gloved hand.

Malory would hear no more of that. She strode out the door to pick up Jade and get on with the day... let the evening be.

Monday mornings seemed to require more coffee than other mornings, and this one was no exception. Malory drank it black and found herself inwardly thanking her drink for containing zero calories.

"Isn't that Paul Wynette staring at us?" Malory questioned Jade.

"Sure is. I wonder what his problem is. We had trouble with him the other night, too, didn't we?"

"Maybe he can't get over how wonderful we look," Malory teased.

"Right. I'm sure that's it. He never did this to me before, so it must be you, Malory."

"Well, I'm going to ignore the man. If he wants something, he should come over and ask. I admit though, I'll feel a little strange in his class today after the way he's been acting."

Jade glanced his way disapprovingly and then turned her chestnut eyes on Malory. She leaned over as if to whisper, practically laying on the table. "Did you talk to Saul?"

"Yes. And I told him about Jill," Malory gestured Paul's way, as he got up to leave.

"Good morning, girls," Paul greeted them as he passed their table. He winked at Malory.

"As I was saying," Malory put good effort into ignoring the man, but certainly was in a quandary over his motive, "I also had collected the pamphlets for him about this place. He'll stop by later to get them."

"Hi, ladies."

Malory was just about to lay some colorful jargon into Paul when she looked up and saw it was Nick.

"You started without us." Paris and Nick slid into the booth joining the general conversation.

Jade told the guys all of the up to date details, and all of them finished a fairly quiet breakfast.

Attending Paul's gym and track session proved to be a little more active. Paul never made any effort to acknowledge their presence which really threw Malory into a tizzy. Just what was his motive then? Malory remained nonchalant even though her better judgment told her she should beware. It wasn't until mid-session that Malory consciously recognized the problem, and then she pulled Jade aside.

Peering over her shoulder, Malory asked Jade, "Did you see *that*?"

"What are you talking about?" Jade cut her short, seemingly interested in getting back to Paris.

"Paul! He dropped a bag of something white out of his back pocket. I'm sure it wasn't baby powder either! Don't look there," Malory cautioned Jade.

"You're kidding! I'm sorry I barked. Paris is on my case about staying out of Dani's business and leaving it to the cops. So, you think drugs?"

"I'd bet my life."

"Are you thinking what I am? That tooter in Dani's room!"

"Ssh! Here he comes?"

"Getting tired girls? Come on. Two more runs around the track, it's good for you." Paul sounded encouraging.

The conversation came to a sudden halt and both girls turned to jog.

Malory trotted at an even gait, still searching her mind for any sane explanation. Okay, so he was on drugs. So what? Maybe she had seen something different than what she thought she saw. Maybe it was really a white hankie that Paul had dropped. Malory wasn't at all sure that she could trust her own eyes these days. She wondered what the place was like before she arrived. Did she really have that suspicious of a nature? Or were these things really happening? One thing she knew for sure was that she'd be the one to keep an eye on Paul, regardless of whether or not he watched her.

*****

Beebee smirked, as he stood outside the cafeteria door, and his face registered a humble morsel of self-satisfaction. Not in his ability to abduct Malory yet, but in his overall effort to create a disruption. He knew by watching her, that Malory had not a clue and that tickled him. Wide shouldered, with a slight hint of tan on his face, Beebee cast his eyes upon the floor waiting for the correct opportunity to arise.

Last night was a fluke. He missed because the bitch called security. He had no trouble, with his mountain climbing experience, getting up to the third story, but those damn windows were made different than what he'd planned... a stupid window with no opening... the damned thing was caulked shut. He couldn't believe it! There must be something he missed, or for sure the place would be cited for a fire hazard. He laughed erotically when he saw the stupid security guard walk out the door, take one look up and walk back inside. What a threat he would be... didn't even spot his rope or anything.

Beebee was impressed with Malory's ability to go on as if nothing was amiss. She certainly had diarrhea of the mouth he thought, as he watched her babble away to Jade. She wouldn't appear so cool and collected if she realized what he had in store for her. What bliss there was in stupidity. Beebee observed the rest of the breakfast ritual hoping for a short time when Malory would excuse herself and he would find her so vulnerable and alone. It didn't happen though... but it would. Beebee was certain that it would. If not today, tomorrow. He wouldn't allow any more leeway than that.

Beebee leaned back against the polished rail that jutted out in the brick encased foyer.

"Hey, a railing is to hold on to, not to sit on," Trixie bellowed at him through the doorway.

He hadn't even noticed her there. Big mouth! Who did she think she was anyway? Beebee remained tight-lipped, wondering how long it had been that Trixie was watching him. Surprised that he hadn't known she was there, Beebee was irritated. He lost all concentration in Malory as he poked his head through the office doorway and talked to Trixie. Silence was no longer his virtue.

"You need not concern yourself with where I sit or where I stand. It's my business, not yours," he told Trixie in a voice as cold as a Magnum trigger.

Trixie was taken aback, not at all used of people talking back to her.

Beebee raced past her door angry as hops. He had the right to expect something better than that. Who'd asked for her opinion anyway? That's what was wrong with women. They thought they could just open their traps whenever they felt like it. Wrong! Trixie would pay dearly for that.

Beebee walked out the first exit he saw, taking in gulps of cool fresh air. He scuffed his feet, angry as a bull in a locked pen. He had to calm down. It didn't matter that his eyes felt swollen into little slits, or that his throat was scratchy, or that his nose was as irritated as he was at Trixie... it only mattered that he needed relief. He took out some extra fine Nose Candy. That would do the job. Then he reached for his trusty little glass tube and it was gone. Now Beebee was knotted with fury. Damn! Thank God he always carried extra little straws with him. But where was his tooter? He couldn't worry about that now. His hands were shaking and his heart thrashing like a beached whale. Warm trickles of sweat beaded on his cheeks... he had to have it now!

Beebee stared across the wedge of acreage that he considered his own. He marveled, as he snorted, at its solitary beauty mostly still untouched by human hands. Virgin land by nature, and if stroked by human hands, would lose its elegance. It was the natural wildness that turned Beebee on. He felt relieved now, out in the environment, away from mortal frailties. He could breathe again... he'd be fine... he was sure he'd be all right now.

CHAPTER 14

Beebee had to gain control before his first session arrived. Everywhere he walked, angry little sputters of hot fumes trailed him. He sat down angled his chair back onto two legs, then tilted his head to fill his gritty eyes with Visine. The tiny drops made his eyes flutter like a victorious slot machine. He glared out at the faded morning sky, leaving muted fragments of an unfocused childhood run reels of pain by him. Beebee shook his head as if to dislodge the unclear figures that filled his mind. They refused to leave.

*****

He was sure at the time of their wedding, Herb and Jillian, better known as Mom and Pop, married with hopes and prayers of attaining the all American dream. But by the time Beebee became familiar with them, dreams had already turned into disillusionments and idealism had melted into reality. Also, Beebee knew all too well the underhanded antics of his older brother, Danny.

By age six, Beebee knew the score. Danny was the angelic, walk in the footsteps of the Lord, child and baby. With the slight Canadian French accent, he let everyone know that Beebee was the no good, make-nothing-of-yourself-but-trouble, kid. Beebee did not take lightly those early prophecies. After all, who was he to argue with knowledgeable elders. Mom was forthright in the community, college educated, den mother of the Cub Scouts, Danny's pack of course, president of PTA, and one hell of an upstanding citizen. Pop was a hard worker, owned his own lumber mill, drank a little too much and was nagged at for the disproportionate flap of skin that hung off of him, better known as his belly.

Beebee held no grudge for unfair treatment, figuring that it was all inclusive of the hard knocks in life. Pop was often mistreated and he loved Pop. The first outright signs of blatant prejudice did not rear its ugly head until the birthday parties of 1965, although Beebee was well aware of it long before that. This marked the first opportunity for Pop to catch her red-handed at it. Danny turned nine that year, with twenty or so guests, red and blue balloons, games galore, barbecue, chips, a two-tiered Danish layer cake, and a brand new ten-speed metallic green bike. Even Beebee had fun until he accidentally broke Grandma Evan's stupid old vase. Beebee missed most of the fun after that, but at night, when Mom let him out of the closet, he still wished Danny a happy birthday. He felt disappointed but certainly didn't tell Danny that. It would have been told right back to Mom that night if not sooner.

Beebee turned seven that year. For days before, Mom reminded him, "Yes indeedy, you're the bad bad boy. Bad boys do not get parties. Do you remember how you spoiled your brother's party?"

Beebee always told her no, he didn't remember, but she didn't seem to hear. Pop suggested that they just have a small gathering and a homemade cake. Beebee thought Pop's suggestion was good, but the day came and went and Beebee never saw a cake or a gift. Danny laughed and Pop said nothing. A few evenings later, Pop came into Beebee's room and gave him a small pocket knife and a piece of lumber.

Beebee saw the hurt in Pop's weary eyes. "Here, son. I thought you might like to do a little whittling. I used to enjoy it. Takes away many long days and nights. Turns em' into fun."

That was the last time Beebee saw Pop. He was killed in a trucking accident the next day. Beebee cried and cried but it did no good. Pop was gone.

He often thought about the kiss good-night that Pop had given him. It was the last one in years he would get, and the only one that ever held meaning.

Life went on as usual and Danny grew more apart from Beebee than ever. Out in public, he wouldn't admit that Beebee was his kid brother. In public, Mom was better at going through rituals. What would her friends think?

By his teen years, Beebee had tired of failure. There was nothing he could do to live up to his mother's expectations, so he didn't. His grades were poor and he quickly developed the pattern of most juvenile delinquents. He started with little things like stealing and progressed to armed robbery. He spent his time, but as with most things, Danny wanted him to pay up double. On one of his '**out**' months, Beebee decided to see if things had changed at home.

He was twenty-seven when he approached his Mom's front porch. He hadn't known she was so ill.

"What do you want?" Danny greeted him.

"I wanna talk to Ma." He tried to push past his brother, who towered over Beebee by a good six inches. Danny stood firm and in the background his mother's sobs echoed.

"Who's there, Punky?" she wailed.

"No one, Ma."

"What do ya mean?" Beebee was angry. How dare he try to stop Beebee! Beebee shoved Danny, not making any headway.

"Who's that I hear?" Mom called again.

Then a woman came to the door, someone Beebee had never seen before. She held a little blondy in her arms and another little guy tagged at her side.

She put a hand on his brother's shoulder. "Come on, Dan. It's not right. He is family."

Danny stepped aside, his eyes piercing blood thirsty bullets through Beebee. "You coward. Don't you dare give her any trouble. She ain't up to it now."

Beebee entered the small untidy room, unsuspecting of what he saw. The once tall sturdy woman, now lay frail and motionless on a twin-size bed. She looked like a bitsy porcelain doll with salt and pepper hair knotted on her crown. Beebee never thought he'd feel sorry for her, but he did. She was so helpless and defenseless. He knew he would not be able to tell her what he planned to.

Instead, he poured a glass of water, aiding it to her baked-clay lips, sorely in need of any liquid. Her hands shook, while spindly fingers, with loosely corded veins, wrapped around the glass until her blue-tipped nails met with involuntary weakness. He wasn't sure this woman recognized him at first. Her slurping sounds made him nauseated and then finally her bleached emerald eyes registered a slight pause of recognition.

"It's you!" she gasped, choking on her own words.

For lack of anything to say, he simply responded, "Yes."

"No good… it's no good," she took the air in through tiny tortured clips.

He should have known, even in this feeble and vulnerable state, she would not give in. It didn't matter now. He left her be.

"How long's she got?" he questioned Danny.

Danny stared sullenly, not offering any bit of information, keeping it sacredly inside of him as he always had.

His wife spoke on Danny's behalf, "It'll be any day now. It's only a matter of hours. Would you like some soup?" She told him her name was Mindy. Mindy was quite pleasant, fixing supper for Beebee and cleaning up after all of them.

Danny paced the floor, said nothing, and periodically went in by Mom. Beebee stayed away but made many unsuccessful attempts at conversation with Danny. Beebee settled for silence filled with an abundance of mixed feelings. He hated Danny, felt pity for Mom, and had an aching loneliness that longed for Pop.

Beebee fell asleep, sitting up in a winged chair. He vaguely remembered Mindy tossing a quilt over his lap mid-evening.

It was the following afternoon that Mom passed away. Beebee didn't cry. The funeral was small and Beebee saw a few relatives that he hadn't seen since high school, but none of them had much to say to him. Danny saw to that. He coaxed, taunted, and belittled Beebee in front of each person. Over and over again, Danny kept making it known that Beebee's presence disgusted him.

Beebee snorted in between appearances, told himself it didn't matter, wasn't important, and worked forcibly to hold his temper. He didn't want to give in to Danny's tactics, still he resented being ridiculed. He planned on cutting out in the morning.

That evening, while Danny was plastering himself with whiskey, Beebee took the opportunity to go outside and skin Danny's brake drums. He chuckled as he worked away, knowing that his brother would be up at the crack of dawn, traveling the road and on his way to his factory job. He felt no remorse, although he hoped Mindy could manage alone. He was sure she'd be better off without Danny anyway.

It happened. Beebee read about it the next evening. Danny had lost his brake power and crashed off the side of Muir Bluff. Beebee snickered and forced himself to send Mindy a card. He couldn't bring himself to attend Danny's funeral.

Several months later, Beebee was tracked down in the east side of Stockton and questioned. He was sorry he couldn't help the nice officers, but he knew nothing about Danny's death other than that it happened. Evidently Mindy gave up easily because Beebee was never asked about it again.

Beebee thought about Mindy often, and just short of a year of his brother's accident, he decided to pay her a visit. She seemed happy to see him and he was surprised to find out that she'd had another son. She was pregnant at the time of Danny's death. Her kids were her life, no other man having entered her castle. Beebee stuck around for two years, hiring out for odd jobs, helping Mindy all he could. In return she gave him good meals and shared her bed.

The time passed quickly and gradually Mindy took on those overbearing obnoxious habits that were characteristic of most women. She began to question his whereabouts at all times, his drug habit was a nuisance, she wanted more money from him, she expected help for the children, and the list went on.

Beebee couldn't live up to her expectations. One day he got up, said he was going to work and left her, spending the next couple of years working here and there, living here and there and staying clear of any commitments. Several times his theory about women had been proven, and he learned to put trust in no one but himself.

Beebee viewed himself as a weak man, very much like his own father. Then something clicked! He wondered why he'd spent so much of his life putting up with that crap from people. He'd demonstrate his ability to deal with life, stand up to women, gain power, hold a job, and still stay out of trouble with the law. It was then that he answered the ad that Dr. Melrose had put in the Daily Times. He filled out the application to the best of his ability, deleting a few minor facts, and adding a couple more in his favor.

*****

Beebee pulled forward on his chair, jilted by the voices and laughter coming toward him. Undoubtedly one belonged to Malory. Another prime example of pushiness in women. His head roared with innate cackles that almost shattered his eardrums. Concealing his private obsession, he greeted the clients comically, never indicating doubts of his normalcy.

CHAPTER 15

Thedy couldn't wait to have Liza work on her hair for numerous reasons. She was anxious to see if Liza toppled on Thedy's prepared drug questions, she enjoyed conversations with Liza, but most of all it was a new morning and after yesterday's excitement she could use a massage of her scalp and temples. Liza was most skilled at this.

Thedy glanced over her notes for things she had to get done on this second Monday of the month. The list was workable so she'd have plenty of time to lull around and enjoy her time with Liza. She took one-half of her Valium tablet, treasuring what little she had until the doctor called her refill in. That was on her list of things to do for today.

Thedy breezed down the corridor, her flowery house dress flowing its generous width loosely around her ankles. She stopped at the glass doors at the end of the hall and opened them slightly for her daily weather check. It was a bit nippy and the sun was still cloaked under the chalky sky. Perhaps later it would peek out. There was slight moisture in the air, but it was feasible that would change.

Liza was glad that Thedy was her first appointment of the day. Thedy was always so cheery, and Liza still had it on her mind to make it up to Thedy for cutting out on her last time when Beebee so rudely interrupted. She planned on giving her undivided attention and she'd even throw in a hot oil treatment. Thedy would be thrilled.

Both girls settled in for a friendly hour or so of conversation, Thedy leaning her head far back into the basin so Liza could gently but firmly shampoo her scalp.

"Liza, I don't mean to pry, but I do hope things are better for you and your guy?" Thedy felt unsteady as she began to chisel away at Liza.

"Oh, don't you worry everything's fine. I was just sorry that I left you hanging."

"No problem. I knew that guy from somewhere though. Must have given you a gift that day."

Liza was suspicious. What the heck was Thedy up to? "I don't know what you mean?"

"Well he seemed angry with you and then he gave you something. Although I suppose it's none of my business."

Damn right it was none of her business. Liza rubbed Thedy's head with a towel and sent her toward the chair. She began tugging the short ringlets with a comb. "It was nothing. Just a friend. That wasn't the guy I was upset about," she lied.

"Oh! Did you see last night on the news, the special that they ran about this area's increasing drug problem? It runs for three consecutive evenings. It was awfully interesting," Thedy continued to rattle, searching for the least bit of discomfort to cross Liza's face. "I guess Cocaine's the biggie, myself, I don't know that much about it. It just makes you wonder what the world's coming to."

Liza agreed, scarcely showing any signs of uneasiness. "Yeah, it seems to be a world full of hate and unconcern. I try to distance myself from it, but that's not always easy either. If I spent time worrying about it, I'd be scared or angry all the time."

Thedy sensed that the drug issue was abruptly ended, while mounds of rationality and some feelings of closeness were quickly disappearing in the silence. She wasn't about to lose her friend and hairdresser over needless prattle. She'd change the subject.

"My Drake, he's all upset these days. You knew Dani Ellison didn't you?"

"Sure, she'd come in here occasionally. But what do you mean by *knew*!"

"Well, Friday night she left. Her husband's here and says she didn't come home. He thinks it's a kidnaping or some such thing. We're trying to help him, but Dani's note said she was leaving and her white Mercedes is gone, too, and..."

"Did you say *white Mercedes?*" Liza's voice rose, while her ears prickled forward with extreme interest. Liza squirted the hot oil from its tube and patted it all around Thedy's wet locks.

"Yes, Dani and her car are gone and no one seems to know where they've gone. Sounds like you've seen her car before."

"Um, well, yes as a matter of fact, I'd noticed it quite often in the lot. I didn't realize that it was Dani's car, though. I suppose her husband is fit to be tied."

"He's a very sweet man and he's got their two children with him here. It's very difficult for all of them I'm sure. Then on top of it, when we took them to Dani's room, one of the girls picked up a little glass tube and then Drake went off yelling about that it must be used for drugs and accusing Dani. Gosh, it's been a long weekend. Feels good what you're doing to my head. I really needed this."

Liza finished Thedy up as quickly as she could, determined to check out more about Dani's car and children. Was it possible that she'd actually ridden in Dani's white Mercedes?

It couldn't be true. It didn't add up. Why and how would Beebee have gotten hold of it? And if it was true, where was that car now? Could it be possible that Beebee knew something about Dani's disappearance? With no more hesitation, Liza cleaned up her station and walked with a fast rhythmic stride toward the front office. The person who seemed to know it all was Trixie, and whatever she knew, Liza intended to find out. There was one thing that Liza knew she could count on and that was Beebee's tempter. He'd be furious if he found her snooping around about the car. She'd have to be very careful with the way she approached Trixie.

Trixie contemplated the work in front of her. A heap of notes and phone calls plagued her otherwise structured routine. They were all calls aimed at the administration and several clients expressing concern over Dani's disappearance. The news had leaked. Were their family members safe, they wondered? Drake refused to answer even one call and so the brunt of the problem fell on Trixie's lap. And it was a problem. How could she be expected to answer something she knew nothing of? How could she answer eerie questions with a positive attitude when she herself felt a trickling of terror? How could Drake believe that she could address what he was ignoring and also keep up with all the tasks identified in her regular job description?

Flustered at the onset of the gloomy day, Trixie felt less productive than ever. She refused to let it show as she began to sort messages in a logical order. She listed her priorities and decided on a lingo in her mind that she could relay to those families that inquired… something that might soothe the agitating facts that now surrounded her. Where was Dani anyway? At first she had truly believed Dani's note, but increasing doubt weighted upon her shoulders each day that lapsed and Dani's disappearance became more of an undisputed reality.

Liza talked directly to Trixie… small talk, the weather, hair, and diet, with an occasional note of humor. Finally, she was unable to stall any longer and decided to pop the question.

"Trixie," Liza fidgeted as she leaned over Trixie's desk with a purposeful hushedness in her voice, "do you know anything about Dani Ellison?"

"What do you mean?" Trixie stiffened, swiping at the edges of her blunt cut.

"Well, Thedy told me that she's gone and that her car is also gone. Is her family here?"

"What? I can't hear you, Liza. Talk up!"

"Her family, are they here?"

"Yes, Richard and the girls are staying in Dani's room. Did you mention her Mercedes? Yes, it's gone, too. She left this note."

Immediately Trixie was unsure that she should have confided in Liza the contents of the note, but gee, no one else around the office would discuss it. Trixie absent-mindedly tossed Dani's file Liza's way. Trixie felt sleeved into the conversation, but quite frankly she needed Liza's ear right now.

Liza flipped the pages of the meager manila folder and gasped when she came across the name **Heather**.

"Heather is Dani's daughter?"

"Yeah. A sweet little kid. Do *you* know her?"

"No, no. It's my niece's name. Just love the name, that's all."

The name! Wasn't that the name on the doll case she'd seen in the Mercedes that Beebee had driven? Liza was sure of it. What did all of this mean? Liza searched for the right words, all the while not being able to ignore the doll case with Heather's name etched on it as well as in Liza's mind. She felt ill.

"Let me know, Trixie, when you need a trim. Here you go, enough of this spooky stuff. It's back to work for me."

Liza gently tossed the folder onto Trixie's crowded desktop, trying desperately to sound unconcerned.

"See you later then. Bye."

*****

Richard was surprised but pleased at Liza's request to have the girls come down and get a beauty treatment. She seemed nice enough and interested. Besides, any friend of Dani's would be fine. He really hadn't wanted to drag the girls with him while he did some snooping anyway and Liza sounded very willing to keep them busy for a while. Certainly Heather and Kristin would have the fun they deserved delving into make-up and hair do-dads.

He delivered the girls personally, one holding tight to each of his hands. They seemed reluctant, but Liza was friendly and quickly guided them, gaining their attention and trust.

"And here we have all sorts of dangle and beaded barrettes. Would you each like one for your hair?"

The girls nodded in unison, but Heather spoke up, "Oh we'd love one of those, but we'll have to ask Daddy first."

"Well your Dad told me that today each of you are special, and it's OK if I treat you to a few things. So, why don't you each pick one you like and we'll work it into your hair-do. I'm just positive that your Daddy won't mind. In fact he'll be happy to come back and pick up the prettiest two girls around."

Liza proceeded to work on Kristin first answering her many questions. Kristin was very intelligent for her twelve years and it was obvious that a beauty salon was nothing new to her. She had a thick head of light brown hair with natural blonde highlights and Liza easily convinced her that a French braid would look charming.

"Your turn," Liza announced to Heather, "Come on over."

There was no doubt that Heather belonged to Dani. Looking into her big green innocent eyes forced a chill down Liza's spine. She hoped Dani was found soon!

"What do you think we can do with these pretty blonde curls? I sure wish my hair was as silky and shiny as this. Yours is really beautiful. How about if we just wash and set it, but let it hang natural? I could pull the sides and top back and clip your barrette up here like this."

Liza gently held the front of Heather's hair in an upsweep position and Heather grinned and nodded yes for approval.

Liza knew her time was running short and her manager politely reminded her that her regular customers were patiently waiting. She left Heather for a moment to catch up on a quick wash. When she returned Heather was playing with a wig she had pinned to a Styrofoam head form. Heather had a few brush curlers dangling onto the ends of the black wig.

"I'll bet you play beauty parlor all of the time with your dolls," Liza coaxed her.

"Yeah. Sometimes I even get Kristin to play, but she says she's too big for Barbies now. I'm not, but I have to get my clothes and stuff from Mommy's car, otherwise I can't play."

Liza's stomach sank. She wanted to hear this, but not really.

"Oh, you left your dolls in your Mommy's car?"

"Only one doll. I have lots more. But I forgot my Barbie's clothes and some furniture. Daddy said maybe he can find it today. I'd rather have him find Mommy though."

Liza tried to push down the persistent lump that kept rising in her throat. She didn't know how to answer the kid, and she knew even less how she was going to confront Beebee with her findings. She would have to make sure her information was accurate and left no room for any of Beebee's benign excuses. Her head lurched into fast forward as ribbons of visions reeled past. Liza rubbed her eyes trying to rid them of the terrible things they suspected. But they would not cooperate. No matter what she did to distract the horrible image, it was Dani's distorted face that came to view. And lightly in the background she heard the distant whining. That God awful whining that she had heard in the cave on Friday. Her head was light with confusion and barely enough strength crept back into her voice to answer the saddened little girl, "Yes, dear. I hope you find your Mommy, too."

*****

Beebee's thick eyebrows raised with restrained expectations, as he watched Malory attempt the exercise he had instructed. She was pretty all right, her red hair dropping to the floor as she bent forward. But pretty didn't matter... she was trouble... and he had to get rid of her. She didn't know that she was safe now and she wouldn't realize until it was too late when she would be in danger. It would be soon though, Beebee was sure of that. This morning he was certain that he couldn't extend her time beyond a day or two. In fact, if she stayed clear of her friends, he may have the opportunity at the end of the session to nab her. Beebee's anticipation rose, leaving him with an undesirable knot mid-chest.

CHAPTER 16

Saul had sent his secretary, Eva Dunlap, out immediately following Malory's phone call to do some extensive searching into the records of Jill Simon. While he awaited her return, he himself had contacted Sgt. Rick Travantis of the Dane County Police Department. He was annoyed with the response he got. Sgt. Rick did not want to be bothered, that was obvious.

Saul clasped his fingers together supporting his neck as he stretched his legs out, resting his feet upon his desk. If Eva were here, she'd have a canary. She'd tell him never, never, never put that chair on only two legs. And he'd answer her, "Yes, mother." Saul gazed out his window, noticing that the sun had finally decided to pop. He wondered for how long. Just then Eva made her entrance, clearly anxious to state her findings.

"Well, she's definitely gone, vanished, disappeared out of nowhere. Could only locate a birth certificate and a marriage license recently applied for. And Saul, looks like she was into drugs."

"Marriage license?" Saul was truly surprised.

"Yes, to a man by the name of Paul Wynette. The family said they'd gone together for only a month," Eva was winded, as she excitedly pushed her sagging glasses back up to her nose.

"Paul Wynette, hmm, that name does sound familiar. I'll ask Malory."

"I'll bet you will," Eva teased.

Saul chuckled and then continued questioning Eva. "What makes you say drugs?"

"The family doesn't believe that part, but they were told that drug paraphernalia was found in the room... nothing else. No clothes, shoes, nothing. The room was stripped."

"Did she have a car there?"

"No. I thought of that, too. But she had also left a note saying that she had to quit the program at this time. All sounds familiar, doesn't it?"

"Too much so."

Saul was confused. It was easy to observe and dissect all the facts in retrospect, but wouldn't the administration question two similar incidents of women just leaving without a real explanation? He was irritated now with Drake's appearance of nonconcern. What was wrong with the man? Unless... no... he wouldn't be involved. Why jeopardize a good business?

Saul picked up the rest of Eva's notes and asked her to make a Xerox copy of them for him. It was time. He had to get back out to Melrose. Perhaps Sgt. Rick didn't care, but Saul sure did. He was determined to know the truth. If two people were truly missing, he feared even more than he had before for Malory's outcome.

Saul would attempt a check of Jill's room although he felt sure it would be hopeless. Some new client certainly would be occupying it by this late date. He'd have to get that check from Sgt. Rick, assuming he did anything at all. Saul's search of Dani's room had turned up negative. Finger prints must have been wiped clean, and he spotted no unusual threads, fibers, or hair to do any checking on. Once again he found his mind caught up in a tug-of-war against a force that is mindless. How do you outsmart a psychopath? Someone that obviously doesn't think normally or carry any sense of remorse for their actions, is not easy to figure for someone so opposite.

Saul arrived at Melrose, smartly clad in his tidy uniform, during the early afternoon hours. He anticipated the long frustrating afternoon to extend into overtime. It often did.

"Hi, there."

"Hello, Sgt. Keller. What can I do for you?" Trixie asked.

"I was hoping you'd be in a very helpful mood. I'm pleased. Actually I think you're the person who can help me," Saul smiled acutely aware of Trixie's crimson blush.

"Anything for the law."

"I'm interested in a note you may have on file. This time the one left by Jill Simon."

Trixie was taken aback, her generally calm exterior seemed to crumble. "Uh, uh Jill Simon?"

"Yes, you remember Jill, don't you?"

"Why certainly, I guess I'm just surprised that you know who she is," Trixie admitted.

"That's my business, Trixie. Any help you can offer would certainly be appreciated." Again Saul gave a winning smile.

"The note that was left by Jill was given to her family."

"Why?"

Again Trixie was shaken. How could she know the answer to this? "I, I really don't know. Drake gave the orders. I followed them."

"I realize you're in that position here, but you seem to have a good working relationship. Perhaps Drake told you why? Or maybe even Thedy?"

"No. I don't know why. And I never asked. I do my work, that's all."

"Do you have a file on Jill at all?"

"Let me look."

Let me look! Saul didn't believe that. He would venture to guess that Trixie knew each file inside and out. Instead of telling her that, he waited patiently as she stiffly walked to the drawer and pulled the one he requested. Quietly, she handed it to him.

He jotted down the family address and phone although Eva had already supplied him with that. He scanned the other information and believed it was fairly standard, nothing stood out as unusual.

"One more thing, Trixie, I'd like to take a look around Jill's old room."

"I can't just let you do that. I'll have to call on Drake."

Trixie winced as she wedged a finger under the telephone system, cleared her throat, and picked up the receiver to get Drake's attention.

"Yes," Trixie answered Drake's question shaking like an old jalopy as she looked up at Saul, her face as white as chalk.

"He'll be right here, Mr. Keller." Trixie looked down to avoid Saul's questioning look. He certainly would like to know what Drake had said to her. He could tell it was no time to ask.

"What's going on here?" Drake asked by way of a greeting.

"For starters, your secretary has been much more helpful than you, but it's your permission I need to search Jill Simon's old room."

"And if I say no?"

"I'll search it anyway."

"You know what your problem is?" Drake fumed silent hisses out of his tightened lips, realizing now was the time to restrain himself. "Never mind, there's the number and key. Knock first, I'd like as little disruption as possible."

"You amaze me Mr. Melrose. Your attitude reeks of guiltiness."

"Meaning?"

"Meaning don't plan any long vacations."

Saul turned abruptly, leaving Drake sputter and bubble his anger minus himself as an audience.

Saul persisted with a thorough investigation of the room knowing full well that its outcome would be futile. It was too late. He walked amongst pantyhose hung in strings of paper doll ribbons over the bathroom shower curtain, contemplating Drake's reasons for contacting Sgt. Rick after Jill's disappearance, and Sgt. Rick's logic in responding to Saul in such a thoughtless manner. None of his speculations seemed to pan out. By rights, Jill's disappearance should have been reported to Saul instead of to her home precinct, where Sgt. Rick also resided. Somewhere along the line he should have been informed, and the fact that he wasn't left even more unanswered questions.

Part of Saul needed to continue an intense investigation, to find out all of the sordid details, to understand the working of a criminal mind... yet, part of him longed to escape his identity as an officer of the law, live in the world of ignorant bliss, and obliterate all need to protect one's self and loved ones from evil forces.

Finishing one of many rounds, the time arrived when Malory had said she'd be available. Saul had no doubt that the next minutes that he could devote to her would be his favorite of the day. He knew he was lying to himself when he tried to convince his conscience that it was out of duty he was going to visit her. True, she felt she needed his protection, but

149

when he thought of her, his ideas were not all businesslike. Even before Malory answered his gentle knocks, Saul could envision her pert little nose and sensuous lips. He had always been attracted to redheads, and he found the combination with her baby-blue eyes intriguing.

Malory invited him in and wasting no time, began to relay all of her disturbing news. As she began to speak she noticed Saul's face was a wee bit flushed. An unexpected surge of adrenalin pumped through her when she met him eye to eye in a brief recognition of explicit attraction.

"I'm so glad you're here," Malory began, realizing how she truly meant that. "Of all things, I walked in the door a few minutes ago and got a very unsettling phone call."

"Who'd you hear from?"

"That's just it. They didn't say. I'm sure it was a man's voice though. He said he hoped I'd be waiting for him and then said something really stupid at the end, almost like it was a joke. He said 'yes indeedy'. Does that make sense?

"No, but that's exactly why I don't like the sounds of it, because it doesn't make sense. Did you check on these windows?"

"The custodians told me a bulldozer would have trouble with them. I'm pretty certain that no one could get in that way now."

"Good and I brought the dead-bolt lock, so I'll get busy and install that."

As he worked on Malory's door, Saul was determined not to show her how disturbed he was by the phone call. He changed the topic inquiring about how her classes at the resort were coming along. He glanced her way periodically and watched her hair flow delicately down her shoulders as she gathered the pamphlets she had spoken to him about.

When he was finished, Malory gave him the leaflets. "I sure thought I'd find something to help in here, especially in the part about all of the staff, but I'm afraid nothing clicked. I shouldn't say this, but I was most concerned about Drake, yet that doesn't make sense, does it?"

"To be quite honest with you, Mal, I'm at a loss myself."

Malory watched Saul page through the booklet, his strong arms seemingly too large for such small papers. The printed material seemed lost in his meaty fingers. She looked again at his masculine jaw line, knowing that it was bound to send shivers through her. He was intent with his work and Malory knew she should not disturb him no matter how much she wanted to.

Saul could see that it would help him to concentrate on the printed blurb on each staff member, but he couldn't do that now. He was just about to close the booklet when he spotted the name, Paul Wynette. He knew now why Jill's fiancé's name had such a familiar ring to it. He was listed as the gym and track instructor. Saul tried not to show any signs of disclosure as he folded the pages and tucked them into his breast pocket.

"I wanted to let you know that I have taken serious Jill Simon's disappearance and I am in the process of working on that also. I need to ask you one more question. Has Jade or anyone mentioned any connection with either girl and drugs?"

"No. Hold it, that's not exactly true. It didn't come from Jade, but from Richard. When they were given Dani's room, one of the girls found a glass tooter on the carpet. Drake had an absolute fit, accusing Dani of being involved in drugs. Richard was obviously upset, not believing a word of it."

"What do you believe?"

"I don't know if I'm the proper judge only meeting Dani once, but, from getting to know Jade and the rest of this wing, I'd say it's unlikely. I don't believe it."

Saul was sorry it was time for Malory to go back to her classes. He felt so overwhelmed with everything he had to do, he'd much rather take a break and play hooky with Malory, but high school days had long since passed and reality screamed at him to move on with conviction. He'd solve this mess yet.

Impulsively, he reached over and kissed Malory on the cheek longing for much more, but it wasn't professional. "Be careful, and call if you need me."

Malory was touched as she simply nodded her head.

Saul left Malory feeling the frustration of controlling his personal desires as well as those of a tedious demanding job. Although he loved the work, Saul understood about its endless pitfalls. He walked into the fresh air hoping that its briskness would somehow clear his head and direct him to the answers. Facts were facts, but they had an odd way of changing when hit in the face with fresh air. It suddenly came to Saul where he might find some answers. He finished wrapping the tooter he'd gotten from Richard in Kleenex and stuffed it deep in his pants pocket. He looked up, realizing that he should have known when he had the first twinge of horror out near the cave that his answers were hidden somewhere amongst the great Sierras meshed unobtrusively with human touches. He felt certain that the answers were only footsteps away from him as he stood outside of Melrose's entrance way. An atrium of power surged through him as he decided to plunge forward and once again cover the surrounding territory.

*****

Saul was positive that the air shimmered with crystals of oxygen, though he was having a hard time connecting them with the tip of his nose. His chest was heavy, heaving up and down with irregular beats. The anxiety he was experiencing was controlling him with tightened arms and he would surely wrestle with its grips of panic in efforts to complete this search.

Saul gave himself permission to skip the cave itself, vowing to line up an organized crew for that job upon the immediate return to his office. It was becoming more apparent all the time how quickly he should and would be moving on this case. He suspected that Malory was in great jeopardy although he saw no need to alarm her more than she already was. He would make it his business to keep good tabs on her.

It was imperative that somewhere out in this vast wilderness Saul locate at least one clue and a variety of speculations. He was now faced with two abductions, instead of the one that at first he questioned. Almost three days had vanished since Dani's disappearance so he prayed to God there was still hope. Each day that passed allowed more confidence to slide downhill and less reassurance to surface. He had to sharpen the tiring cogs of his investigative clock, not allowing time to grind away at its notches until it slipped beyond his reach.

Saul knew he should be seeing it, but he couldn't. He felt too stupid or not sadistic enough to interject his own thoughts onto those of a sick man. Was he sure it was a man? His eyes mounted each tree, branch, rock, or growth within seeing distance. His pupils were hurtled into eternity in a game that he was destined to lose. What was wrong with him? He was disgusted at the thought of giving up. It was unlike him and Saul suddenly rumpled his voice into a snarl. No way would he allow this animal to dictate him, deceive him or thrust any more harm upon Malory or anyone else. He'd allow wisdom and the hands of God to intercede. That monster better be ready because Saul was ready to submerge.

As he suspected the late afternoon mist was beginning to transcend. It draped its willowy branches overhead choking off any signs of a spring-blue sky, winding its tentacles around each and every growth threatening to strangle it with one little whip of the wind. Saul continued to nose around, ignoring the endless lack of air.

Using a long stick, Saul poked the ground repeatedly and combed the entire circumference of the outside edge of the Melrose property. Saul knew the area was rich in soil and loaded with underground streams and caves. He wound his way through to a wooded cliff and saw a gigantic dog staring him in the face. He was taken aback by this beautiful creature crudely shaped by hardened lava, so unique of this Sequoia area. He trailed his weary feet a few more steps to allow a peek over the edge. The ability of the human mind to create images was astounding and perhaps even alarming, especially in time of necessity. Saul was sure he was peering across into a rotund pool of green rippled water, when instead he leaned forward to thousands of swaying evergreens, deep and immense. He stared for only a moment and then he saw it! Tire marks! The unexpected clue he was seeking. He knelt down to touch the shallow impressions, already partially destroyed by a rainfall. They must have been ankle-deep or more at one point and he was not certain enough was left for a positive identification... still they were there, proof of the foul play that was now so visible.

CHAPTER 17

The day had ended as dreary as it began, with only a few hours resembling the spring season that Malory ached so to see. The sky had faded from its washed out blue shade to a dull gray, filled with waves of rolling fog. Her exercise routine had seemed to invigorate her and she was looking forward to spending an evening with Jade, Nick, and Paris. It was unbelievable that she'd known them for only a matter of days and still she knew more about them than she did her coworkers at the office, some of whom she worked with for four years. She was sure their conversation would sway to Dani and all that they had shared in so little time. She hoped it did anyway, or she would see to it. Malory was anxious to voice her own concerns and surmise in group effort any other considerations they may have.

Malory had changed from her sweats into jeans and strode into the crowded cafeteria hunting for the familiar threesome.

"Over here," Jade motioned. "We've been waiting for you."

"I'm starved. I sure hope they believe in healthy portions tonight. I'm not quite in the mood for a carrot stick or two."

All were in agreement with Malory, but when dinner was served it included a thin slice of rare roast beef, a smidgen of seasoned noodles and the infamous carrot sticks. They all laughed.

During a sugar-free dessert, the conversation on Dani finally began.

"I noticed that Sgt. Keller came to see you this noon? Anything new?" Nick asked.

"Not really. Although one thing happened to me that I'm concerned about. I had an anonymous phone call. That was at noon and in fact I had two during the time I left you guys, while I was getting dressed to come here. The final one was a bit of a threat."

It wasn't difficult for Paris to see the darkening creases in Malory's brows. "What do you mean by threatening?"

"Well, I haven't even had the time to tell Saul this, but the man on the other end seems to think I like to listen to his heavy breathing and hysterical laughing. To tell you the truth, it's scaring the heck out of me."

"That's it? Breathing?" Jade asked, while the other two sat silent.

"Not really. After that, he said **yes indeedy, you'll see Beebee real soon!**"

"What's a Beebee?"

"Got me. I have no idea. Maybe this isn't connected to Dani at all. It's just that I have an awful feeling about it."

"I can see why," Nick attempted to console Malory by putting his arm around her shoulder, "I think you should tell Sgt. Keller about it right away."

"Saul."

"Right, Saul."

"Nick's right, Malory," Jade said assuredly. "And I also have some suspicions about Dani's abduction and I don't like them at all."

"Speak up, tell us what's on your mind," Paris told her.

"I have two people on my mind lately, Drake and Paul."

"How could you think Drake?" Nick asked.

"I really can't see Drake wanting to ruin his business with crime. Though I thought of him, too," Malory continued as she reached over to get a packet of Equal for her coffee, "but it doesn't feel right. I know he's acting strange or maybe unconcerned, but I'll bet it's his way of coping."

"Seems to me it's not coping," Paris corrected her.

"I suppose, but there are so many possibilities. Like Jade said, what about Paul? And Dani's own husband could even be a suspect."

"Richard. Oh my God!" Jade was beside herself with disbelief at what she was hearing, "come on. Richard wouldn't hurt a flea."

"It's not a flea we're talking about, besides I didn't say he did it. I meant that no one could be ruled out at this point."

"I guess so, but Richard is so, gosh, husbandly. I can't imagine that he's anything but concerned. In fact later, Malory, I want you to go with me to see him. I want to see how he's holding."

"Sure, Jade. I'd like to know if he was able to track down clues or information of any kind."

"As I think about all the people here, staff and clients, I can't help but go over and over in my head anyone that had any even slight reason to be upset with Dani."

Jade looked into the space in front of her with a blank stare, obviously upset and waiting to see if the rest were as bothered as she was. The tears began to roll freely.

"I'm sorry," she continued, "but there's still one incident that I can't seem to shake. Do you guys remember one day, oh about two weeks ago, when Bart was giving Dani a hard time during our tennis session? I know he's short with us often, but that particular day he was downright rude. And I remember him saying to Dani that she could work her tail off to get thin but nothing could change the fact that she had a stupid name and that she was a low-life woman. It's probably nothing, but I was real tempted right then and there to go to Drake and Dani wouldn't let me."

"Maybe you're right and it meant nothing. Both Bart and Barry are curt most of the time they speak. It's their way."

Paris cushioned his word with a kiss. Trying everything within his power to console Jade.

Come on, why don't we all lighten up. Paris, how about a few rounds of tennis while the girls visit Richard?" Nick was enthusiastic as he jumped up from the table, filled his chest with a fresh tank of air, and motioned to the doorway.

*****

Richard did not answer the door promptly and both Jade and Malory began to wonder if he and the girls had left. Before too long Kristin slowly opened the door calling, "Daddy, Jade is here."

They walked into the room and found Richard plopped across the rumpled turned-down bed, apparently exhausted. Richard rolled over dangling his feet and hands over the edge of the mattress and squinted up through a set of slitted eyes. Almost as if in slow motion he forced himself to a sitting position and then managed to arrest all movement.

"Maybe we've chosen a poor time," Jade began, "would you rather we came back at another time?"

"No. Please stay. Just give me a minute."

"How about if I get all of us some coffee. I'll be right back."

When Malory returned, Richard looked a little more alive than he had. He and Jade were talking avidly and coffee was sure to hit the spot.

"I don't understand it, Jade. Dani's disappeared off of the face of the earth and it's like a nightmare. No one believes it."

"Who doesn't believe it?" Jade bluntly asked as she poured two packs of Equal into her cup.

"I spent a good part of the morning with Saul Keller and I'm not even sure he believes it. Then I picked the girls up from here and did tons of phone calling, friends, relatives, you name it. Many were willing to come up here and help. If I don't get answers soon, I will take them up on their offers. I don't know where to turn. That's the big problem. Actually that's not it either. I really think someone from right here, besides you, Malory, must have seen something. I'd like to ask around, but I'm not sure how it will sit with Drake."

"I think you should do it anyway," Malory offered. "What can it hurt? Drake could only get angry and he's that anyway. Just be discreet."

"Sure, make yourself available in the cafeteria and all over and soon people will come to you. You'll be able to ask all the questions you like. Although really, Richard, I can't imagine it's anyone that works here, I hope." The tinge of doubt in Jade's voice was all that Richard needed.

"It's hard to imagine any of this, but let's face it, someone is responsible and I aim to find out who. This is moving too slow, as I pointed out to Saul. This is already Monday evening and he doesn't have so much as a clue."

"Maybe."

"What do you mean **maybe**, Malory? Do you know something?"

"No, Richard, but a cop isn't going to discuss all of his findings. That wouldn't be kosher."

"Yeah, I guess that's right. I feel so helpless though. And I want Dani back, unharmed."

"We all do."

"I've got an idea," Richard spoke rapidly in a higher than normal pitch. "Would you be willing to stay with the girls for a while? I want to start right now with talking to staff and clients."

"I don't mind. If you see Paris, though, let him know where I am and if you find out anything, come back and tell us right away."

"It's a deal."

Richard's fatigue was nowhere to be seen as he excitedly hopped up from the chair, pleasantly said good-night to his children, and darted forward toward the door, bound and determined to complete his mission.

*****

The chilled air insisted disagreeable pain on Liza's fingertips as she waited impatiently for Beebee. She was already irritated with him, so he'd be wise not to push his luck. He should have been here fifteen minutes ago. Liza danced up and down on her tip-toes and wove her fingers into tight little balls, while she listened to the wild breeze in the distance, hooting the awnings and whipping the branches in harsh rhythmic strides.

The wait was endless and Liza was perturbed by the remote but continuous hollow groaning. Was it a sick animal? Where was Beebee anyway? She could just pop him in the head, she was so angry. But she was sure he'd look at her with those big cow eyes and she'd melt. It didn't matter though; she'd vowed to herself that regardless of how she loved him, and pitied him, she would find out what it was he knew about Dani's car.

Beebee was out of breath. "Sorry I'm late," he gasped.

"It's freezing here."

"Why didn't you go farther in? You knew I'd be here shortly."

"I don't' like those noises I hear. Do you think it's an animal?"

"Perhaps. I'll be back in a minute."

Liza watched Beebee sink deeper and deeper into the cave. When she no longer saw his light, she curled up against the wall trying to benefit from the fire she'd begun. In no time at all the warmth permeated the immediate area and she actually had to discard her jacket. Liza cringed at the whining and for a split second thought it was a baby crying… and then there was dead silence. The stillness was almost worse than the merciless sound.

It was then that Brisket trailed across the dirt and stopped in front of her. Was that who she heard? She beckoned him to her and like an obedient pup he came. She felt sorry for him noticing his limp toward her and realizing how far from being a pup he was. His straggly fur was moist and matted, but he wagged his friendly stump of a tail anyway. Liza noticed something blue around his neck and attempted to yank at it, but Brisket wouldn't allow her near it. He bolted out of the mouth of the cave almost as if he knew it would be a mistake. Liza quickly forgot about Brisket when she spotted Beebee heading her way.

"It's okay, Babe. It was an old hyena and I ran him out."

Liza wondered where he ran out to, but she left it drop, not really caring, just glad the moaning had ceased.

"Come here now, it's cozy." She guided him next to her, aware that her own fire was burning now. She was anything but cold and completely unaware of the blustery weather outside.

Beebee moved his experienced fingers around her waist, unsnapping her jeans and gently tugging her chiffon blouse over her head. She reached for the quilted sleeping bag to cushion her bottom as Beebee mounted her. In this state, Liza felt guilty knowing that she fully planned to drill him for information later. She had to know. For the time being, however, she pretended he was the best... the master... the only satisfying man to come into her life. It wasn't really a lie, as Liza found Beebee far superior in his performance most of the time. Tonight was no exception. The struggle would come in separating Beebee her love from his mysterious side. Liza felt certain he was hiding something.

The way to approach the subject did not come easy as Liza laid next to Beebee dabbing at his sweaty forehead. She was apprehensive knowing that it would probably cause an argument. She trailed her fingers across his strong cheekbones noticing the dim view of a smile on his face, somewhat derisive. The man could be impossible at times. What was on his mind now? It didn't matter, because Liza would dare to ask her question and surely shatter any thoughts he had.

Resolutely, she began, "Did you make up your mind about the Mercedes?"

Liza swallowed hard and could tell faintly that Beebee was squirming under the blankets. She tipped her hand to shield the light of the lantern from her eyes.

"I thought I told you not to worry about that car," he snapped, controlling an idle snarl caught deep within his throat.

"Well, I'm not worried, I just wondered," Liza managed to keep her voice even though she felt unattractive welts of anger invading her lead-weighted tongue.

"Don't wonder, Liza. The subject is closed."

Weak with fright, Liza couldn't let it drop. "I thought how nice it would be, a fairly new car and all. You know," she grabbed him purposely where the sun doesn't shine, "I mean it'd be much more comfortable than this old dirt and blankets."

Beebee was white with anger. He felt the temperature drill through his heart like a hot poker. He sat up holding his hands and gritting his teeth. Suddenly he swiped out at her grabbing her neck from behind, leaving no doubt what would come next. Liza scooted her butt back trying to loosen his grip, but it didn't work. His other paw descended with a heavy thud upon her shoulder, taking her by surprise. Liza knew he had done this before many times. In a blind rage, with his flat eyes fixed on her he graveled to grasp a clump of her hair by the nape of her neck and drew the lantern close to her face.

"I'm going to tell you only one more time," he sputtered fire into her vulnerable eyes, "don't ever mention **that** car to me or to anyone again. Got it?"

Liza knew her voice was gone but she nodded slightly. Beebee's malignant manner challenged her to dispute his words or actions. She was sure if she did, she'd be dead. Had he really gone berserk? He positioned her long, bony extremities for easy access. Liza could taste her salty tears as she winced at his jerky animalistic pushes that ripped inside of her again.

CHAPTER 18

Mondays have a way of turning into Tuesdays, and this one was no exception. Richard kept the girls close to his side, feeling that a walk in the brisk fresh air would do all of them some good. The grounds were vast and he felt his sense of loss twofold in such a huge area. It was vacant, like his life, these past few days. He was somewhat fearful of bringing the girls along, just in case… there it was again, his negativism. He had to stop it, for his sake and that of everyone else. It wasn't fair. He had to be strong and he had to believe Dani would be found alive.

Richard believed it when Saul told him that he found nothing out here when he searched the grounds, he only hoped there was some small detail that was overlooked. Richard had to see for himself. It was kind of like the fat lady at the circus or the nine foot tall giant, one just had to look on their own. The phenomena was unbelievable unless your very own eyes took it in. Richard's eyes had to see the *nothing* that Saul talked about in order to accept its truth.

Gradually Kristin walked slightly in front of Richard and Heather, anxious to see what the land held for her next.

"Daddy, what's that?" Kristin pointed to the hard form under her boot.

"Looks like limestone. This place is loaded with all sorts of growth and rock formations. Be careful, you almost tripped there. Besides, the ground is soggy."

"Okay."

"Daddy," Heather tugged on Richard's khaki jacket, "are we almost done?"

"Heather, shh," Kristin told her. "We just started to look."

"Look for what?"

Richard felt knots gather in his stomach and tighten upon that thought. How could he tell a little child, his own no less, what he was really looking for?

"Honey, we're looking for anything that might help us find Mommy."

"Are we looking for Mommy?"

"Yes."

"In these weeds?"

"I thought maybe Mommy got lost."

The sky was not nearly as overcast as Richard's gloomy outlook and Kristin shot him a knowing glance. If Heather started in again, he'd have to quickly exit from the conversation. They walked thirty or forty feet more when they heard a bark coming nearer to them and then Richard recognized the old fix-it man. Tom Tinnley. He limped toward the residential building and hollered at his dog to keep near. There's one person whom Richard hadn't the chance to speak to.

"Is that the dog Thedy said we could play with?" Heather asked, interrupting his thoughts.

"I believe so."

For some reason, Richard could not shake the image of Tom limping across the field. He made a mental note to find the old guy later and see if he knew anything that would help. It briefly crossed his mind how good a dog might be on a

165

search, but again the idea was cut short by the never ending questions.

"Can I climb one of them trees, Daddy?"

"No. That's not a good idea. That type of tree isn't even a good climber."

"Look at all the pine cones. Can we collect some?"

Typical, kids rarely wait for the answer before another question oozes out of their mouth?

"Sure, fill you pockets."

Was that actually a few minutes of quiet that Richard heard? He took full advantage by reflecting last night's conversations with some of the staff members. He couldn't say any of them had devastating news, but he felt he learned something by watching their mannerisms in an uncomfortable questioning session. Paul Wynette never looked him in the eyes. Tia Jovan was very apologetic. Bart Bante was your typical wise ass. Neely Orth was overly concerned and Liza Kipper was in a big hurry.

Although none of those observations would fare well in a court of law, they were interesting and one couldn't help making them. He still had many more to talk to and he wanted to do it soon before word got back to Drake. Drake was bound to put the cabash on it.

"Daddy."

There it was again. Richard was trying to be very patient, though he feared it was running on the thin side today. He had to laugh however, when he looked back to see both girls coming at him with pockets so stuffed that they could hardly walk.

"I'd say you have plenty of pine cones. What was it you wanted, Kristin?"

"Is that a big hole over there?"

"Where?"

"There." She pointed to a hump covered thick with branches and surrounded by rock.

It seemed obvious, but unobvious. Certainly someone took great care to make the cave entrance look inconspicuous. That idea alone bothered Richard. He really didn't want to go in it, or let the girls near it.

"Come back here, girls. Daddy's going to go tell Sgt. Keller about this. As the words came out of his mouth, Richard couldn't help but wonder why Keller hadn't told him. What else had Keller forgot to mention? Or was he so blind he hadn't even noticed a cave?

*****

Saul leaned over the morning newspaper disappointed to find an error filled account of Dani's disappearance as front page news. He had hoped to avoid this, as it always made his job more difficult. He was sure the culprit for its print was Richard. Saul supposed he couldn't totally blame him and so he smiled grudgingly.

The drive to work was relaxing as he rolled along the winding road at an easy speed. Today the weather was a fooler; it looked sunny and bright, although Saul guessed it wouldn't last, still the cool air hit with force. Spring always tried so hard to emerge to be endlessly slapped in the back of the head by winter. It seemed uncanny and Saul sure hoped Friday evening had wrapped up the end of the snow business. He didn't mind the heavy spring rains though he hoped they waited until after today. He had an expert going out to Melrose to take a look at the tire imprints and he knew they could not withstand a great amount of rain. In fact he felt proud of the plan he had now set in his mind to search for Dani.

The arrogance that Saul had felt just a second before was blasted when he turned into the precinct parking lot. In no time at all he came face to face with Richard, as Richard huffed out of his car and up the cement slab. His walk was a definite *I want to see you now!* walk. Saul hadn't even the chance to grab his morning coffee. What a day! He could feel it already.

"Hi there, Mr. Ellison. What can we do for you?" Saul greeted politely and opened the door for Richard as the two of them entered the building. "How about a cup of coffee?"

"Not right now. I want to talk first."

"What's on your mind?"

"My wife. What's on yours? The same I hope."

"You seem upset about something. Why don't you just come out with it?" Saul motioned for Richard to sit as he spoke.

"I took a look around this morning. You told me there was nothing out there."

Saul swallowed hard. Had Richard seen the tire marks?

"First of all, I said I saw **little** out there. What is it that you're wondering about?"

"The cave," Richard's voice pierced through the tiny cubicle they sat in.

"Settle down, Richard. You certainly must know from your short time in this area that caves are not unusual? Yes, I saw it and plan to have it searched. But by evidence or unusual findings, we refer to those as things that are unnaturally placed, you know, they don't belong."

"And you ignore the most obvious?"

"I don't believe that having the cave searched by experts could be called ignoring it."

"When? When is this being done?"

"It's scheduled for first thing Friday morning."

"Why don't you just wait another week? That way you can be sure Dani will be dead somewhere." Richard's sarcastic tone shot through Saul's chest like a bullet. *Couldn't he see that Saul was doing all he could?*

"I think that's very unfair of you. After all, it wouldn't do much good to do a search if the right people weren't involved. I had to set a time when certain skilled officers were available and I have two of the top speleologists in the state coming here to help us out."

Saul took out a large rolled piece of parchment paper which contained a blue-ink sketch of the cave.

"This was done by a university professor and an inexperienced crew of spelunkers, college kids. They combed many of the surrounding caves two summers ago. It's the closest thing we have and it's really very important. Surely you're not of the idea that a person should walk in and explore an unknown cave alone, are you?

"That's not what I meant. But Friday will be one whole week since Dani was taken."

"If Dani was taken, and I do believe she was, it was late Friday and remember you and I were not informed immediately. Until I discussed it with you on Sunday, I couldn't see a reason to line up an investigation crew. And like I said, being that a cave may be involved, both you and I are at the mercy of the experts. Besides, I have volunteers and officers working around the clock to hunt all the encompassing towns and fields along with twenty-four hour surveillance. I'm doing all I can and I'm sorry if you're unhappy with that."

Richard couldn't get over the simplicity with which Saul was able to explain what needed to be done. It was hardly even a dilemma to him. One minute Richard had a wife, and the next he didn't. It was so simple for Saul. It was the same kind of inane logic that anyone not in the situation would use. What if it were the doctor's wife that had inoperable cancer? Or the fireman's dad that was trapped in a ten-story skyscraper in blazes? Or the psychiatrist's mom that was schizophrenic? Or the police officer's wife that was missing?

Richard cupped his forehead in the palm of his hand, squeezing his eyes tight and wrinkling his nose helplessly, "I thought you could help, that's all." He got up slowly and calmly and turned to walk away.

"Don't do anything foolish, Richard. I *am* trying to help you."

Richard not only looked pathetic, but felt it. What did Saul mean by foolish? An attempt to save his wife could not be considered foolish even if it meant entering a cave at his own risk. He had to take the chance.

The drive back to Melrose was in a daze. Richard's head throbbed at the temples as if in a vice, and his neck felt stiff with shooting electrical currents running through it. He jammed the car in the lot at an awkward angle and began to jog toward the back of the lot. The entrance of the cave was not too far away.

His breaths became more shallow with each step he took, and practically came to a halt when the sight of the cave came into view. He had to do it... for Dani... for himself. The warning that Saul had given him played over and over again in his pounding brain. Was this really the right thing to do? What if something happened and he couldn't get help? What about the girls? Was it fair to them if he were to be missing also?

Richard couldn't seem to stop his feet from heading forward. He tried to tell them to turn back, but they possessed qualities of their own and they wouldn't listen. Only a few steps inside the cavern, and Richard was overwhelmed by blackness. A sudden chill traveled from his head to his toes. He felt he was losing a battle of tug-of-war with the cave. He wanted to keep going but something inside was telling him that he'd gone far enough. Then he heard it… a low groaning and moaning. Was it some type of animal? It began to cry in a voice that sounded evil, like the devil. Richard's heart began to pound wildly, and without another doubt, he did an about face and fled.

*****

Richard had left Saul to do some real honest to goodness soul-searching. Was he indeed doing all that was possible? He couldn't see a stone unturned, and other than occasional time he deserved spent on thoughts of Malory, Dani was all that he thought about these days. As with any prominent case, he reviewed endlessly thoughts of suspects, evidence, procedures, and interviews until he was blue in the face.

At this point the list of suspects was still large and enough holes could be shot through each theory so that the only thing left was a blank page in which to start all over again. Saul's talk with Paul Wynette was inconclusive. He was engaged with Jill and still distraught over her disappearance. He was also resentful that nothing was done about it. He named Sgt. Rick as the chief jerk in that mess. After Saul confronted Sgt. Rick, he couldn't agree more with Paul if he wanted to. It seemed that Sgt. Rick found no evidence of foul play and dismissed the case, assuming that Jill left of her own free will.

Saul went over the list daily and didn't feel free to dismiss anyone at this point right down to Drake and even Richard. Although he didn't feel comfortable with most of his speculations yet, they were nonetheless necessary. Even Jill's family were disappointing. They were resigned to accepting Sgt. Rick's lazy accusation as the truth.

A breather came when Saul took a few healing moments to fancy Malory. In all of this puzzle, the one piece he was certain of, and absolutely sure of the perfect interlocking fit to his own, was Malory. He wanted the case solved because he knew it was a horrible crime, and also because it would leave him free to be with Malory.

The pamphlets Malory had given him had been very helpful. As Saul paged through them now, he realized that he still had a few people he should talk to. He stared at the picture of a younger Tommy. This old guy appeared very nonchalant, but also very aware. Perhaps he should give him another try. Someone like Trixie was never much help; even though she had knowledge of most happenings at the place, that's the exact reason a criminal would stay clear of her. He'd even like another turn with Thedy.

Somehow whenever he considered Drake or Tommy or anyone in their age range, it came to him that it must be a male, but someone more in their thirties. An image of a young man running across the grounds of Melrose would come back to him. For awhile Saul wondered if he'd dreamt this scene, and then he vaguely remembered on one of his first visits to Melrose, he'd stepped outside for some air, and he saw some young guy run along the side of the building and enter it. He had been sure at the time the guy had been running, perhaps exercising, and also sure that he had come from the back fields. He tried now to recapture that person but he remembered there was a hood over his head and he had just started to pull it down when Saul had spotted him. He sat back trying to relax and recreate the scene. He suddenly had an urgent craving to know exactly who that man had been.

CHAPTER 19

Above, the hoot owl sang its familiar chant and below, Paul sauntered the area still partially numb with some slight tingling sensations appearing at gaited intervals. A feeling here, a memory there, but still mostly deadened by the absence of Jill. He was amazed at the fuss being made over Dani, wondering where the concern had been just weeks before when Jill was taken. A dream dressed in satin and lace was gone, a treasure of a lifetime of keepsakes stolen, and Dani's disappearance brought it back to a non-existing presence.

Paul was sick about the publicity and had half a notion to tell Malory to shut her big mouth. It only brought him pain that twisted and gnarled within the depths of his torso. He tried so to forget, but out here among the land that Jill loved so, her spirit lived. He remembered vividly the last sprint across the snow they had taken together. Jill was gratefully pleased with her weight loss.

"Hey, look at this! I can run, I'm free," she giggled and waited for him to tromp through the fluffy white blanket to catch her, "and I have *you.*"

He remembered smiling at her bubbly youth. Paul thrust forward with open arms to capture his blonde princess. They fell, laughed, and kissed until they couldn't any longer. Her rosy cheeks glistened in the gentle wintry sunlight. She tried to form a snowball, but it wasn't packy enough, so they both laid flat on their backs and flapped their arms like wings, to make angels in the snow.

Paul posed himself now at the very spot, the one where they had been happy sculpting snow angels.... only three yards away from the cliff that had swallowed Dani's Mercedes. The ground heaved with accumulated drizzle and Paul's fleecy sweats were soaked to the seams, but it didn't matter to him. He leaned over, plagued with anger, not allowing himself the luxury of a comfortable spot. He wanted to rectify all that had happened... he needed time to think... what had gone wrong?

*****

They hadn't returned until almost midnight. Paul had taken her to a popular restaurant, Dell Monaco's.

"Only the best for you, Madame," Paul teased, as Jill cozied up next to him and freshened up her lipstick before they entered.

"Tell your parents yet?"

"Sure did. I called them yesterday and my mom is at this very moment coming up with a guest list, so you can't get out of it now."

"I had no intentions of getting out of it, although I hear the ball and chain can get pretty heavy," Paul said, flashing his flirtatious eyes above the half-filled wine goblet.

"No way, mister. I don't need bondage methods to keep my man," Jill giggled at the very thought of her talking in this manner. She leaned over, exposing slight and supple cleavage.

Paul winked and looked directly into her bosom, "I have something for you," his wanting eyes stared directly at her chest and gradually moved upward until they landed smack even with her own. He pulled out a small gift-wrapped box with a bow on top made out of tiny pink loops.

"Thank you," she said as she skinned the wrap and slowly uncovered a large marquis-shaped diamond, surrounded by several chips set in a swirl of delicate silver. "I love it!" Tiny tears pattered down the sides of Jill's freckled nose as Paul slipped the beauty on her finger.

They enjoyed the rest of the quiet peaceful meal, speaking softly and intimately. At last the evening ended with a long embrace and many endearing kisses outside of Jill's room door. She longed to stand there forever, but sleep was inevitable and so she unlocked her door and went inside. She read the digital clock still in the dark and knew it was 11:43, shortly before midnight.

Jill turned to reach for the light switch, when something stung her from behind. She reached down to grab her ankle, wondering where that pain had come from, then fingered her ankle coming up with a warm wetness that she could now feel trickling to her foot. She flicked the light on to see her own blood briefly before a looming figure snapped the light off and Jill felt thick thumbs upon her throat. He pressed her neck cords tight again and again, leaving her to hear his babbling in between her gasps for air.

"Yes indeedy," he growled in a slow low monotone, "I have plans for you, Miss Simon." He gagged her mouth and turned her face-down on the bed, instructing her of the note she was to write and sign. He demanded that she look straight ahead as he provided the light from the lamp next to her bed. As she wrote, he held the gag not allowing any side movement of her head, sat on her back, and held her left arm up her back, her own fist formed between her shoulder blades.

The tears rolled onto her pillow in puddles, but he didn't seem to care. Although he was right on top of her, he was distant in her mind. He grunted and groaned, and she could feel her chicken rising in her stomach at the dank and sweaty smell of him. He kissed her bottom lip and neck full force with liver breath and Jill wanted to vomit. When her arms were free, she attempted to push him away, but her weak and frightened limbs were lost in the bulk above her.

Every cell was shrieking for air and Jill was positive that her brain had drifted out of her skull, and headed for the world beyond. Her throat was long gone, constricted beyond recognition even to herself. It had dried up and shriveled away but still she seemed to hear his roaring respirations and the crinkle of each of her own mortified joints. Her ears were still intact. Her eyes blurred so that all she could see was a dark obscure shape thumping and pumping his thumbs into her esophagus via her ripping skin. Her gaze was finally drawn away from him, as she forced herself to take one last look at the sparkling ring upon her finger, now dulled by only distant moonlight.

Beebee loaded the corpse in a thick black body pouch, grabbing her just under the knees, and hoisting her over his right shoulder. Overlooking the back ramp, he took her down one flight and out the rear exit, traveling along the edge of the tar far beyond the tennis courts. What a lug! When he hit the field he dropped her and pulled the bag by the long attached strings. She slid easily now along the icy path.

Periodically looking back, Beebee headed straight for the cave anxious to settle his victim in. He tugged her far beyond the entrance of the cavern, and quickly unzipped the bag. Taut from the suffusion of blood, her blueish purple face practically popped out at him. Muscles riveted in and out of place as he worked to remove her completely. He wondered momentarily if he should take off her jewelry, but he knew better. It would have been traceable so no good to him. Leave her have it, he thought, chuckling aloud.

Beebee worked mechanically in a state of diffused delirium. He chanted as he labored, "in came the doctor, in came the nurse, in came the lady with the alligator purse. Yes indeedy, Uncle Beebee will take care of you." He stared down at the swollen mass of skin lying limply spread eagle on the dirt floor. He was baffled by what it was that fascinated him with a dead body as he squeezed her throat one last time, jerking it in the direction of those who passed before her. His senses remained completely undisturbed by the stench around him.

By and large he was compelled to seize another snort. Changing his mind, Beebee prepared a needle, burner, and syringe. He hadn't the patience to wait for the effects of a snort. "Liquor is quicker, candy is dandy, but nothing gives a zing like a little speedballing," he cackled at his nonsensical rhyme as he began to draw the clear liquid through the syringe. Instantaneously, he felt his heart explode and he began to float to the ceiling, as his beats excelled in fierce succession.

The sorry night passed without further episodes, and Beebee awoke with burning anticipation about the excitement Jill's disappearance would evoke. But it didn't happen. Through Trixie's grapevine, he heard about the note being left and given to the family. He also got wind of Sgt. Rick's shabby job of investigation. The good Sgt. suspected no foul play and so there was none. Jill's fool family accepted his unfounded claim.

Beebee had no idea how to deal with the reaction they gave him, or rather didn't give him. On many occasions he approached friends of Jill's and although they were somewhat concerned, their worry couldn't begin to match reality and he was at a loss on how to make it do that. Then it occurred to him that he had to strike again.

*****

Paul broke a short limber branch in fourths and added them to the pile that he had constructed over the past hour. He still had none of the answers that he sought. His mind was fogged with disturbing thoughts, leaving no room for rational responses. One thing that became very clear was his desire to talk to Jill's family personally. He had not been able to bring himself to do this yet. He could not allow them to overlook her disappearance any longer. She never left of her own free will and they needed to know and accept this fact. He planned to see them this very evening.

CHAPTER 20

Drake paced the immaculate floor beneath him with sad defiance, recounting inwardly the many infestations that had been bestowed upon him due to the new found notoriety. Angrily, he envisioned Melrose as a quiet peaceful resort, purposefully built in this secluded location. Shocking though it was, Melrose was undoubtedly becoming a household name and that fact poached Drake's much needed privacy.

Trixie's buzzer demanded his attention but instead of complying, he stomped toward the door whizzed it open, and shouted, "What do you need?"

The pitiful look on Trixie's face embarrassed him that he could no longer control his emotions. He had to get a grip on it now!

"I'm truly sorry, Trixie. What can I help you with?"

"Maybe this is a bad time; I wanted to speak to you."

"It's as good a time as any. Come on in," Drake flagged his arm out straight and hand motioned her into his office, "here, sit down."

"These last days have been quite hectic," Trixie began as she rolled her fingers in and out of each other, playing with the tips of her nails.

"Definitely. How long has it been since Dani has gone? That seems to be the beginning of our problem."

"Yes. She left Friday night, I guess. But I think our problem started even before that, Drake."

"What do you mean?" he looked down at the pen he continued to tap incessantly on his desktop.

"Well, I'm also getting a number of calls concerning Jill Simon. I don't know, Drake, if I'm equipped to handle all of this. I'm a secretary, not a detective."

"What are you trying to say, Trixie? You don't like your job?"

"I do like my job. But it's not my job anymore. I've considered looking elsewhere."

Drake jutted out of his seat and began to pace the floor, his face tomato red. "How could you do that to me?"

"I haven't done anything yet," Trixie bubbled the words from her quivering lips and continued to sputter, "I can't take this kind of pressure. I don't know if I'm even telling the people and the cops the right thing. And you don't help it at all cause you sit in here and fume and won't say a word to Thedy or me."

Trixie stared at Drake's washed out blue eyes, clearly burdened with melancholy thoughts. She wanted to reach out and touch his graying temples to console him, but Drake was a private man.

"So, Thedy's unhappy, too?"

"I didn't mean that. I don't know, but I am."

Drake respected Trixie for her straight forwardness; it was one of the qualities that he considered when he hired her.

"Look, Trixie, this sounds like a hasty decision to me. Let's try and work it out… give it a little time. I've put myself first lately and I've been wrong. Do you know I've had staff call in sick left and right which is almost unheard of around here, so I've been busy taking over classes which is not my cup of tea.

Forgive me, and I'll try harder. Please, I can't afford to lose a secretary, too."

"Okay, Drake, I'll try. But I will need your help."

"Sure thing. Call me when any problem comes up, and I promise you I'll deal with it. I won't take it out on you, honest." He smiled genuinely, and for the first time in several days a hint of the old Drake peeked through.

*****

The phone rang off the hook throughout the afternoon and Trixie gave it her best shot to keep up with all clients, their families, the press, the police, the public and unwanted cancellations. She was exhausted and took a few minutes to sit back, stretch her legs, and order her mind to go blank. She slowly sipped some water to accommodate two coated aspirins down the old tube.

She took advantage of the few moments she found to let her mind wander and when she did a rolling cluster of juices churned in her stomach, realizing that she of all people would have had contact with every person in this building, if indeed foul play was an issue... she must know the assailant.

Trixie's well-bred ways did not allow her to stray from the job for long and soon she was back to answering phones and typing. Goose bumps marched up and down Trixie's arms following the next ring. Her mother had always said she had an eerie way of knowing what would happen next, and mom's were usually right.

Trixie blew off the ominous feeling and put the receiver to her ear, "Good afternoon, Melrose Resort. May I help you?"

"I'm sure you can. I've been watching you. Yes indeedy, you need to quit running your lips or I will have to take care of you." It was a low sultry voice that left Trixie weak.

"Who is this?" her inflection demanded an answer long after her brain was cognizant. The pictures on the wall ahead of her blurred as her breathing temporarily halted. The line went dead.

She hardly had time to regain her strength when the phone rang again. Her shaky hand picked up the brown receiver from the cradle and wobbled it toward her head.

She'd forgotten what to say; "Yes?" she managed.

"Trixie?"

"Yes."

"I mean you!" He laughed with a power driven shrillness that cut through Trixie like a toothed hacksaw.

Thedy picked up speed when she saw Trixie slumped over her desk.

"Are you okay? What's the matter?" Thedy reached her arm out and encircled it around Trixie's shoulders. She gently shook her, watching Trixie struggle to focus.

"Come on in here," Thedy led her into Drake's office and over to the couch. "Rest here for a minute and then tell me about it. I'll get you some water."

"You know, women get faint for all sorts of reasons, low iron, pregnancy, nerves," Thedy handed Trixie the paper cup, and told her to sip slowly.

Pregnancy? Was Thedy nuts, too? Trixie's color began to return to her cheeks and she carefully sat up to sip the water. Her jaws felt tight and she was uncertain if she should relate what happened to Thedy or if she should purposefully not engage herself in a conversation at this time… after all, he told her not to talk.

Forget him! Trixie would not allow herself to be dominated by some dumb jerk on the phone, even though he made her stop breathing and almost killed her in the process.

"I received a very frightening phone call. Some man told me that he'd been watching me and that I should shut up or basically that he'd shut me up. Then he called back and laughed a horrible laugh. And he used this goofy expression, 'yes indeedy'." Trixie sounded out of breath as she rapidly relayed the horrifying conversation.

"Oh, forget about it. I'm sure it was a prank."

Thedy was probably right. The last few days have been so loaded with awful things that she must have let her mind run wild. The call had nothing to do with Dani or Jill and Trixie knew she needed to rest, forget about all of it, and certainly not resolve herself to fantasies... she hoped. Still, the sinking feeling had not left her stomach and she couldn't help but think that the dreadful voice she'd heard had a peculiar familiarity to it.

*****

Thedy spent the afternoon trying to ease her disturbing thoughts about Liza's boyfriend and worrying silently about Trixie's anonymous call. She continued to check on Trixie and each time, Trixie was busy filing or taking inventory. Thedy decided a hot cup of black coffee would do her good, so she headed for the cafeteria only to find Nick and Paris sitting alone at a table. She joined them.

"No sessions for you two?"

"It's our break time," Nick offered, "and the girls went into the clothes boutique, so we ended up here. What about you? Trying to keep out of trouble?"

"That's kind of a tall order these days. I find myself either in trouble or troubled," she laughed, attempting to present a false happiness.

"What's bothering you?" Paris asked.

"Anything and everything. Hey, do either of you know the guy Liza is dating?"

"That's what's bothering you?"

"Kind of."

"I don't really know Liza all that well, so I have no idea. How about you, Nick?"

"Oh, I've taken a few ganders at Liza, but I've never seen her with anyone. In fact, I thought she was free," Nick chuckled, raising his eyebrows a notch or two.

"I think she's too old for you, Nicky," Paris chided, "I'll bet she's forty."

"I'm very capable of handling a woman at any age, besides ten years isn't all that bad."

Paris observed Thedy deep in thought, gaining no particular pleasure from their teasing back and forth. "Why are you bothered by who Liza's going with anyway?"

"Oh, just a hunch about him. I don't think he's good for her. And another thing, Trixie just received a prank call and Lord knows we've had enough going on around here without jokes."

A dark expression loomed over Nick's face. "Maybe it's no joke. Malory got a call that scared her one day, too."

"I wonder if I should say something to Drake."

"Couldn't hurt, if he'll listen," Nick answered. "It's time for us to go back to work."

Thedy sat for a minute longer, teetering on the last words Nick had said. He was right! She was not sure that her own husband would listen, and evidently the rest were getting the same vibes from him. Her wifely response was to wonder what she could do to help him, though she had some intuition that it went much deeper than that. Thedy hoped it wasn't too late to give Drake the support he needed.

*****

Work was finished for the day and Beebee had no time to waste. The law was really moving on this one and he feared his clock was running out. He turned rigid when he thought of Liza and how furious he was with her. How dare she question him on anything? She was companionship, however, and perhaps she would leave with him. She'd probably end up to be a pain in the ass like all women, so he'd have to consider whether or not she was worth his trouble.

He decided he could hold a double funeral. He'd bring Malory out by Dani and end the two of them together, then split. He pounded his fist on the table and stared up at the ceiling as he thought of the mistakes he'd made with Malory. He couldn't miss... this time he had to have a fool-proof plan... no errors allowed. He remembered how easy it had been with both Jill and Dani. Maybe Liza would help... no... couldn't count on a woman... only for one thing, and she didn't even seem to enjoy that lately.

Beebee plunked himself down on the cement slab that jutted out about three foot from the side-door entrance. The sky was a menacing blue, still not permitting spring to take over. The air was sharp and hit Beebee's already irritated nose with the sting of a bullwhip. The hair in his nostrils stood on end and he felt the usual trickles of blood. He fumbled in his pocket for a hankie and as he wiped, gave his eyes a squirt of Visine.

He blamed his emotional turmoil on Liza, feeling both compelled and justified in snorting a few lines. Beebee lined the powder up and squeezed the tube in his experienced fingers promptly. He sniffed in tiny brief breaths as he zoomed the tooter up and down the round little mirror, and stopped for a fleeting moment to take a look around. It took only seconds to jam the stuff back in his pocket, so he rarely thought about getting caught. It really didn't matter. It was his business what he did outside of working hours. Besides, he could easily stop any time he chose to.

Beebee scooted back to the brick and rolled his back against it waiting for the rush of adrenalin. As he sat there he people-watched, hoping to see Liza come out to her car. Usually he finished before she did but today he'd wait for her. Then, he closed his eyes and began to mellow out, deliberately slapping his legs straight out in front of him taking up the majority of space. The palpitations began with slow rhythmic jerks and escalated to a rushing flood of liquid sputtering through warm veins under his flesh like twin shuttle rockets. Beads of perspiration dripped down him forcing his palms to slap away at it as if he were applying after shave.

Then it quit, almost as magically as it began, and Beebee got up and walked away completely forgetting that he had planned to watch for Liza. Dani was on his mind. On his stroll to the cave, the persistent smell of waterlogged pines wavered in the wilderness around him. Once again the infuriating drops of blood began seeping from his nose. This time he pinched his nostrils together between folds of linen. He tossed the cloth into the tall brush when he neared the entrance, hearing Dani's wails. Why was she so damn loud? The dingy coppery dirt flung into the air from the weight of his sneakers hitting the ground, and his contemptuous howls echoed the cavern walls as Beebee headed straight for her deafening mouth.

CHAPTER 21

"Richard, Richard," Dani wailed in a laggard gritty chorus and then began to cry. She was sure she had heard his voice as clear as if he'd been standing right next to her. Why did he leave? She hadn't time to call him, for in a flash he was gone. He yelled something she couldn't understand and then screamed "Oh no!" and was gone. Had Beebee hurt Richard also? Her sobs stuck like mashed potatoes in her throat and suffocated the words about to spill out of her mouth.

Dani knew she had to stop the noise, but she didn't care if he killed her or not. Streamers of photos floated by her eyes, detailing pictures of her children from birth to when she'd last seen them. It wasn't fair that she couldn't hold them tight and give them little pecks on their noses and chubby cheeks, or read them a bedtime story, or Band-Aid their minor cuts and kiss them better, or... she stopped and listened to running. Richard?

Wobbling like a large cube of Jello, Dani stretched her tired muscles upward and swiftly melted to the murky earth. Just then Beebee darted ahead, thumping his extended palm flat on her face, clamping his thumb and pinky into her jaw-bones like a vise.

"*You* shut your big mouth, understand?"

If she felt any spunkier than a wet noodle she'd have told him **no** she didn't understand a thing. Instead, she nodded her head fighting off the impulse to bite his smothering hand. Dani was sickened at the sight of Beebee's bloody nose and tearing eyes along with the ever-present musty cave scent. She wished he would just give her the pills and put her out of her misery for a wonderful while.

"So, your hubby was looking for you. Well, he won't find you. He's a chicken shit like the rest of them, **Dani**. You know," he continued to rattle as he prepared her drink and medicine, "I really hate your name. Danny was my brother's name, and someone killed him. Good thing, though."

Dani couldn't believe her ears. There were so many things she wanted to know and questions to ask. Beebee's face was not hindered by any signs of intelligence and Dani wasn't at all sure he was capable of answering her. If he wasn't strung so blessed high on drugs, perhaps, but as it was she would never find out all of the whys. Why her? Why Jill? Why jeopardize his job? What was Liza's part? Were Richard and the girls okay? The list went on but Beebee would take no chances of hearing anything from her. He swished the water in the can almost with as much pride as if he'd mixed her a Bloody Mary or a super Martini. He allowed her to take the pills on her own, and Dani didn't argue.

While she prayed that drowsiness would infiltrate, Dani slid her icy hands in the gravel below, searching for a dry patch that might be remotely comfortable. Beebee paced the ground weaving his hands in and out of each other, chanting his familiar phrases, and bellowing tirades that made no sense to Dani. Still, even as she became sleepy, Dani perked her ears his way hopeful to hear something that would give her a clue.

"I wish you'd pay attention," Beebee leaned over into Dani's face and continued, "I'm going to bring Malory out by you. I sure hope she'll be in good enough condition to be company for you." He sneered and then began a maddening laugh that began at the bottom of his feet. He danced as he chuckled and began the nightly ritual of emptying his alligator bag, "In came the doctor, in came the nurse, in came the lady with the alligator purse."

Malory? Malory would really be here" Dani dropped her weary head wanting to shout for joy and at the same time hoping that Malory wouldn't be harmed. Breathing was more labored now and Dani was almost ready to drift off when the horrible thought struck her... could it be possible that somehow Malory was involved?

*****

Liza wrapped her scant tanned body in between the warmth of an oversized terry-cloth towel, patting her skin virtually dry. She sank deep into the springy cushions of her sofa, determined to apply oodles of moisturizing crème and body lotions. She refused to grow old before her time. She then shook her head and fingered the damp ringlets to hasten the air-dry treatment. It was nearly seven-thirty and she hadn't even begun supper.

Each time a car drove by an odd sensation rippled through her. And each time Liza would hop up from the sofa, yank back the ruffled curtain, and pray to God that it wasn't Beebee. She actually felt guilty about avoiding him, but tonight after work she exited through the rear door, afraid that he might be waiting. Liza set out to color her nails with short gentle strokes, but each vision of the man he was last evening left her blood bubble, and she started to jab at her nails, eventually missing them completely. She exhaled fiery breaths out her nose like a dragon, huffing and puffing contempt at every image of last night's horror she recalled.

Had Beebee lost his mind? Had he actually gone mad? Irritated by his strange cold symptoms lately, Liza began to wonder if he just didn't feel well. Confusion crept into every joint, even her fingers, as she worked hard to rectify the mess she had made of them. Glamour from a bottle... she wasn't at all sure about anything. Liza was still devastated by his appalling response to her inquiries. He had turned so violent. And why wouldn't he tell her about Dani's car? Why had he gotten so upset about the tooter she'd mentioned? It wasn't like she accused him of anything. She had simply been curious, that was all. He was the one who took her in the car, and by God she knew it was Dani's.

Standing by her open closet door, Liza tried to decide what mood she was in... silk, teddy bears, or flannel. She chose a toasty warm flannel gown, her favorite to wrap up in with a good paperback. She was not much in the mood for a heavy meal, so she headed to the kitchen to whip up a light salad full of cucumbers and tomatoes, and a touch of creamy Italian dressing.

Liza toted the remote control in one hand and balanced her salad in the other. Before she sat, she took one last look out her front drape and if Beebee called she would plead sick. The thought of his demanding voice brought shivers to her back, and deceptive though it may be, she couldn't face him tonight... if ever again.

The thermostat read eighty but Liza rubbed her icy nose and slid the bar up a few more degrees. Her eyes bulged and her throat ached with jabbing pains. She tossed the rest of her salad and concluded that a cold was on its way. No wonder she felt so lousy... and lonely. Liza really ached to hear a voice, some understanding soul, whom she could spill her guts out to and they would listen. Knowing that her conversation would have fourteen tracks all headed in Beebee's direction, she was at a loss as to who she could talk to about him if she really wanted to. She didn't want him any angrier at her.

A wave of heat hit Liza in the back of the head with the force of a hard rocket ball, coercing her to the window to capture a few deep breaths of air. She wondered if she had a temperature or if she were just that stressed. Like magic, breeze filled her lungs and her foggy head cleared. She stood there a moment longer looking out her apartment window, awaiting some semblance of movement... a sign of life. The night was dead and Liza ached for another human being, not caring if she got him out of a Cracker Jack box whistling Dixie out of his ass or if she found him under a rock, clad in nothing but a fifth of whiskey. It didn't matter, she needed someone.

Unpredictable forces led her to the phone to call her younger sister. Their relationship was all but tragic, and Liza realized she was hitting bottom if she considered talking to Jen as speaking to a human. She was relieved when there was no answer.

Almost as if he had ESP, Beebee chose the correct time to call.

"Hi doll. Where were you?"

"Hi. I finished a little late. I must have missed you," Liza cleared her faltering throat.

"How about tonight?"

Her palms were sweating now. What if he wouldn't accept her reply? "Oh, I thought of that, but I don't feel well. I'm sure it's a cold."

"Come out and see me."

"I'm sorry, Beebee, but that cool night air wouldn't be good for my throat. Let's make it another night," Liza casually told him, feeling a sudden chill at his persistence.

"I'll come by your place then."

No, she wanted to scream. Her heart began to race wildly and Liza was weak with fear. She didn't want to see him... she couldn't trust him... he wasn't the Beebee she once had loved.

"I don't think that's a good idea. I told you," she insisted with an even voice, "I don't feel well."

The click on the other end hit hard, still ringing in her sensitive eardrums a few minutes later. Now she was terrified! Would he come over anyway? How could she avoid him? Liza wanted to run at an uncontrolled gait out her door, and run and run until she dropped, as long as she didn't drop near Beebee. Instead, she securely latched her only door and walked to and fro each window to assure herself they were locked. Then she turned off all of the lights and curled up on the sofa with the phone only a reach away. Lying in the pitch darkness, she felt rather foolish for the actions she'd taken, yet something present in Beebee's tone told her she had no choice. He sounded cold and demanding as he had last evening, and she was not looking for a replay of that.

The calm was alarming and Liza twisted her head from side to side in suspicion of a forced entry. She closed her eyes, then opened them, then wiggled to blanket her legs, then uncovered them, and finally began the whole charade again. When she couldn't stand it any longer, Liza bolted up to a sitting position and made up her mind who she would call. She flicked one lamp on very dim, and raced her fingers through the phone book, hunting for Melrose's number. She would call Thedy... she was positive Thedy would listen.

*****

Paul glided his Jaguar into the space along the curb, behind Jill's blue Tempo. It sent shivers up his spine to see her car parked there empty... he hadn't even given a thought as to what had happened to her car. Once again it reaffirmed the necessity of his visit. How could a person who left on purpose leave without her car? It didn't make sense.

The house looked exactly as Jill had described to him, an English Tutor set slightly off the road, the yard neatly manicured, bushes trimmed like round clouds of green floating above a dimmed lawn trying its darnedest to recover from the winter blast. The luxury presented itself in no uncertain terms and through his tinted sunglasses, Paul could picture a much younger Jill romping and turning somersaults across a zig-zagged cut lawn into her daddy's longing arms. How could that daddy be so unconcerned just a few short years later? Jill had idolized her father, waited on him, cooked special meals for him, even read the paper to him.

Paul rang the bell and was invited in by a young man, about sixteen years old, and he assumed it was her brother Jerry.

"Could I speak with your folks, Jerry?"

"May I tell them who's calling?"

"Paul, I was, uh, am your sister's fiancé."

Jerry's eyes lit up as if he wanted to tell Paul something, but instead he turned to exit the room, laying down the book he had in his hand first.

"My Pop's here. I'll get him."

A tall man, dressed in a colorful silk brocade wrap-around, double knit dress pants, and a pipe full of cherry tobacco, introduced himself as Mr. Simon. The stately gentleman offered Paul a seat.

"I hope you don't mind my being frank, young man, but I wondered when you'd get around to see us."

The statement took Paul by surprise, "I'm sorry, this is difficult for me. I don't know quite how to respond to that. I am still not over the shock and I really came to see if anything is being done."

"Being done about what, Paul?"

Paul's palms began to sweat bullets of moisture. What was wrong with this family?

"To find Jill... are efforts being made to find Jill?"

"I don't believe my daughter wants to be found." He crossed his legs and brought an oriental ashtray forward to empty his carved pipe of unwanted ashes. He tapped away, irritating Paul as much with his actions as with his words.

Jerry strode back into the gloomy room and stoked away at the dwindling embers, appearing to deliberately eavesdrop. Paul sat back trying to relax and think of an appropriate response. He gazed outside, watching the Weeping Willow tree lash its lengthy limbs against the metal awning. Somehow, Paul felt like the awning.

Well, right to the point, what the heck! "I thought perhaps you might have the note that Jill had left. Could I see it?"

He said nothing to Paul. "Jerry?"

Jerry left and quickly returned with a slip of paper which he handed to Paul. Immediately Paul noticed the shaky signature, so unlike Jill's normal writing. His stomach sank to depths he didn't know were possible and the only word that entered his head was *force.* Jill had written her name under duress. Couldn't her parents tell that?

"Could I show this note to Sgt. Saul Keller?"

"Too late, my boy, it's been done. Sgt. Keller beat you to it. This is only a copy."

How could a man's voice be so flat when his daughter was missing? What made him think that Jill wanted it this way?

Paul stood up, anxious to leave this dismal atmosphere, "Thank you for your time. I do hope Jill will be found soon."

"Perhaps with your help she can."

CHAPTER 22

Malory had exhausted every muscle in her body and decided to retire early for the evening. Nick insisted that she attend Nelly's nutrition class as planned, but Malory declined. She yawned and rubbed her eyes, burning the mascara around each watery lid. In a sluggish motion, Malory managed to manipulate her fatigued body in the direction of her room. Her arms hung heavy at her sides and she could still smell someone's stale smoke lingering in the hallway.

The walk seemed longer than usual without Jade's cheery voice for company and Malory was aware at once how desolate the place was. She had cut out on the expected routine and was very alone... too alone. Perhaps deserting the crowd was not such a smart idea after all. Her tired body, now in a mild state of panic, picked up a rapid pace with her once heavy arms in a fast back and forth jogging motion. She longed to be inside of her room door... safe.

With every one of her senses now in full gear, Malory heard a soft whining paired with a low haggard growl at the tail end of the hall. Who was there? Before she had a chance to answer her own question, a black-gloved hand jutted out with the figure of a man leaping in the air in front of her, making a great attempt to obstruct her door. The next thing she knew, Brisket came to her rescue, snarling his large set of canines and tugging at the man's black sweat pants. Brisket sank his teeth into the man's calf. The man slapped his beefy hand at Brisket's head and yelled, "Damn dog." It was then that Malory recognized him, and fumbled impatiently for her keys. Brisket pulled and pulled, gnawing continuously at his leg, while Malory jarred her door open.

Stunned, he whirled about the hall, cussing the dog up one side and down the other. In that instant Malory called Brisket into her room, slammed the door with double bolts, and crumbled to the floor. Breathing with furor, Malory knew she had to call Saul... she had to identify the man.

Malory was afraid to move from the door... afraid that if she did he would burst through the wood and come for her throat. Brisket thumped his heroic tail on the floor, permitting a small piece of blue paper to fall from his collar. Malory snapped up the tiny slip, and read the crudely printed word **Dani**. There was no time for incompetence as the relentless lights kept blaring in her sorry eyes. Saul... she could only think of Saul.

It took every ounce of effort for Malory to drag herself up from the flooring. She was about to dial Saul's number, when her phone let out its piercing ring. She reached her quivering hand out to answer, and then quickly pulled it away, not being able to shake the image of the hooded form clad in black looming over her. What if it were Saul on the other end? Malory hesitantly picked up the receiver.

"Hello," her voice emerged in barely a whisper.

Malory coddled herself holding Brisket in a snug grip against her chest, terrified to listen in return. Relieved to hear Thedy on the other end, Malory heaved a sigh of relief.

"Malory? It's me, Thedy. Are you free, honey? It's imperative that I talk to you now. I'll come up, okay?"

Malory's only thought was to get to Saul, but Thedy wasn't allowing any slack. She'd said her piece and hung up the phone and Malory was certain Thedy was almost to her room by now. By her statement, Malory knew Thedy's visit would be well-meaning, still, she didn't want to leak any of what had happened to her... she'd call Saul the second Thedy left.

The short interval it took Thedy to arrive, seemed like the clock had stopped to Malory. She directed Brisket to the rug in front of the fireplace, and he appeared rather casual there. Malory hadn't quite decided how she'd explain his presence there. Tears welled in her aching blue eyes, when she heard Thedy's knock, once again afraid to open up and also craving to tell Thedy all... but she knew she couldn't.

"Thedy, is that you?"

"Yes, dear. Open up, there's a draft in this hall."

Thedy's brows raised in question when she took a look at Malory's pale expressionless face, commonly associated with fear or illness.

"What's the matter?"

Did she look that bad? Malory was stunned at Thedy's bluntness, and for a brief moment wondered if Thedy could be trusted. The thought only added to her tedious anxiety and sickly demeanor. She had to get her strength back and take control of what was happening... no matter how upset she was about the truth.

"Nothing, I'm just a little tired. What's up, Thedy?"

"Maybe I shouldn't upset you now, but Nick thought perhaps you wouldn't mind talking to me about some things that have to do with Dani. I need to confide in you some information that has been brought to my attention." Thedy stopped cold, obviously waiting Malory's approval.

Glad that at least she had the consideration to acknowledge Malory's feelings, Malory smiled and told Thedy, "I'd be happy to discuss it with you, Thedy…"

"I know I've interrupted your sleep, dear, but I want to warn you to be very careful. I was told that you received an evil call, and so has Trixie. Not only that, but Liza's been talking to me some and her boyfriend has lost his marbles. She even suspects that he has something to do with Dani's car disappearing. Not only that, but the guy that called Trixie, said **yes indeedy** and I know I heard Liza's beau use that expression also. I'm so nervous about all of this and I can't seem to find Drake. Anyway…"

"Hold up a minute, Thedy," Malory held one hand in the air as if she were a traffic control cop, to put a temporary halt to Thedy's speech, "Sorry, but let me ask you, what exactly did the guy say to Trixie?"

"He told her to shut her big mouth or he'd shut it for her."

"And you think this is Liza's boyfriend?"

"Yes, and Liza does too, but she won't say his name, other than Beebee. If she does, he'll kill her."

"Liza said that?"

"Yes," Thedy sadly looked down at Brisket, for the first time paying any attention to the fact that he was in the room at all. "I thought of calling Sgt. Keller, but I made a promise to both girls that I'd keep quiet. Do you understand my problem?"

"Yes, I do. And you're right, so I'll call Saul. I was going to anyway." Malory's head was spinning with details, not knowing which thing to tell Saul first.

Outside, the rain began its show with an introduction of tiny droplets, increasing to a burdensome downpour with intermittent zaps of electrical lighting amid the booms of thunder. Malory patted Brisket's nose in comfort, when he began to trot from window to window panting in anticipation. She tossed a slipper his way, trying to interest him in an informal dog retrieval trick game, but he insisted on guarding the weather.

Malory didn't know which way to turn. Having Thedy here was a God-send, still she couldn't talk freely to Saul if Thedy stayed. In the background Malory was aware of Thedy's chatting, but her mind was full of so many bits and pieces of information she was in the midst of a general overload, simply unable to compute any more input. As her concentration dwindled, Malory glanced to see Thedy's pinched nose zeroing close to her, "Malory? Malory?" Thedy's voice finally registered.

"I'm sorry. What did you say?"

"I must leave now. But you call me if you need to, no matter what the time is… and Malory, be careful," Thedy bent over to give her a quick hug and peck on the cheek.

The night continued to persist its threatening conditions over Melrose, jolting the sky with streaks of lightening that practically jumped inside of Malory's window to do a short two-step before exiting. For once, Malory was glad to have the blackness interrupted by flickers of white.

The phone was only a matter of feet away and Malory's brain told her to move, but her bones were constipated with emotional fears. If she'd have been an ice cube, it wouldn't be possible to be any more frozen, both movement and temperature-wise. Her internal system of checks and balances was out of whack, the amount of contributions was not in sync with her outflow and she felt jammed.

After a few deep breaths, action seemed to regain its meaning. Malory kept a vigil on the ominous windows around her, held Brisket in view, and headed for the phone. Her fingers shook so hard that their touches were choppy as the punched out the number for Saul's home phone. The room spun in circles and Malory anchored her arm around the foot of the bed as she clung for dear life. Then it happened... the most horrible sound that she ever expected to hear... an obnoxious buzzing, telling her that the line was busy.

*****

"Saul, the car report is in, both the tire prints and the prints on the car itself give a positive identification. You'd better come in right away to see who and what you're dealing with. By the way, the prints match some of those found on Jill's note, as well as Dani's. Hurry up."

Eva didn't even have to say that much to get Saul out the door. He had wondered all day if his hunch had been right. As if sent to him by God, he had been able to clearly envision who it was he'd seen enter the building that first day at Melrose and now he'd finally see if he had been correct. He couldn't take all the credit if it turned out, because it was Malory who had thought of and supplied the staff brochures.

Saul zoomed up his engine and found his mind racing as fast as it was. His eyes quickly adjusted to the glare of the wet pavement, this being the first time in ages he set his siren to blaring. His intuition told him many people were in jeopardy. He veered the car into the lot and ran to the door holding a magazine over his head to shield himself from the shower. The bolts of lightning shot a path mapping the way to the entrance. Saul's heart leaped with excitement in hopes that it wasn't too late, although secretly he had some doubts.

Before his dripping plastic poncho even hit the hook, Eva was beside him, "Malory has called several times. She sounded rather rushed, but said it was urgent that she speak with you."

The two scurried toward the stack of reports piled on Saul's desk. "So this is it!"

"Yes, it's what we've been waiting for. You don't think I'd be here this late myself for nothing, do you?"

Saul shot his friend an admirable grin and paged through the papers at a rocket's pace. In light of the last half hour's frenzy, Saul stared vacantly at the given name before responding. It's just what I expected."

Eva handed him a cup, filled to the brim, of steamy hot mint cocoa, "Did you read the previous jail records? It all fits, doesn't it?"

"All too well. I'd better give Malory a quick call, and see what she needs."

Saul moved with mild shock, finding himself wishing that through some puzzling fluke the guy would have been a stranger. He sat with all the proof he needed only an arm's length away speculating, as Malory's line jingled, when and how he'd tell her. Now, he only wanted to hear her unharmed voice.

Saul remained dumb-founded all the while Malory perpetuated the many events of the evening. He was especially disturbed by the note she'd said came from Brisket. Could it be possible the note actually did come from Dani? If so, was Dani still alive? He tried, though difficult, to pay attention to Malory's details but his mind always strayed back to the note. Where would Brisket go, that Dani could be? The place had to be unlocked... and like a thud, it walloped Saul right between the eyes... the cave. Queasiness lined his stomach and began to agitate his cocoa with a slow sickening motion.

"I want you to make sure to keep your door locked. I'm going to request extra security there, immediately."

"But Saul, what about Trixie and Liza? They're not in this building."

"I'll take care of them. Just make sure you do not, I repeat, do not answer your door for anyone."

"I hate to sound like a baby, but you're scaring me."

"I don't want you to be frightened, but I want you safe."

"There's one other thing I haven't mentioned, yet," the twist in Malory's voice spiraled Saul's diverted attention.

Even in the middle of a crisis, Saul had left his mind wander to his desire to help Malory, to hear her voice, to lover her. At the end of all this hustle and duty, he wanted to be reassured that Malory would be there for him.

"What haven't you told me, Mal?"

"I recognized him, I know who it is."

Not in his wildest dreams had Saul expected Malory's answer. He had paid so much attention to the note, that he had missed how close she came. Not only embarrassed, but apologetic, Saul quietly listened to Malory tell him what he should have told her.

"I'm sure it was my tennis instructor, Bart Bante."

She correctly said it right out and now he was in a real predicament. Should he set her mind at rest with the facts, or should he wait until tomorrow when he apprehended Bart?

"Malory," Saul cleared his throat, "Um, please don't say that to Jade or anyone. Have you? I'd rather you not do that, until I get there to talk to Bart?"

"Talk to him? Saul, didn't you hear me?" Malory's increased volume demanded a satisfying answer, "talk to him nothing, arrest him and find Dani!"

"That's what I plan to do."

"What? You knew this?"

"Malory, you're pushing. I shouldn't be discussing it with you. Yes," he gave into her, "I found out this evening. We have proof of prints and other reasons to suspect Bart…"

"Suspect?"

"Mal, I think you're tired. Please call if you need me, otherwise I'll be there first thing tomorrow morning. Do your usual thing, trust me. And Malory, I love you."

Malory tossed all evening with uneasy feelings about harboring Bart's guilt mingled with appeasing thoughts of Saul.

*****

Paul stepped up his pace, afraid his weak knees wouldn't carry him as far as his car. What had her father meant? Did he suspect Paul of something? His cynical remarks haunted Paul all the way back to Melrose. Paul's intent had been to line up a search, or go with her father to see Sgt. Rick; anything constructive might ease his helpless feeling.

Back at Melrose, Paul felt both defeated and angry. His long face showed complete disappointment and Trixie was the first to notice.

"What hit you?"

"Oh, nothing, I guess. Why are you here so late?"

"The work never ends these days."

Paul wanted to ask Trixie what hit her. She was actually pleasant, something that he hadn't seen in all the years he worked at Melrose. His weary eyes drooped and he didn't have the energy to pursue Trixie, but a major decision overtook him, and he realized it was time he confess to Drake.

CHAPTER 23

An unrestrained pounding, loud enough to wake anyone from the dead, sent Drake pattering to his door at 4:00 A.M. The booming rocked the walls and Drake could not unlatch the bolt quick enough for the soon-to-be perpetrator. Thedy jolted from the bed, wrapped herself in a blue silk robe, slid into her matching slippers and followed in Drake's footsteps. The both of them clamored for identification and looked at each other with disbelief when they were told it was Richard.

"Yes, what do you need?" Drake's eyes had adjusted to the dim light and Thedy had reminded him to be nice.

"I need some answers from you."

"At this time in the morning, most people need sleep. Huh, but you need answers. Wonderful!"

Richard pushed the room door open wider than Drake had intended. Seeing this, Thedy quickly suggested that they all go to the cafeteria and she would make some wake-up coffee. Drake hot-footed it behind Richard and Thedy, completely fed up with Richard and his demands.

Sitting face-to-face, Drake glared at Richard, twisting his under-the-nose fringe. "You've got our complete attention, and I don't mind telling you that there are many more appropriate times for this sort of thing."

"Really? I haven't exactly noticed you putting yourself out any and there have been many times when I've called on you, and I've been told you're not available."

"I'm sorry about that, but I'm rarely available when I'm sleeping either."

"Count yourself lucky, you can sleep. Some of us have wives that are missing. That tends to cut down on your wink hours."

"Men really," Thedy bluntly cut in, "this kind of discussion isn't going to go anywhere or solve a thing. Let's get on with what's important. Obviously, Richard, you came to see us for a reason. What is it?"

"I want to know who this Beebee guy is that works for you?"

"You got me out of bed to ask me about someone I never even heard of? We do not have anyone on the staff named Beebee."

Thedy felt a twinge of guilt and bit of betrayal knowing she had spilled the beans to Richard earlier. She thought it would help him, not make him angry.

"Then you need to check your records because a reliable source says you do."

"Who's your source? I won't answer until you do."

Thedy's frown practically met with her chin. It would be easier to crawl in a hole and never come out than to admit what she'd done, but she had no choice. She balanced her head in one hand trying to discover the right words to say. There were none.

"I was his source, Drake."

"*You?*" The single word cut through Thedy like a sword. She couldn't help but wonder if their life would ever be the same again.

Drake's head pounded and he had the impulsive urge to tip his coffee over both their heads, but it wouldn't do any good. He had to admit to himself that somewhere along the line he had allowed too much space and he realized now that he must be losing his grip. In the past, Thedy never would have confided in someone other than him.

"Well since you two are the only ones that know what you're talking about, one of you had better explain it to me."

Richard took over, filling Drake in on Beebee being Liza's boyfriend, about the phone calls that Trixie and Malory got, as well as the note that Malory had shown him.

"Then Dani must be alive?" Drake sighed with disbelief and wiped his brow with a tiny white napkin sitting on the tray in front of him. "I'll be honest with you, Richard. Up to this point, I had my doubts. I guess what we need to do is call Sgt. Keller."

"Malory was going to do that after I left her last night."

"Then Keller should be here shortly," Drake surmised.

"I'm sure he will be," Thedy agreed.

*****

Reluctantly Beebee came out of hiding shortly after they left. His muscles twitched visibly in his upper arms and face. He smirked when he thought of their asinine conversation. Who did they think they were fooling? They knew nothing and he'd be gone before they could find out anything. He clamped his fists tight and then loosened them several times. He needed a fix in the worst way.

The soft mist felt cool on his face as he left the building and jogged toward the cave. His blood ran cold when he thought of the trouble Malory was causing him. There had to be a way to solve the problem without a trace. His footprints made slight indentations as he scurried along, glad that dawn was not yet ready to break. He remembered that they talked about him as Beebee and turned red in the face when he thought of Liza the traitor. Spit flew from his tongue and lips, his demonstrative way of letting Liza know what he thought of her. The sprinkle landed in a small ditch and he cackled as he hurdled over it.

Beebee was still baffled by the note they were talking about. What note could that be? He made sure Trixie took care of the one he wrote. He wouldn't worry about that now. He had too many other things to accomplish. He rushed into where Dani was half sitting up.

"So, your sweetheart's causing a fuss. Thinks he can outsmart Beebee," he laughed as he cupped the mirror snugly in one hand. "What a laugh! You listening to me?" Beebee snorted, then wrinkled his nose and peeked out of one eye at his audience.

Dani looked up solemnly, just enough to satisfy Beebee. She continued to hang her head over and bat her eyes, in hopes that he'd give her less if any pills. She'd never considered herself for show business, but perhaps if she were able to stay coherent for a better length of time, she could think clearly enough to know what she should do. Obviously, the note she had tried was in vain.

He pushed her head back to look at her fluttering eyes, "Hey, you don't look so hot. I got things to do."

Beebee left as quickly as he'd entered and Dani wanted to stand up and cheer. He didn't give her any pills. It worked! Before she could hold her private celebration, he strode back in grinning from ear to ear.

"Gee, how awful, Uncle Beebee almost forgot about you, his most prized possession."

Beebee went directly to his alligator bag, did some neck stretching exercises, and turned to Dani chanting, "In came the doctor, in came the nurse," he cackled like a wet hen, "yes indeedy, how could I almost forget my favorite patient? Pure negligence, Dr. Bante. Do you want to be sued?" The penetrating pitch of his voice frightened Dani all over again.

She thought she'd noticed only one pill this time as he pried open her jaws to administer it, and sloshed the water in her entire face. She gulped to feel a breath of air, terrified that this time it wouldn't be there. She slid down, hankering for her own brass bed at home with Richard holding her tight. In the distance she could hear him shuffle off.

Dani had always thought that caves were quiet places, but it was amazing to her how many sounds a lonely person could hear. Sometimes she wondered if she were just imagining them. Dani ached to be pain free, at home, and clean... all of those wishes making her feel foolish. Shouldn't she just feel lucky she was alive? Dani didn't think so. She reached up to touch her once soft and silky hair, only to find thick, matted clumps of stringy clay in its place. Her skin was clammy and surely her eyes bulged out at least an inch or so. She must look a sight! There was no comparison as to how hollow and void she felt.

Brisket bounded in, taking Dani completely by surprise, one which she had no objection to. As much as she loved the dog, he painfully reminded her of her flop idea... the note. Dani called Brisket near to her, wishing she had some treats to give him. Brisket claimed the space next to her for his own, and Dani patted the bristly fur letting her fingers stop at his collar. The note was gone! Elated, she kissed the old pooch thanking him inwardly. Maybe her attempt had worked...

maybe Richard was on his way. Dani felt a shaving of satisfaction before she drifted off to sleep.

Beebee went along on foot until he hit the main highway. He graciously tagged along the sparse traffic, thumbing each time the opportunity arose. He needed to get into Ridgecrest, the next tiny little town away. It was there that he would spend the day, gathering the things that would be necessary, and mapping out his next moves. A semi pulled along the gravel edge of the road, and Beebee cordially accepted his assistance. He sat quietly next to the driver, swallowing back titters of anger and anticipation. Did Malory actually believe she could cross him up this often and get away with it? He shook his head in disgust and the truck driver looked on as Beebee began to laugh out of control.

*****

Liza rubbed her damp hair with a dry towel. She plugged in the blow dryer, and rounded the heat all about her head. Just before it was completely dry, she spritzed the top, puffing it up in straight wisps across her crown. She put a handful of gel along each side and fashioned them in an upsweep motion. All set to run out the door, she stopped to answer what she hoped would be a brief call… she was already running later than usual.

"Hi doll, I got something I want you to do."

Liza nearly froze solid when she heard Beebee's voice on the other end. She hadn't slept through the night fearing his arrival. She fumbled now, the phone in her iron grip, as to how she should reply. She felt like a blemish in the midst of her stark white kitchen. Somehow, she felt sure that somewhere out there Beebee was watching her… keeping a vigil. She peeked out her kitchen windows, stirring the starch white curtains slightly out of place, half expecting Beebee to jump up and stare her in the eyeballs.

"What do you want, Beebee?" she answered without any indication of her true feelings.

"I want you to come with me," he said casually. He stood in a dingy roadside diner, looking over the clientele mostly donned in leather jackets, jeans and sunglasses.

"Come with you. Where?"

"I'd like to find a new job and move, ah, maybe southern part of the state, Chula Vista, or around that area."

Liza wanted to say, 'you mean Mexico', but she didn't.

"I'm really very settled right here. I thought you liked Melrose and me for that matter."

"Babe, you know I love you. I need a change, that's all."

"Even if I wanted to, Beebee, I'd have to take more time with such a big decision. My family's in this area and all."

"But you don't like your family, remember? Come with me. We'll be good for each other."

"Beebee, I'm late as it is. Can we discuss this later?"

"There's no time, Liza. I'm on my way **now**. I didn't figure it was too much to ask my girl to come along," he wasn't getting his way, and his voice began to show signs of childish pouting.

Liza knew at that moment that she never would go anywhere with Beebee again. He'd frightened her, and the chilling coldness in his tone reminded her that there was something not very human about him. In fact, she couldn't honestly recall what had ever attracted her to him in the first place. Right now, she only wanted out of the relationship completely, but she knew for her own good, she had to handle him with the gentlest of kid gloves.

"Beebee, I really have to go. I can't consider leaving now. But you can keep in touch. I wish you would," she lied.

"You know, I can't believe you. All you Goddamn women are alike. I busted my ass for you and this is the thanks I get."

"I'm sorry, Beebee. Really, but I can't go. Good-bye."

The words lingered longer than they should have and Liza found herself afraid to go out to her car. What if he were there? She couldn't trust that he didn't call from somewhere very close. She locked the door behind her, happy that the mist had lifted, and she could see her way clearly. Liza slung her purse into the passenger's side and looked over the head rest to reassure herself that the back seat was really empty. Funny, she thought as she drove along, how unexpectedly love could turn to a suspicious hate. What if she were wrong about Beebee? She couldn't stop herself from wondering, if he planned to escape to Mexico, what had he done with Dani? What a jury she'd make. She had him convicted before being tried. Just because he knew about Dani's car, didn't mean he knew about Dani. She couldn't shake all of the little things, especially the awful groaning sounds associated with the cave. Could it be that Dani had been right under her nose? Liza refused to believe it.

She rolled into the designated employee parking spot making absolutely sure to peal her eyes out for a dark curly head or someone in a black jogging suit. Hesitantly, almost as if she dared her soul, Liza popped the car locks, got out and ran toward the salon entrance. Her heart would not settle down until she was inside surrounded by other people. Beebee was nowhere in sight, and as she took inventory of her supplies, counting scissors, bottles and sprays, Liza felt the world lift off of her weighted chest.

CHAPTER 24

Saul left at precisely 7:30A.M., pleased with the fact that it would all be over soon. Only five days later, and he would be able to apprehend the suspect with overwhelming evidence in the state's favor. Many a case did not happen so smoothly and although it's been a long few days for Richard, Saul was satisfied that soon he'd be under lock and key and Dani's outcome would be ascertained. A cop's intuition told him not to be too hopeful, still Malory had found a note that may have been written by Dani... only may have. The possibilities were many and Beebee could have even written the note as a ploy. He was not nearly as confident when thinking of Jill. It made him shudder to consider any other likelihood.

The fog had lifted and all that was left were traces of moisture that he could slightly detect on his windshield. The sun was trying to peek out, still partially buried between the blanket of scribbly white fluffs overhead. He decided the best step would be to inform Drake first, and then apprehend Bart before the sessions got rolling. The address listed on his application didn't exist, so this was the easiest and by far the most inconspicuous way to seize him.

Trixie was not at her desk, but Drake was just around the corner and spotted Saul.

"Can I help you Sgt. Keller?" Drake's suave walk was indicative of a man who knew something was up.

"Yes, I'd like to see you in private for a moment."

The two men entered Drake's office, and the slightly gray-haired man offered Saul a cup of black coffee.

"Do you use cream or sugar?"

Saul was stunned at the man's graciousness, an impression that he had not yet seen.

"I was awakened rather abruptly this morning by an irate husband, and I was going to give you a call about that."

"I'll save you some time then. Let me go over this quickly. I believe our man is your tennis instructor, Bart Bante. In fact that is why I'm here now, to arrest him."

As if a chameleon, the tanned man turned white standing weakly in front of Saul. He shifted his weight to one leg and Saul wondered if Drake were going to fall flat on his face.

"Arrest one of my staff? What are you talking about?"

Saul very directly summarized all the facts and his intention for Drake who was visibly shaken by the whole idea. Drake took hold of a chair by one arm and slid gently back into it.

"You're sure of this? No mistake?"

"I'm very sure and although no one is guilty until proven so, I don't believe this is a mistake, Bart's our man."

"And what about Dani and Jill?" Worry lines creased Drake's burly brows and his set jaws still contained a brief flicker of skepticism.

"I can't say. That information would have to come from Mr. Bante himself."

"Let's go," Drake began issuing instructions, "the staff has coffee in the cafeteria to start the morning and Bart is usually with them."

They wasted no time and went directly across the hall into the smell of ripe fruits, home-baked bread, and freshly brewed coffee. Chatter and laughter arose from the table that the men approached. A shadow crossed Saul's face when he noticed that Bart was not present.

Drake faced his comrades, and politely asked, "Has anyone seen Bart?"

"Not yet," Paul spoke up, and then laughed bitterly, "I told you the other day, Drake, the boy's been having a little difficulty telling time lately. I've had to cover for him often."

"So you did. I had forgotten that."

"Geez, a cop and everything. What's he up for, murder one?" Paul snickered and the gang roared.

The quiet was unbearable when the grave officer simply replied, "I hope not."

"We could try the machines. Many of the staff work out first thing in the morning and if he's not there, the tennis court is right next door. I'm sure he'll be there at eight or shortly after."

"Let's go," Saul responded although he wasn't as hopeful as Drake. Could it be possible Bart got a tip somehow?

"Sounds as though Dani must be okay."

"What do you mean?"

"Richard told me about the note."

"How did Richard know?"

"Malory, I guess."

Saul did not answer. Why would Malory tell him? Saul's liveliness had left. He was fairly sure of the outcome by this time. Bart was not in the gym. The first session of tennis came and went, and Bart never showed. Drake left to call in a replacement for him.

*****

Liza toed the floor nervously and was alerted to the windows and door at each new arrival. She had already finished three heads when she was paged. The movement clattered loudly in her ears this morning and she could barely hear above the din of the dryers. Drake wanted to meet with her as soon as possible in his office. It must be about Beebee. She hung her lavender jacket on the hook, promptly creating a large knot in her stomach and mounting pressure between her temples. What could she tell Drake? She stopped briefly in the ladies' room wishing she could hide out in there forever. Liza began to sweat profusely when she entered the office, noting Saul's presence.

Liza raised her eyes to the ceiling, profoundly aware of the uncomfortable heat. She had information they wanted. She looked elsewhere around the room, scrutinizing the arrangement of framed oil paintings, scattered pens and pencils and even Thedy's photo on his desktop. Then the questioning began.

"Liza, I understand that you were dating Bart Bante?"

"Yes." She was had. Beebee would call her a blabbermouth, but what could she do? He was a cop and all.

"When was the last time you spoke to him?"

"This morning before I came to work" she said coldly. Liza didn't know why she felt the sudden need to defend a man she was scared to death of. All she knew was that she felt defensive, like the poor judgment she used in choosing him was sticking out like a sore thumb.

Saul couldn't have been more shocked, "Just this morning?"

"Yes."

"Did he give you an indication that he wouldn't be at work today?"

"It never crossed my mind," Liza twisted her hands in her lap and then the tears began to come, "I'm sorry, I'm afraid to say anything. Yes, he wanted me to go away with him. He said to southern California, but I suspect Mexico. What's he done?"

"We'd like to ask him questions about Dani's disappearance."

Liza knew the answer and had no idea why she felt the need to have her own convictions verbalized. Then she began to volunteer information, telling Saul how she had recognized the doll case when she was taken to dinner in the Mercedes.

While Liza talked verbosely, he wrote, appreciating the honesty with which she spoke and understanding how difficult this must be for her.

"Liza, where did Beebee stay?"

"Name some places you can think of."

Liza named the Kingsway Motel but was hesitant to mention the cave. How did a girl lower herself and tell a police officer she went out to his wonderful filthy palace mainly to have sex with him? Liza's cheeks lit with crimson color, and Saul stopped for a short while, requesting some coffee from Drake, who gladly obliged.

When they had sipped several times, Saul noiselessly scrambled for his pad of paper and continued.

"Did Beebee ever stay anywhere right here on the grounds?"

Damn it, he knew. "Yes."

"Come on, Liza, we really need your help. This may involve murder, and for your own safety…"

He didn't need to convince her any longer, she knew better than he about Beebee's mean streak.

There is a cave in the field that he'd stay at sometimes."

"Do you know where this cave is?"

"Yeah sure, I've been there with him, lots of times."

"You've been in the cave?"

Drake's enthusiasm peaked. A cave on his land? *He wasn't even aware.*

"Yes. Lots of times."

If Liza had been there, then Dani wasn't. The search in the cave would still continue as planned, but Saul saw no need to rush it any. If Liza had been there, certainly she'd know if Dani was there. He'd concentrate instead on apprehending Beebee. If he were in the cave, he'd have to come out soon, and when he did, Saul would be there.

*****

Liza was such a dope, Drake reflected, and yet how could he criticize her when he was on his way to Tia's room? His thoughts quickly faded from Liza to Tia's long sleek body, silky hair and soft spoken voice. How could he tell her what he had to? A couple of times Drake suspected it would come to this, but he had truly hoped it would be after his lifetime.

Methodically, he rapped twice on the door, identified himself and walked in. He caught her smile, full lips glaring him succulently in the face, as she leaned her elbows on the table while she conversed on the phone. He could hardly await her savory kisses.

Tia held up her index finger. I'll be with you in a minute," she mouthed.

The day had dragged and Drake was totally relaxed now as he tucked a throw pillow under his wavy locks and leaned back on the sofa, eyeing up her cleavage from across the room. As he examined her in a sensual way for one last time, he agonized over how he would break the news to her.

Tia laid the receiver back carefully on top of its cradle. She took long strides, her hair flowing as she walked and Drake couldn't help but notice that the hem of her tight shorts barely covered her rump. He leaned up and reached to caress her buttocks, pulling her directly on top of him. His thick hands squeezed in moderation and rolled circles around her hind end, pushing and releasing. She tipped her chest onto his, rubbing enough to ease his buttons open, all the while slithering her tongue up his chest and neck eventually landing in his ready mouth. The passion was as strong as ever, neither taking time to stop or think. When she felt his fullness deep inside of her, Tia detected a slight distinction in his lovemaking. At that moment, she feared his true reason for coming to her today.

She sat up, leaning against his thigh, and pushed her moist hair out of her face.

"I can tell you're troubled, Drake. What is it?"

He was distracted by the profile of her beautifully carved body and found it even more difficult to speak.

"What can you tell me about Bart, Tia?"

"Oh that. I heard Sgt. Keller was looking for him today. He's not a pleasant man. I told you that long ago."

"But do you think he'd be capable of maybe even murder?"

"Who's to say? How does anyone know what another man is capable of?"

He too, sat up, and slowly began to dress. He fluffed the pillows back in order, suggesting that he hadn't been there.

"Drake, we've known each other too long for this. What's really on your mind?"

The tears welled up in Drake's eyes. Tia was right, he could no longer live on a pretense, a stupid game of cat and mouse, which neither of them deserved.

"You've got to leave Tia. It's best."

"Don't tell me what's best for me, Drake, although I do believe it will be better for you."

"It won't be better, but it has to be. We both knew it would come to this, though I wish it hadn't. I'm no good for you or anyone this way. You know that."

He turned away so she could not see his puffy pink eyes and all the doubt that her leaving would be an even exchange for his lonely life. It couldn't be.

"It'll be alright, Drake. I do understand. I will pack and leave in the morning," she rubbed her fingers from behind along both jaw lines, carefully turning his heavy-hearted face back to her, "I will always love you." Tia then kissed him and held his head between her bare breasts for several minutes.

She pulled his chin upward, "Drake, what will become of your place if Bart is guilty?"

It was just like Tia to worry about him and not herself. He also was concerned more about what would become of him without Tia.

"I expect time will heal, as they say. Business will decrease for a while, and then pick up again when the news moves on to something else." He kissed her breasts and then her lips passionately.

"And then again," Drake spoke softly, "the whole thing could blow over. Liza said he's on his way to Mexico right now."

"I hope she's right!"

Tia pulled her comfortable robe snuggly around her slim waist, and belted it tight. The phone rang just as she picked up her hair brush, and the noise cut through the air like a knife.

Drake backed out of the room, looking at the same scene of a beautiful lady hovering over the telephone, as when he entered. It was almost as if nothing happened between the two of them for that short interlude.

"I'll be back before you leave," he told her, and closed the door gently.

CHAPTER 25

Liza could not convince her heart that she did the right thing. She had many good times with Beebee, although lately the bad times did not balance out the good. Somewhere between Melrose and home, she had to rid herself of this fear and collect her thoughts. What should she do next, if anything?

She grabbed her winter jacket, still rubbing in hand cream to prevent chapping, and tried to maintain her thoughts enough to drive home. Her concentration had dwindled since Sgt. Keller's interrogation. Liza looked every which way, afraid of where Beebee may be lurking. She tried to satisfy herself with the idea that he had left for Mexico, but that thought did not stop her from slowing up at corners, checking the back seat of her car, or craning her neck to see each passer-by.

Over a cup of steamy hot cocoa, Liza examined the day's events. Step-by-step she recalled each horrid little detail. It wouldn't surprise her a bit if her blood pressure zoomed right off the thermometer. No matter how hard she tried to escape it, every event brought Beebee to mind. Even during her hair-cuts or perms, she found her mind straying to how Beebee's hairline was starting to recede or how wavy his head still was.

The car was roasting and even turning the heater down didn't cool it quick enough. Liza swore it was a hot flash. If a bucket of ice water would have been next to her, she was sure she'd have leaned over and submersed her head into it.

Instead, she rolled a window down and yanked her jacket off with her only hand left on the wobbly wheel. It helped. She drove along and decided to go through a fast-food place and pick up a quick hamburger. The thought of cooking turned her stomach. She hadn't the ambition tonight to so much as boil an egg.

Her appetite improved immensely as she picked up the all-American aroma. She ordered a double cheeseburger, onion rings, a hot apple turnover, and a double root beer float. This was a girl with boyfriend problems? Perhaps she planned to eat herself to death, or maybe it was true depression. Regardless, she planned to eat each and every stinkin' calorie.

Darkness descended earlier than usual, and Liza figured it was due to the mist caused by the ocean effect. The dark gray sky was compatible to the gloomy time of the year. She watched the pine needles shiver in the breeze and listened to the wind whip through the stately branches. It wasn't often that she paid attention to the size of the taken-for-granted Sequoias, but tonight they loomed over her causing a forlorn feeling.

Liza took four steps back in disbelief once she turned on the light to her apartment. She stepped into the long living room taking into account all of her personal items that were now ruined, ripped or broken. Wooden bookshelves were upturned, two table lamps laid broken on the floor with both lampshades ripped to tatters, the curtains had been slashed, and a pile of ashes which appeared to be her clothing scattered the center of the room. On top of the heap was a large white piece of paper.

Shaken beyond control, Liza walked forward, swallowing continuously without relief. Goose bumps traveled up and down her spine, and she tipped her hand slowly to touch the note. In huge blood letters, the note read, 'Yes indeedy, you'll be sorry'. Liza's teeth chattered as she shivered involuntarily. She had to sit. In amongst the broken hodgepodge, Liza plopped herself on the floor before she fell there. She sobbed her mascara into tiny black streams running down her ghastly cheeks. As she laid flush against the itchy wool, Liza spotted an antique bisque doll that had belonged to her mother. Fringes of its human-hair wig were twisted with blue glass eyes that crackled. Surely if she were to lift it now, it would crumble right out of her fingertips. Liza's heart sank and her tears rolled more freely as she noticed the small hairline crack had grown into an irreversible fracture. It was the only keepsake she had, and Beebee had destroyed it.

Laughing bitterly, as she thought of all she had given Beebee and acutely aware of what he offered in return, Liza pulled herself by the arms, as if her bottom half were paralyzed, and literally dragged herself to the phone. It was not until she had the receiver in her hand that she felt the breeze of the front door she'd left flying open. Panic shot through her. What if Beebee was still here? Even through the buzzing of the dial tone, Liza heard the door thump against the siding, as if someone had a life-saving grip on the knob and was purposely banging it. She screamed with all her might, as she dialed the operator, but all that would escape her lungs was a tiny eke that carried in the wind without as much as an echo.

*****

Malory snuggled under several layers of toasty warm blankets comforted by the thought that Bart was probably in Mexico by now. She was also secure with the fact that Saul would find Dani, one way or the other, good or bad. Soon, the whole ordeal would be a thing of the past, and that suited Malory just fine. She tried to fend off any negative thoughts, dismissing them as irrelevant. Malory needed to put effort into her future at Melrose, her weight loss, the reason she was here at all. She secretly hoped her future would include Saul, and that was worth ousting terrifying ideas out of her head.

Malory tossed and turned from midnight until two-thirty, before she finally got up to get a drink of water. Her throat was parched, probably from the anxiety-filled day. On her way back to the bed, she picked up her jacket and shoved it into her closet door, visibly a catchall for any sort of material. She flicked off the nightlight and put one knee onto her mattress. Malory felt a tug on her ankle. She kicked her leg vehemently, trying to shake off the clearly defined black glove that hung tight to her ankle like a tourniquet.

With a grapefruit size lump in her throat, Malory listened to Bart's dead even voice, "I'll bet you thought I forgot about you. Wrong." And then the resounding of laughter throbbed at her temples mercilessly, and she had no choice but to hear his stormy temper.

He pulled her to the floor and the burst of Ether hit her nose with the fury of an inflamed car and she was out... her mind vacant.

Beebee's eyes narrowed to slits as he trudged along the back of the tennis courts, fighting the misty rain lashing at his face, holding Malory by the deadened ankles. She was a heavy one and part of the time he was forced to drop her on the ground and drag her. He watched her head flop up and down, the ends of her red hair turning muddy brown, and her face repeatedly spattered by muck. He stared ahead at the faded cave in the distance, cackling at Keller's incompetence.

Beebee couldn't help but wonder if the man was on a plane to Mexico. Dumb ass.

Malory felt the intermittent tugs and thumps of her head. Surely she had died and donated it to the National Ping-Pong Association. It ached so deep inside, she thought it must be nothing but a black hole by now. Malory tried to yell but only little gasps of air would push out. Her empty eye sockets must have caved to rest on the back of her skull, and certainly her brains were trailing far behind her actual head at this very moment. If they could only catch up to her, perhaps she would be able to think clearly. Her arms stretched far above her head, and she had visions of fingering the strings of brains back together and encasing them once more inside the frame of her head.

The edges of her mouth filled with a gritty substance, much like she imagined the taste of stale bitter chocolate pudding. It drizzled down her chin in tiny clots, and splashed into her eyes at an alarming rate. Between the turmoil, she could still see flashes of the towering figure dangling her at life's loose end. Even if she had the energy, she wouldn't want him to know she wasn't dead.

It seemed like miles until Beebee pulled her across the murky floor of the cave. Her eyes followed the beam of his flashlight and she could see very little. Occasionally, she'd hear the wings of tiny bats, the hoot of an owl, or the sound of scratching feet, perhaps a hyena or... she hoped not a rat. Malory pulled what was left of her neck muscles forward, trying to avoid the endless abuse to her head.

He finally dropped her. Using his flashlight as a source of light, he found and lit the old lantern, probably of forties-vintage, and the entire space around them illuminated. Malory laid still on her side, allowing her throat to click its disbelief when she saw Dani, secured by heavy metal chains, slumped almost to the ground. Was she still breathing? Malory searched her mind for clues. She could tell that Dani wasn't stiff dead... but was it possible in his recent rage of mind, that she had just been killed? Dani hung, her chin snug between her bosom, not permitting or not able to move a muscle.

Malory watched and listened as Beebee carried on his usual ritual and chant. Something was severely deranged inside this man's obviously malfunctioning brain... and it didn't take a professional to figure it out. He snorted a few lines and then took a bottle of alcohol and poured it over the gashes that Brisket had so kindly marked on his leg. Beebee yelped like an injured pup at its sting and tossed the empty container just missing Malory's eye by a narrow margin.

Malory caught herself groaning, at least she thought it was she, when the blood burned through her veins like a roller coaster of hot pokers. She took a deep breath, trying desperately to maintain a frayed speckle of sanity. She remembered reading somewhere that the body went first and at this particular moment, she wanted to know the bloody truth of that statement. Could it be possible that her body was gone and only her thoughts lingered? Then she spotted the other body!

Malory observed the decomposed remains, partially covered with leaves, branches and dirt. Was this Bart's distorted way of hiding evidence? Malory shuddered. She felt certain it was Jill, although she'd never seen or met the woman.

Beebee crossed in front of her, his filthy sneakers scuffing more dirt into Malory's face. He took a long-handled shovel and began to pitch dirt from a spot very near where Jill laid. He sang as he went along, almost as if it added to the pleasure of what he was doing.

"Wouldn't want you young ladies to have to look at this for long. No, no, Uncle Beebee will see to it that your stay is enjoyable. Yes indeed, we don't want any sad faces," he rambled on as though this routine were part of life... nothing out of the ordinary.

"Did you hear me girls?"

Who was he talking to? Was Malory supposed to answer? There was only one of her, so was Dani alive then? Surprise and optimism popped out of Malory at once.

"Awe, too bad Jilly... got all gussied up and nowhere to go but in the hole," he snickered and laughed so hard he began to snort, as he dug away methodically at the coffin-size cavity he was creating in front of him.

He worked determinedly until enough dirt was up that he was able to kick the corpse into the pit. Malory flinched as she watched his absolute imprudent behavior, and her anger quickly turned to hate. Beebee slid some dirt back into the hole and then happily splashed water on top as if he expected it to grow. With her own pain increasing by leaps and bounds, it wasn't surprising to Malory that it became more difficult to watch this sick man. The last Malory saw of Jill, was her thin and mousy looking strands of hair that still stuck up above the fresh grave.

It seemed on impulse that Beebee grabbed for Malory's already tender ankle. He twisted and pulled on it until she wanted to die, sure that he was ripping it apart from the rest of her leg. She squeezed her eyes tight and grit her teeth, trying to create a larger amount of pain than he was, but it was impossible. Another good technique... in theory. He finally secured it in the cuff at the end of the thick metal links, the same one that Dani was attached to.

It was then that she could actually look up at Dani's face. Her eyes were closed, still Malory swore she saw them twitch, almost as if she were trying to keep them closed in spite of all the tragedy that took place around her. Malory reached out and touched Dani's knee. It was reasonably pliable and warm... she was sure of it. Malory pushed harder on it... again and again... finally Dani gave her the sign she had so longed to see. Malory met Dani's pleading eyes straight on... open, moving, and alive as she was. Malory found enough solace in Dani's effort to lay back and heave a heavy sigh of relief.

Chapter 26

Sometime during the night, Jade had kicked every blanket off the bed, and now when the alarm chose to buzz in her ear, she was left with nothing to pull over her head... to suffocate the noise... a blatant reminder that a new day arose. She rolled over and pressed the buzzer off, snapped up the quilted blanket that had fallen to the floor and stretched it over her large frame, for just a few minutes longer. Jade forced her sleepy lids open and stared at the swirled plaster ceiling. It was Thursday. In so many ways the week had been endless, and in other ways, it was difficult to believe that tomorrow evening would mark a week since Dani's disappearance. Was it possible that so much time had elapsed?

Yawning was a monotonous part of this morning that couldn't be avoided. When she could stall no longer, Jade swished her legs over the end of the bed allowing her feet to dangle a while. Good for circulation, she told herself, and not too bad of a way to procrastinate the inevitable, either. The quicker she got her morning brew, the better, she supposed.

While she waited for her curling iron to heat, Jade showered and dressed in her everyday sweats and sneakers. She flipped a curl through her sparse bangs and gathered the rest in a knot barretted to the back of her head. She then walked down the hall to call for Malory. No answer... that was funny because last night they made specific plans.

Malory had probably forgotten and would meet her in the cafeteria. Jade's steps hastened when she spotted only Nick and Paris.

"Hey, where's Malory?" Jade's raspy voice caught attention from several onlookers. She wiped back a piece of her silky black hair that had fallen from the barrette.

"We thought with you. Make up your mind you guys," Nick teased.

"Seriously. She didn't answer when I knocked. I thought perhaps she left without me."

"Not here as you can see. Maybe she was showering and didn't hear you."

"Yep, you're probably right," Jade told Paris. She began breakfast feeling a bit uneasy and really couldn't explain why. Tense from all that had happened, she guessed.

It didn't occur to the men that anything was wrong and Jade felt a little foolish for getting jumpy over nothing, but as the breakfast neared its end, and Malory still hadn't shown, Jade demanded that they all go up and check. The guys obliged and Malory was nowhere to be found.

"Let's get the key from Trixie," Nick suggested.

"You do that, Jade wait by Mal's door, and I'll check other parts of the building," Paris moved rapidly, but for Jade's sake, showed no true concern in his expression.

Jade tapped her foot against the carpet and periodically knocked on the solid wooden door, verifying Malory's absence. Surely, if she were there, she'd answer. Jade considered calling Saul, but decided to wait until all avenues were explored, in order to have something concrete to tell him.

"For once, can you believe this? For once," Nick repeated, "Trixie didn't give me any trouble." Nick flagged the shiny brass key in front of him as he jogged down the hall.

Neither Jade nor Nick were too surprised that Malory was not inside of her room upon their inspection.

"I don't understand where she would go?"

"Look, Jade. That seems strange to me, does it to you?"

Nick pointed to the unruly bed coverings that started from the side of her bed and extended across the room, ending about three foot from the door, almost as if she held onto them until she couldn't any longer.

"You mean because the sheets aren't on her bed?"

"Yes."

"I don't know about you, but I sleep like that all the time. I guess to me that doesn't seem unusual at all."

Nick thought he found a starting place, but he could see that it was probably too simple and a little far-fetched besides. Nothing else was out of order, in fact, quite the opposite.

"There is one thing I want to see," Jade opened the closet and a nylon jacket popped out at her.

"She's not in any of the other buildings, and I talked to Thedy. They haven't seen her in the office either," Paris rushed into the room, squinting at its brightness. After the past few days and nights of gloom, the sun finally decided to make its show.

"I wish I had better news. What **are** you doing, Jade?" Paris' trailing thoughts were disturbed by watching Jade yank items from Malory's packed, but organized closet.

"Look at this!" she concluded as she plopped down tennis shoes and a sweatsuit.

"What?"

"Her clothes! Can't you see, these are the things she wears for work-outs. They're still here."

"Come on, hon," Nick began, "that's stretching it, too. Certainly Malory has more clothes. That's not conclusive evidence, I'm sure."

"Maybe not to you, but it indicates a problem to me," Jade stormed out of the room in a huff.

"Now what?" Paris followed her. "Where are you going?"

"To my room," she yelled, "I'm phoning Saul, no matter how crazy you all think I am."

By the time Nick and Paris entered, Jade had Saul on the other end, convinced there was a problem.

"What?" Jade glared at the men as she hung up the phone, "What's wrong? He's on his way."

"Nothing. It's good that we're all concerned. It's better if we check it out," Paris looked at her approvingly. He was not about to disagree. The look on Jade's face assured him that it wouldn't pay.

Eight o'clock was their regular time to begin sessions, and it was now eight-fifteen. Jade glanced at the clock.

"Why don't you two head out, and I'll go to the office to meet Saul. I won't be long, but I do want to talk to him myself."

Jade choked back every emotion that boiled up inside of her. Once again she brushed her long dark tresses, twisted them and set them back into the barrette. Nothing was going right today! She shoved her vanity drawer shut, glanced at her owly reflection in the mirror unable to reverse its direction. Jade was certain she had reason to be disturbed.

*****

Thedy was upset at even the slightest implication that Malory couldn't be found, but she had something more pressing on her personal mind. Where was Drake? It was the third morning this week, along with a few evenings that she could not account for his whereabouts. What if he were involved somehow in this Dani deal or in some other kind of trouble?

Trixie had no idea where Drake had gone, so Thedy took it upon herself to find out... enough was enough. She roamed the halls, clad in one of her many floral gowns, pink slippers, and a cup of hot piping black coffee. It wasn't long before she spotted him coming out of the second floor conference room. Drake's back was to her, and she was just about to call him, and then it struck her how stupid that would be.

Thedy watched and followed as Drake locked the conference door, looked both left and right, dropped the key in his pocket, and strode on. She felt foolish spying on her own husband. Again, he stopped mid-way down the corridor, looked both ways, and finally knocked on Tia's door.

One of Thedy's hands covered her open mouth, while the coffee shook violently in another. When he opened the door to walk in, Thedy distinctly heard the low cunning voice on the other side say, "Come on in, Drake. I've been waiting for you." And the obstruction of the door closed Thedy out.

Unable to move, Thedy stood like a statue at the very corner, hoping it was all a big mistake... assuming that he had business with Tia... wishing that he'd exit soon... and all the while sure that her suspicions about his recent change, were materializing right under her nose.

Determined to stay there until Drake retreated, Thedy forced her legs to become flexible enough to carry her to the sink to dump her coffee and take a few sips to settle her dry pulsating throat. She then leaned within eye's sight and waited the longest wait of her life.

Scads of treasurable memories crossed her mind, and not one was without Drake present. Could she ever live without him? She began to get weak in the knees, imagining all sorts of horrors. The next several minutes, she spent recounting their courtship, marriage, and many years of hard work and happiness. Thedy glanced at her watch wondering why Tia wasn't teaching her class.

She stopped cold when the door opened, appalled at what she saw next. Tia stood bare-assed in a flimsy nightie, her arms hugging Drake's neck. Thedy stepped far enough out of sight, but continued to watch the spectacle he was making of himself, as well as a fool out of her. He rounded his hands about her buttocks and kissed her passionately. He then took a breather, long enough to check the hall. Assuming it was empty, he continued to embrace Tia. No words were spoken, only looks given that made Thedy ill.

Drake closed the door for Tia, sadly shutting off another chapter in his life. He turned to see his wife facing him in the middle of the hall. Tears streamed down her cheeks and she put her index finger over her mouth, as if to hush any words he might try to say. Drake looked sheepishly into her eyes and tried to reach out for her, but she pivoted and ran.

Stunned, he scurried to follow her, but what could he say? "Thedy, wait, listen."

She heard his muttering, but kept on going. Thedy didn't know where to run, she just knew that she couldn't stop. She didn't want to wait and she didn't want to listen. She knew that for the moment she was too hurt to look at Drake.

*****

Today the drive to Melrose was more unpleasant than ever. For once the weather was cheerful, sunny and a bit cool, but Saul was distracted by Jade's call. He hoped she was excited over nothing and that by the time he arrived Malory would come out to greet him. He knew that if she were missing, Beebee's cry to Liza was only a miscue and that wouldn't be at all unusual. What it meant to him, however, was that the man had really flipped his lid. And of course that was not good for Malory.

It tore his insides apart, realizing that perhaps he'd made a poor judgment call. The cave had only been under suspicion though, the same as every other part of the grounds. It was not beginning to look like it was the only possibility. He had it under surveillance most of yesterday, and when Jade phoned, he attempted to move the search ahead. But it was to no avail, the experts could not arrive at Melrose until morning. He thought of going in anyway, but it was no use. He examined the map that had been given to him, and the pathways were extensive. It made no sense to jeopardize more lives. News of Malory's absence was beginning to register and Saul wore the guilt like an angry bull. Why hadn't he been able to see this would happen? If Malory were hurt, or worse, he'd never forgive himself.

The squad pulled into the reserved space and before he could put it in park and turn the key, Jade came out to greet him.

Saul hesitated to ask, "Malory hasn't shown yet?"

"She's not here. I'm sure of it. Saul, you've got to do something, please."

Jade's plea only made him feel more inadequate. "Jade, I'm working on it as hard as I can. You know I wouldn't sit back and leave something happen to Malory, or any of you. These things can't be predicted or anticipated. We knew, and Malory knew, all along that someone was out to get her. Remember? That's why she called me."

As he spoke, Saul tried to convince himself as well as Jade. He was no psychic and had no inside tracks with the Lord, he could only do his best. Right now, with Malory gone, his best was not good enough.

"I'm sorry, I didn't mean to sound like that. I know you're trying. I don't understand, that's all."

"For one thing, he was just identified. And he's a man without wheels, which is much harder to track. He also may have been smart enough to use an inaccessible place to most of us for cover. A cave, if that's correct, is not something to take lightly."

Jade listened, and in turn offered Saul all of her many observations, unsure as to how they could help him. Saul watched as Jade jogged in the sunshine to attend her classes. He remembered how uneasy he was coming to this place at first, and now he appreciated its value and fully understood his attachment to it was not purely business... he had to find Malory.

Saul contemplated where he had gone wrong. He used his knowledge of laws and procedure, not his heart. Richard had been right! He had to think of a way to make both of them work. Saul's mind was void of answers. It only had room for the images of Malory which he could not, and did not want to, shake. It finally came to him... there was a way... and he knew exactly who would go that way with him.

CHAPTER 27

The dim lighting and musty odor cut through Malory's nostrils like a shot of Ammonia. She found herself aching to get even the slightest recognition from Dani's often shocked and vacant gaze. Dani's war wounds were obvious. She had fared well in the most difficult battle of her life… she was still alive. Being terrified is expected, standard issue, but torture has an eventual different effect… a distant numbness that one can only identify through experience.

Restrained without consent, Malory could not walk over and tap or prod Dani. Instead, she made noises until she found one that alarmed her, regardless of the stupor she was in. Malory assumed Dani was drugged, and if that were true, she could somehow manage to get through to her. Tears rolled down Malory's cheeks when she remembered her first night at Melrose. Dani's friendliness was overwhelming, and then Malory remembered that awful misty evening when she had seen Dani being towed away. Her own head throbbed with a dull sluggish pain that ran up her spine and landed like a thud on the back of her head.

"Dani, look at me!" Malory demanded as she turned her pounding head towards Dani's drooping one. "Dani… Dani…" Malory cleared her throat, whistled, and whooped like a wild Indian. After several minutes, she saw Dani's head wobble and finally lean her way.

Dani had been certain that Beebee hadn't given her a big dose, still she was unfocused. She had unclear visions of some woman trying to bring her out of the tunnel, calling to her in a gruff voice. Had she done something wrong? What if it weren't a woman, and it was that nasty old Uncle Beebee again? Her jelly-like neck muscles would not cooperate, dipping her head from side to side and weaving it all around like a drunken sailor. Dani screamed at her neck, but it probably couldn't hear above the woman's bellyaching. Dani tried to move her head toward the circle of light ahead of her, but the stubborn thing would always hang back down, cutting off the little air she had. When it rocked to one side, Dani swore she had a glimpse of Malory, but she knew what the effects of strong drugs could do. Why would Malory be out in this dump?

"Dani… Dani…" the voice kept calling to her. Should she answer it?

Malory watched, her body rigid from the tension, as Dani tried to gain some assemblage of reality. Dani's voice was the low guttural monotone of someone coming out of a coma. Was that possible? Malory remained on her side, annoyed at her own stringy damp hair that kept slapping her in the mouth.

"Dani, look at me. It's Malory," once again Malory slid along the dirt bottom to reach Dani's knee. Her legs ached terribly and she could feel warm trickles of blood ooze into the cold rusty mud below her, making the mixture staining her nightgown look like a jar of wet cinnamon blotted onto it.

Malory could not give up, "Come on, Dani. It's okay, Bart is gone. Wake up and talk to me. I need you." She patted Dani's stiff filthy jeans and couldn't help but notice purple swellings on Dani's forearms. Her face looked like healing bruises, but was marked with a bitter gauntness that did nothing to conceal her private agonizing wounds. Dani had been through hell, and Malory felt on the doorstep of that horrible pit herself.

Reaching up to touch Dani's face, Malory used her sleeve to wipe back Dani's matted blonde hair. It looked like an old musty doll wig and Malory couldn't help but recall vibrant curls that once bounced up and down lightly. She wondered if she touched it, if it would fall off in a big clump right to the ground.

"Malory," her gravel-filled voice eked out, "I can't believe it's you." The slow words came cautiously and then her sunken eyes began to tear.

"I want you to know, Dani, there's a police officer and Richard and many others that will come and look for us. They already know it's Bart."

In between the muddled words, Dani felt a sense of relief... at least they knew... now she hoped they'd come in time.

It was strange, but Malory held great belief that her reason for being here was to help Dani. She wanted to give Bart no credit whatsoever... she kept faith that somehow she and Dani would both be found alive, and he would be doomed to pay for what he had made Dani and Jill go through. Jill... being taken forcibly made one attach an unspoken allegiance to another person, although she never ever knew her.

"How's Richard and my girls?"

For a moment Malory was shaken, "They're all fine, Dani. Of course they're upset about you, but they're holding out, and you need to do the same," Malory reassured her.

"I will, but I hope it's soon."

God, how Malory hoped the same, though she chose not to tell Dani. She believed with all her heart that Saul would soon be there.

"It will be. I'm sure," Malory smiled and touched Dani's hand gently, painfully aware of the grip the metal cuff had on Dani's swollen skin.

*****

"In came the doctor, in came the nurse, in came the lady with the alligator purse. Yes indeed, ladies, guess who's here?" Beebee's grand entrance shook Malory, but had a stoic effect on Dani, who never moved a muscle.

Malory began to wonder what would happen if she moved or talked. She didn't have the chance to find out before Beebee continued with his crazy unimportant act. Typical, Malory thought, of a madman. She quickly dismissed the passing thought in her mind as to what a person this mixed-up could be capable of. She'd seen one example of that already with Jill.

"We're moving on to where they'll never find us. Yes indeed, those mountains will hide us forever," his volume rang throughout, only intensifying Malory's headache.

The girls watched as Beebee pulled two bandannas from his sack, a thirty to forty foot thick rope, more chains, a knife, and a plastic bag of white powder. There were so many questions Malory had for Dani, who was finally semi-alert, and now it appeared to be too late. Was Beebee really taking them into the mountains? The only good thing about that, was that he certainly wouldn't drag dead cargo. They would be alive, and if alive, there would still be hope.

He enjoyed prattling away with his lean backside to them. He swayed with his chants and laughed at his rhymes, and although he'd address them now and again, he really didn't seem to know they were there. And then he turned, and immediate horror told Malory that he was very aware of their presence.

Beebee's blood-red eyes narrowed to beady slits that seemed to flow from temple to temple, his brows furrowing in a downward slant barely a half inch above. His smile had weakened to less than a frown, the edges of his mouth grooved into his chin. He was deviously quiet as he held the red bandanna taut in front of his wide expanse of a chest. He cocked his head to one side and Malory noticed that his usually thick head of brown curls were slicked down as he let one end of the kerchief drop. He took deliberate long strides forward and it was then that Malory recalled descriptions of this person. It was from her clients, those who had dealt with rapists or killers. Beebee's was a face void of any feeling, carved from stone… the face of a murderer.

"Oh, please no," Dani's wail was unrecognizable, except that Malory watched her lips move.

"Shut up," he spat as he walked up to her, threw her head back, popped something in her mouth, and ordered her to swallow as he offered her muddy water. Malory wanted to vomit.

It was obvious he was not bothered by Dani's harsh, sharp gasps as he snapped her mouth open and secured the bandanna tightly around her head. Only muffled noises were possible now and Beebee was satisfied as he looked into her bulging eyes. He uncuffed one hand, and then he fastened a new one onto her ankle.

He then turned to Malory, his flare of anger not yet subsided. She wanted to scream, but the voice wouldn't come. It was stuck down as far as her stomach and every muscle seemed to bar it from entry to her vocal cords. The pills stuck in her throat like plastic and the slithery bitter mouthwash did nothing to ease her constriction. Beebee only laughed as he chained her in the same fashion. By the time he was done, Dani and Malory were chained together, yet each had one arm and one leg free. He pulled them onto their feet. "We're moving on," he poked at them until they hobbled deeper and deeper into the echoing depths of the cave. Malory had not yet decided what the rope and knife were for. She was dizzy and began to feel as if she couldn't walk but Beebee insisted. In her haze of thoughts, she was certain that soon Saul would be on his way. He'd save her and Dani... she knew he would... he had to.

*****

Where in the hell was that cop? Richard leaned against the cold rock that sat in the entrance way. Saul was late. Richard was sure he said to meet him here. He had left the girls in Trixie's care and told her he wouldn't be long. If Saul didn't hurry up, Richard was ready to run in and check for himself. How complicated could a cave be anyway?

Saul walked out beyond the parking lot, turning away from the sun glare of the pavement out to the foreboding fields. He sure hoped Richard was out there already. He had glanced briefly at the map of the cave that lay on his office desk, reassuring himself that the first section of the cave was not at all dangerous. He'd already warned Richard that he would go just so far. Once again Saul questioned his judgment. Should he really be doing this? Especially as a rookie, with a rookie.

Saul spotted the medium built man in the distance, noting his shortness in comparison to Saul's tall stature. Richard, wearing an emerald bulky knit sweater, was pounding his fist against the rock and every few seconds scanned the area.

Either he was afraid Bart would show up, or he was ticked off that Saul was late. Saul guessed the latter.

"Where the hell you been?" Richard shouted as soon as he so much as saw Saul's shadow.

"Sorry, business." Saul could hardly admit to another man his apprehension in entering a cave.

"Let's get with it. I've got my girls with Trixie, and I don't think she feels babysitting is in her job description, Richard spoke rapidly in a deep Bostonian accent.

"Yes, but remember now, we're going to the head of the cave only. This one goes deep and it's a winder. Lots of trails."

"Yeah, you told me that."

Reluctantly Saul followed. As much as he wanted Malory, he couldn't stop his heart from pounding the minute he was enclosed. Daylight did not affect the obscure, almost nonexistent lighting inside. Only a few feet from the entrance and totally dependent on flashlights… it gave Saul the creeps! Bigger things than bats knew his vulnerability and if any touched his feet, Saul knew he'd run like a trooper. He kept visualizing Malory's plight, knowing that was the only thing keeping him inside this God-forsaken place.

"Hold it. Flash the light that way again, to your left," Saul instructed.

"I'll be. What do you make of that?" Richard asked.

"Looks like a camp out, doesn't it?"

Richard waved the light slowly up and down and back and forth, making sure to hit every nook and cranny.

"Blankets, hay, a campfire and an old lantern."

"Doesn't work," Saul told Richard as he inspected the lantern. "Hey look! Two bags of white dust, Cocaine."

"Someone was just having a party here."

"Maybe so, but they were still here. Bart has a record with drugs, Richard." He looked to see Richard's face strain.

"I guess maybe I'm stupid, but I want more. Let's go farther."

Saul wanted to back down, but his intuition told him there was more to see. The effort was painstaking, but he continued to follow Richard down the unfamiliar trail.

"We should have thought harder," Saul began, "if we had rope, we could be dropping it all along to point our way out."

"We aren't that far in, Saul," Richard was irritated, "and I'm not your professional spelunker."

The air was heavy and the odor began to change from that of moist clay and dirt to what? Saul's nose stung from the bite... to death. His hands wet with sweat, reached out to hold on to something, but there was only space.

"Stop here, Richard?"

"Why?"

"Give me the light."

Richard handed it over, not realizing why Saul was so determined.

"God, it reeks in here."

"Yeah, that's what I want to check. That ain't no stale wine you're smelling."

Saul flashed the light along the cavern wall and stopped it dead when he saw the chains. He eyed the contents once again, and then the light filtered to a sunken circle. Saul slowly walked toward the spot, with Richard at his heels. Next to the round impression was a black sweatshirt. That didn't bother Saul, but what did was the human bones and traces of human hair, not a lot, but enough to shake any cop he knew.

"Think it was an animal?"

"He's an animal all right, a sick merciless animal. Come on let's get out of here, Richard."

Before he left, Saul bent over to pick up a beautiful Marquis diamond ring. By the description he was certain it belonged to Jill.

CHAPTER 28

She wanted to offer more to Heather and Kristin, some love and comfort, but Thedy felt only enough energy to bring them tall glasses of milk, chocolate chip cookies, and a squeeze of affection.

"What are you drawing?" Thedy asked Heather.

Heather got up off of her knees, pushed back her blonde ringlets and brought her pad of paper over to show Thedy. She politely told her, "This is my house, and that's me jumping rope. Over here is my Mommy and Daddy kissing. They're kissing cause Mommy made it home." Heather smiled thoughtfully and walked back to the chair where she had been coloring.

"That's a nice picture. I think you should save it and show it to Mommy. What are you busy with, Kristin?"

"I'm just thinking."

"Sometimes thinking gets hard, doesn't it, dear?" Thedy tugged the young lady's neatly braided hair.

Thedy's heart went out to both of them and she couldn't take herself away from watching their wonderful youth and innocence, even during such a troubled time for them. She longed to have that back, not wanting to deal with an unfaithful husband and heart-wrenching decisions.

"Aren't they good girls?" Trixie asked. I'm not used of that! My sisters' boys are something else. They could turn anyone against having children."

"It was nice of you to let Richard keep the girls here for a while, Trixie," Thedy pulled up a chair next to Trixie, noticing Trixie's unusually calm way with people lately.

"I know I didn't have to, but I feel very bad for all of them. And now I can't believe Malory is gone, too."

"All of this makes your job harder, dear," Thedy patted Trixie's sleeve. She remembered Trixie telling her about shopping for that sweater. She'd gone out in a blizzard to get the sale price. She had carefully selected it before the holidays but refused to pay the mark up and told them so. Thedy would miss Trixie's companionship if she chose to leave.

"What's wrong, Thedy? You're crying."

"There's too much tension around here these days, that's all. Trixie, would you tell Drake I'd like to see him in his office, please?"

"Sure."

Thedy closed the door behind her, Trixie aware of her lack of enthusiasm. She wished she knew what was really wrong, but she didn't want to pry. She paged Drake and when she told him Thedy was waiting, his face went white.

"Hi," he came directly to the sofa and sat next to his wife, his head tilted in a downward slant.

Thedy looked at her husband, his wavy hair having a tousled messy appearance and his bleached-out blue eyes wearing the lines of age and grief. She loved the man, there was no denying, and it was almost pity that she could identify as her own emotion. He jiggled his legs and attempted to sit tall and lean, still donning a sheepish expression, he prepared to take what he had coming like a man.

"I don't know if I've settled down enough to say the right thing, Drake. I'm going to miss you and this place, but I need to leave for a while. I've talked to my Aunt..."

"Thedy, please. Give it some time. I know it's my fault, but you have to believe that I love you. I'll always love you. Stay and reconsider, please. It's been many years, Thedy. I know this hurts, but I don't think I've been bad in the past."

"It's not the past, Drake. I can't relive that. I need a future, and in that future, I had counted on you."

He could barely look at her, his stomach flip-flopping at the remembrance of the painful look on her face. Now he could see a sense of rightful disappointment and he realized that Thedy had never been disillusioned with him before. How could he expect this perfect woman to stay and understand his human error? He really did love her, and true to any prophecy he'd ever been in contact with, upon the threat of losing her, he realized just how much.

"I wanted to tell you, so it wouldn't come as a surprise if you see me packing."

He knew she meant like the surprise he gave her... it was so unfair of him. What could he say to make her stay? He was at a loss.

"I'm glad you talked to me about it, Thedy. But I truly hope you'll think it over. Stay. We can work it out, honest." Trust would be hard to regain, but Drake would work at it the best he knew how.

Drake sat still for the good part of the next hour, wishing it was kosher for men to cry their eyes out, call up a friend, or simply throw a tantrum. Instead, he casually walked out his door and talked to Trixie.

"Are things better with you?" his sad eyes tore through Trixie's heart.

"Yes, but it's so hard for me to believe that Bart did it, and he worked **here**!"

"It's a puzzler." Drake's soft voice lingered.

"How did we miss all that on his application? That's what I don't get."

"Do you remember when he came, we were short of help? Well, I needed the position filled and he used Paul's name as a reference. Just the other day, Paul came and confessed that when I questioned him about Bart, he'd only just met the man. Paul's a good teacher and a good man. Obviously, he feels sick about the whole thing."

"Yes. Who would ever guess something like this of anyone?" Trixie shook her head and then picked up a pen, quickly jotting down a reminder.

"Trixie, I'd like to dictate an ad that I want you to have printed in the Journal for a week."

"Sure. Is it for Bart's job?"

Trixie followed Drake and turned to Heather and Kristin, "Girls, I'll be in here if you need me," she pointed to the door. "I can't get over how good and quiet those two are. Now, back to you. Is it for Bart's job?"

In a sullen voice, Drake explained, "It's for two positions. Yes, one is Bart's and the other is for Tia's job."

"Tia?"

*****

Tommy carried Tia's suede bags, and she asked him to stop in the office first so she could bid farewell. He set the load next to the glass doors, Brisket fast at his side, and watched the two little girls busy coloring.

"I'll be right with you, Tommy. If you like here's my car keys." She handed the old man a set of keys, bound in a circular ring with a large gold letter **D** for decoration.

"Trixie, it's been fun working with you. I'm sure Drake has told you that I'm leaving. I'd like to say good-bye to Thedy and Drake. Are they busy?"

"Drake's in his office. I'll buzz him."

Tia sat her perfectly shaped body, now emphasized to perfection in a skin-tight black suede dress with a loose fitting overcoat, into a chair next to Heather and Kristin. She picked up a magazine to glance through, crossing her lanky nylon-covered legs. She could easily be a model, Trixie thought, trying not to stare at Tia's show of diamonds as well. Trixie hadn't noticed how beautiful she really was, when she saw Tia most often in baggy sweats.

Tia stood almost as tall as Drake. He stood, holding both of her hands in his, and said how much he'd miss her. Trixie wondered why he didn't call Thedy, but didn't ask. It was agreeable to both of them that Tia leave, and Trixie was dying to know why. He must not have fired her. Drake walked her to her car and Trixie watched through the slats of the vertical blind as Drake kissed Tia's cheek, waving as the car backed out of its space.

It was possibly the hardest moment in Drake's life as he watched the metallic blue Jaguar pull away. It tugged at every muscle in his body, and he made a vehement effort not to let it show. There would never be another Tia... Drake knew there couldn't be.

On his way back into the building he caught a side-glance of another person watching her departure. Thedy stood in the bay window of the second-story hall, her head held down and the Kleenex in her hand kept drifting to her eyes. Drake had not told her that he asked Tia to leave.

*****

The quiet in the cafeteria was similar to the alarming calm before a tornado. Everyone wanted news, but didn't want news and most table conversations focused on the cave search, the biggest one ever to be held in the area, scheduled for Friday morning, tomorrow. What, if anything, would they find? Men were making conscious efforts to walk the women to and from classes or to their cars. Life was becoming group oriented more so than ever at Melrose.

Jade's table held the same conversation, but the void of Malory and Dani's presence was astounding. She watched the maintenance crew vacuuming the pool and recalled vividly the first day Malory swam in it. She passed out with weakness, afraid to tell Jade what she knew about Dani.

"Did you notice Richard's girls in by Trixie? I wonder where he went."

A frown crossed Jade's face, "He never gives up, you know. He told me the other day, he drove two hundred miles, combing all the near-by areas, and recruiting surrounding counties to do the same. It's heartbreaking to see him return, with the news that nothing showed up."

"It wouldn't make him feel better, but at least if there has been anything a person could do, Richard's tried it. No matter what the outcome, he did his best," Paris offered, taking a large spoonful of sugar-free orange sherbet.

"Let's hope that the search tomorrow will help. I have mixed feelings about that cave though."

"What's that, Nick?"

"It's right under our noses, for one. Wouldn't we know if someone were going in and out of there like it was a home?"

"Bart was right under our noses, too," Paris reminded him.

"Besides, when it's even a slight remote possibility, I feel they should check it out," said Jade.

"I guess I think they're long gone from the area by now.

Jade skimmed the top of her cup with a spoon, "I have a feeling they're not so far at all, and it gives me the willies."

"Hi, mind if I sit?" Paul slid into the booth next to Nick. "It's the first decent day we've had outside. Too bad this place isn't filled with sunshine, too."

"We were talking about the cave search," Nick told him.

"It's about time. If you ask me, it should have been done weeks ago, when Jill first disappeared. Then perhaps we wouldn't be two less people now," Paul held up his hand and waved it, "I know, I know. It takes time to do these things. I got the speech from Saul already… spare me."

"I wasn't going to say that," Paris was blunt, "but I do agree that it isn't worth risking more lives. As far as Jill goes, that wasn't Saul's blunder, was it?"

"No. You're right, he's helped. There's always roadblocks and I'm tired of them."

"We all feel like that, Paul. It's your fiancé, Richard's wife, Jade's friends and our friends. It's difficult on all of us, and we do understand that you love Jill. We love Dani and Malory, too. We all want to see this thing come out well," Nick gave Paul a pat across his broad shoulders.

For a while, the quiet eased its way back to their table, each one trying to seek a level of understanding that would allow them to go on… carry on in a normal fashion, concealing any private pain or useless worry. That was expected, but so very hard to do.

"Anyone else for Sherbet?" Paris asked over the rabble of curious on-lookers. He stood up, about to get seconds. He was angry with himself, but this was a good example of his food problem. Right now he was eating nervously, he wasn't a bit hungry.

Jade wanted to caution Paris, but she was also having a difficult time devoting her mind to diet and exercise. She sat with her chin cupped in one hand, fighting off invading visions of her two companions. She couldn't help but wonder how they looked this very minute? Could they talk? Were they hurt? How could she help them? All the talk around was only a matter of suppositions, and like the rest of them, Jade wanted the truth.

"I'm going out for some air. Want to come along, Paris?"

"Yes. Let's go."

The breeze slapped away at the branches, still bestowing a whoosh of badly needed fresh air. Overhead, the sulky sky indicated gaps of sunshine, and it was evident a storm was in the making. Jade sat on the edge of the cement planter taking gulps of raw free air.

"Are you okay?"

"Just a little light-headed. I'll be fine. It was so stuffy in there."

"Look!" Jade pointed to the field, "Here comes Richard and Saul!"

"Wonder what they were up to?"

Paris and Jade watched the two men huff and puff through the high weeds, heading straight for Saul's car. Saul jumped in, said something to Richard and high-tailed it out of the lot. Richard stared at the car as it jerked in gear, leaving a puff of smoke as it raced away.

"Richard," Paris yelled to him, "What's up?"

Out of breath and red in the face, Richard hobbled their way, "Don't repeat this, but we went a little way into the cave," he could barely spit the words out. Richard took a deep sigh and continued, "they were there. We found Jill's diamond ring!"

CHAPTER 29

Saul was kept awake all night, between the pelting splashes against his window and the relentless nightmares of bones, skulls and jewelry. He finally gave into it, got up and perked himself a pot of strong black coffee. Saul crashed down on the living-room couch wrapped in a thick woolen blanket. As he sat sipping and listening to the crashing sounds above, he couldn't shake the images of Malory and Dani pleading with him to come and find them.

He checked the clock again. Only three fifteen. If he called the lab one more time on the ring, they'd surely fire him. Still, he slid the phone next to him in case. They were all to meet at the cave by six A.M. It would do him no good to dress now. He got up and paced the floor, going through every feasible outcome once again in his head. He knew he should rest, but it seemed an impossibility.

Through his kitchen window, Saul could see the streaks of lightning bolt to the ground, illuminating probably all of California. He tried one more time and was able to catch a tiny catnap, when again another boom from the heavens jolted him awake. He finally gave up, showered and dressed heavy in thermal underwear, jeans and a flannel shirt. He put on two pairs of wool socks and then hunted for his high-top rubber boots and raincoat. Yesterday he froze in the cave and it was a fairly decent day out.

The lab called and confirmed prints on the ring as Bart's and got the jeweler's confirmation of the purchase, as well as Paul's. There was no doubt that the ring had belonged to Jill. Within two minutes of the call, Saul was out the door, fighting off a good old-fashioned electrical storm.

Richard met Saul in the lot.

"I'm coming along," he told him.

"I don't think that's a good idea, Richard."

"I don't believe I asked. If you don't let me, I'll only follow and that'll be worse," Richard said determinedly. He said no more but followed Saul through the spongy field exactly as he said he would.

Saul recognized Dr. Jonathan Edgars, an expert speleologist from San Diego. He'd been on many expeditions and was currently working in computer technology in relation to cave study. Dr. Jon introduced a fellow speleologist to Saul, Dr. Edward Mills, from the Los Angeles area. The introductions were short and they went inside the entrance to wait for the officers to arrive. Saul had given each a map to and from the cave. He stood at the edge, just realizing the truck load of equipment the men brought.

"I probably shouldn't mention this, Saul," Jon told him, "but your jeans are not the best attire for this type of traveling."

Saul noticed the men were dressed in looser clothing, hardhats with headlamps attached to them, gloves, and sturdy boots.

"What's all this stuff?" Saul asked.

"All the gear any wise person entering a cave should take; compass, first aid kit, rope, and lots of high energy snacks. Anything else you want to know?" This time Ed answered.

"We aren't planning on moving in there or getting lost, are we?" Saul's eyes squinted into a skeptical twist.

"Something like that is never planned, but anything is possible and should be prepared for."

Saul watched as Ed lashed his rope around the tree trunk right outside the entrance, and then wound it around a metal spool that was tied to his waist.

"What's that for?"

"In case we have to climb, this acts as a brake. It allows me to control the rate of descent."

Logical, Saul thought, but he wasn't about to climb. No way! He saw the other officers arrive and they too were dressed in sturdy but loose attire. Saul felt foolish thinking that his jeans were perfect for the job. He then watched Jon and Ed fill their pockets with raisins, candy bars and peanuts.

Saul continued to watch the men put on gloves and gather various other items. While he stood there listening to the crackle of the thunder, he spotted a piece of something white sticking out from the rear tire of the truck that was backed in. It was a handkerchief and Saul carefully took his tweezers and extracted it from its position into one of several plastic bags he carried.

"Okay men," Jon began, "Sgt. Keller has put us in charge so we mapped out little jobs for each of you. Perhaps we'll find what you're looking for early in the game, if not, this cave contains many crawlways, slippery paths, loose rocks, streams, sloping walks, needless to say I could go on forever. Using our common sense is most important," Jon stopped to hand one officer a roll of orange tape. "Here you go. This is luminous tape, when I tell you to mark, simply take a four inch strip and tear it off and stick it to the cavern wall."

One officer was given a measuring tape, another a carbide lamp, and still another an inflatable raft. Saul was given a waterproof container carrying matches. He was completely overwhelmed as they began, his stomach in his throat, still he already had great respect for these men and now great hope that if this were the place, Dani and Malory would be found.

Within the first lap of the race, Saul was aghast at how many interesting cave features he hadn't even noticed last time. Richard agreed.

"Look down there," Ed told them, "it's a natural ice box. All the cold air sinks to the bottom and glaciers form, it's an ice palace."

It was an awesome sight. They'd already passed both sites that Richard and Saul had explored. Saul admitted to himself that the further they went, the more beautiful it became. It was a whole world in and of itself.

"Do you know there's not much air in here?" Saul asked.

"There's plenty of oxygen. What you're noticing is the stillness, the lack of air currents," Jon explained.

Above, the arched ceiling seemed to get farther and farther away until the great old walls were towering overhead. It was much lighter this time and Saul could actually see the chiseled strange shapes continuously etched on the cavern walls. Unfortunately, he could also see some crawly things that made him shiver.

"Can those hurt us?" Saul was beginning to wonder why he left his pacifier at home. He just hoped no one else wondered the same.

But Ed didn't seem to mind explaining, "Most of the life within won't hurt or attack you. Those are isopods, I call them white centipedes. Harmless. Over there," he pointed to a spot on the shallow rivulet that looked like floating sawdust, "those are Springtails. They're wingless insects that jump. Again, harmless."

He made it sound so easy. They trudged along through a tight crawlway and down into a large space with many options.

"Now what?"

"This is where we stop, consider what we're looking for, and check out the map. Any path is a possibility," Jon pulled the map from his hip pocket and unfolded it. "I doubt he'd go this way, it's a complicated pattern full of lava tubes and side vents. Really doesn't go anywhere."

"How about this one?" Ed suggested, scratching his brow, "it's about a mile long, filled with streams and a pretty straight shot. Not a lot of ups and downs."

"Let's try it."

The path was slippery, with constant trickles of limewater mixed with valdose water. One was white and the other streaked with iron, resembling long hanging strips of lean bacon. It was narrow and Saul began to feel the throngs of claustrophobia. He distracted his mind by admiring its beauty and asking questions.

"Makes you wonder how these things are made."

Jon never passed up an opportunity to teach, "Very simply by phreatic water, that is drainage patterns. Look there," he pointed to a section of the ceiling, "looks like a loaf of bread. The crosslines of the water spills divide it into slices, so to speak."

Saul tried to listen, but the sealed in feeling of under ground darkness made him woozy. On top of that a daring bold bat came down and swooshed over his head. He jumped back and fell to the ground.

Saul looked up sheepishly, "I know. Harmless." He attempted a laugh.

Ed reached out a hand to help him up, chuckling, he told him, "Not always, but most of the time. Some of those silky little characters are blood suckers with razor-sharp teeth, but unless they're rabid, very uncommon, they still won't really hurt you. That one looked like a little pink devil, a lump-nosed bat. Nothing to write home about."

Saul had just about lost his sense of humor when the path swayed slightly and all the men jogged to the obvious spot where Bart had spent some time. His mind went from cave jargon to hard-hit evidence of murder.

Dani and Malory were nowhere in sight, at least Saul hoped it wasn't them. At the bottom of a slight decline, running along the murky stream's edge, were decomposed bodies, he approximated five of them, partially covered by the red earth, and partly submersed in the iron-filled creek. One particular one caught his eye. Its wrist and fingers stuck straight up in the air, lined with faded gems of various sizes and shapes. All indications pointed to Jill. Saul was not the only one to retch.

Next to a silver chain were some vials, needles, a mirror and three glass tooters. Just beyond were some wrappers from candy bars, raisins, crackers and peanuts. Looks like they met a match. Bart seemed to know a little about caves himself.

"Richard, come here. It's okay. These bodies are too decomposed to be Dani. There's still hope," Saul reached out to console the man who'd turned fright white.

"I can't go on in here," Richard told Saul. He looked away, his thick hands shaking, as if he would be next to lose his cookies.

"Don't worry. I'm going to collect some things I need, then two of the officers, myself and you will go back."

Color came back into Richard's dead face, but he still turned from the scene, not caring to observe the insanity it reeked of.

"Sgt. Keller," Jon summoned Saul, "we've looked over this map again and it appears that somewhere in this general vicinity, there may be an opening."

"Another way out?" Saul's interest was apparent by his immediate takeover of the map. "Where?"

"Right around here. My guess is into the rugged mountainside."

"Then there's little hope?"

"I wouldn't say that. The man must know what he's doing."

"If he does, he may be with two women who don't. What are their chances?"

"I can't answer that."

*****

Exiting the cave was like being reborn. In this realistic, though often disappointing world, was where Saul functioned the best. The men headed resolutely for Melrose, beating off the pellets of rain that insisted on whipping them every chance they got.

"We need some help out here quick," Saul spoke bluntly into the receiver, "I want crime lab and air patrol, pronto."

Saul paced with the phone, not wanting to hear the answer he got. "No, it can't wait, rain or not. If you don't send help, I'll go higher up. I'm sorry, that's the way it is."

Trixie kept her nose pried to her file cabinet, but Saul knew her ears were connected to him.

"So let the choppers wait, but only till the rain subsides, I want everyone else immediately. They can begin, and I'll hang back and go in the chopper. Fine." He slammed the phone down, wincing at his own disrespect.

"Sorry, Trixie."

Saul was scared. The sight they'd seen made him understand how valuable time was. He knew the helicopters couldn't navigate in this weather, yet he had to make it imperative that they wasted no time later. He'd wait… he had no choice. Now that he had a chance to think, he wondered why he hadn't suspected that the cave had another way out. In retrospect, it was so obvious.

The weather had let up a little, though nothing that would help his situation. The forecast was gloomy, but he knew the rain wasn't supposed to be an all day affair. Saul ambled back and forth until he heard the familiar hum overhead. He called Richard from his room and they were off for an incredible ride.

Richard had never been up in the air, other than perhaps to hurdle the high jump. He white-knuckled the back of the seat Saul was in, not venturing to guess how many thousands of feet off ground they were. The chopper flitted in and out of spaces Richard couldn't even see. He leaned over barely seeing anything but a flock of green. How would they ever spot something as small as a person in amongst the soaring pines?

"What's that?" Saul said excitedly.

"I don't see a thing."

"Look! Go back, go back over there. By that clump of lower trees."

Richard stared at Saul in disbelief. Saul insisted they recircle the area four times and Richard couldn't see so much as a dot, other than branches of pine needles.

"There! There it is… slow up."

The helicopter swerved in sideways narrowly escaping a slap from the great Sequoias. They floated for a moment nil of any direction, and Richard peered over the edge not really knowing what to look for.

Then he saw it... he was sure... he hadn't forgotten... sitting in a small opening, looking like specks on a blanket of green, a man and two women.

"Dani... oh my God, it's Dani."

CHAPTER 30

Malory sat on the wet grassy patch about four feet from where they had exited the cave. She curled her knees up to her chest and wrapped her arms around them trying to gain a remote sense of warmth. She shivered and shook, her brittle bones chilled to the marrow. Beebee had long ago unchained them knowing there wasn't the slightest chance they could escape. Her stomach cramped at the thought of the muddy stream water with protein additive that he forced down her throat. She hoped she would never in her life see another raisin, Mars bar or peanut... for strength he said. She preferred to be knocked out on Valium, though she knew she hadn't made a good walking partner then.

Malory looked at Dani sitting just another few feet away. She had regained some of her color, but she still needed medical attention, the sooner the better. She seemed vacant and Malory couldn't detect if she had gone into a depression, lacked the right nutrition, given up hope, or all of the above. By the tears streaming down her cheeks, Malory guessed she'd just had enough.

Malory wanted to offer Dani solace but her own arms were too tired and stiff. She couldn't seem to make her mouth form any words that were sensible, and each time a thought would arise it was diverted by Beebee's obnoxious hooting and dancing.

Above, the weak gray sky seemed content with its aura of gloom... there was no light... no hope... no life. Around them only the trees moved without command. None of God's creatures were present to witness their entrapment amidst the haggard cliffs and stagnant mist of air. They were morsels of human life never to be heard from again. Malory tried to shake her pessimism, but it was only amplified by Beebee's actions. He continued to slip and slide in the slicks of muck that neatly accumulated. Malory found her spiteful mind wishing he'd roll right off the end... over the embankment and out of her mind.

Her ears continued to play nasty tricks on her, and Malory tugged at them to rub away the loud rumbling engine that thudded overhead. A frightened mind could do that... surely she was hallucinating help on its way. Dani slid closer, not saying a word, but took Malory's chin and pushed it up to the sky. It was help... a black and yellow helicopter tilted its nose almost into the side of the mountain. Then they heard voices, still Malory was afraid to believe it.

Beebee began to pace in and out of the cave, chanting his verses and talking nonsense. His evil eyes, carved in a stone expression, refused to look anywhere but straight ahead. He did not acknowledge the man that was attempting to climb down a rope which was slung out the side of the chopper.

Malory watched as the man, bound in heavy rope around his waist, climbed half-way down the swaying ladder and began to holler. Were her eyes playing tricks on her, too? His brown wavy hair was blowing off his forehead and his broad shoulders clung to the rope for dear life. It was Saul.

"Malory, it's okay now. There's more help on the way."

His words seemed to echo and get carried away with distance. Beebee ran to the edge of the cliff, waved his arms like a maniac and yelled at Saul to leave them alone. He told Saul that he didn't stand a chance. He slid down to the mud earth and grabbed a branch to balance his footing. He continued to scream obscenities and orders threatening to go back in the cave.

"It's over, Bart. Besides those of us in the air, another crew is working their way through the cave. They should be here any minute."

Bart turned in a huff toward Malory and Dani.

"You two belong to me. If I can't have you, no one will."

Beebee took the large switchblade from his pocket and popped the blade out to show his authority. He began to lunge forward but in haste and anger, he lost his balance and landed flat on his stomach. The knife flew forward and Beebee pleaded for help as he tried to grasp the slippery tall grasses that lined the edge of the cliff. The shrubbery ripped under his weight, the girls watching their assailant fall to the depths below, his mouth opened wide expecting a welcoming reprieve.

"Look up girls. Listen hard. Mal, can you hold on longer if I take Dani in first?"

"Yes. Get Dani, she needs help," Malory yelled convincingly. Her stomach bounced in anticipation, happy and scared at the same time. Would they really come back for her? Malory knew better, she only hoped they hurried.

"Stand up, Dani and as soon as I get close, grab for the ladder. I'll hold on to you." Dani obeyed, standing as tall as she was able, hunched slightly. Her hands shook as she reached for the ladder in motion. The helicopter paused to allow its new passenger time. Saul quickly secured a rope around Dani's waist and held her tight.

"I'll be right back," he called, "faster than you can count to one hundred." Saul motioned the chopper and carefully it exited the area, heading back to Melrose.

Malory sat numbly for a moment and then let her mind get the better of her. She was caught up with the image of Beebee's mouth open and eyes as big as saucers. She imagined him clinging to the mountain's edge and scratching his way back up to get her. It was easy to be frightened out in the middle of nowhere. She had to stop sabotaging herself and think about what Saul told her... he'd be back... count to one hundred. She buried her tucked head into her knees and arms and silently began the rote, as if beginning a game of hide-and-seek. She was it.

The sound was muffled but beautiful, and she looked up to see the ladder dangling within arm's reach. In the distance she heard a siren, certainly must be coming to the resort. Malory reached out and clung tight to the ladder and her man. Saul smiled and she felt secure in his arms. Nothing could hurt her now... not Beebee... not the height... nothing. She relaxed her head on his shoulder as the chopper softly jerked in gear and they soared high above the majestic pines.

*****

For the first time in weeks, the sun radiated its gentle warmth upon the redwood resort. The early morning shower dried with only a few small puddles as a reminder of its wrath. Now spring was only a few green buds and early blossoms away. Malory wanted to scream with a new-found freedom when her feet finally touched the blacktop. Saul grabbed a blanket to throw around her. Jade, Paris, and Nick came running out the front door.

"Where's Dani?"

"Don't worry, Malory. She's all taken care of. Richard went to the hospital with her. He'll call us when he knows anything."

"What about Paul? Does he know?"

"Worried about everyone but yourself?" Saul teased.

Then he added, "Paul knows…"

Malory walked into the office and sat down, quietly aware of all the hustle about her. Saul called for a doctor to come out to the resort to see her. Trixie offered her coffee with a smile, and Malory smuggled a giggle. What a nice switch. Malory thanked her. And of course Thedy and Drake were also in and out. Malory sensed a tightness there that she had to check into. It was like a homecoming, the best she ever had. She felt sorry for Paul and Liza, realizing they were the real losers, but an eager sense of pride when Heather and Kristin peeked through the doorway and Malory knew their happy ending.

Malory thought back to the first time she'd seen Saul, the attraction was immediate. His job was over as far as she was concerned, but the feeling in her heart and the tender look in his eyes, told her that he was far from finished with her. He sat down and drew her close, gently stroking her hair. The time had come when he was no longer only her strength through fearful times, but her pillar in life. He would be around for a long, long time.

CPSIA information can be obtained at www.ICGtesting.com
Printed in the USA
LVOW11s0028130614

389832LV00001B/34/P